DARK HEART, VOLUME 1

A MANHATTAN MONSTERS NOVEL

ELLA JAMES

Dark Heart, Volume 1
Ella James

This book is a work of fiction. Any resemblance to actual events or persons, living or dead, is entirely coincidental.

Cover design by Najla Qamber Designs
Formatting by Jamie Davis

PRELUDE

All the world's a stage,
And all the men and women merely players;
They have their exits and their entrances,
And one man in his time plays many parts …

—William Shakespeare, *As You Like It*

CHAPTER ONE

Luca

"Dude, you look like fucking Zorro."

Alessandro holds a big-ass tray of *chiocciole* between us as he makes this proclamation. His brown eyes are wide, and he looks earnest, because Alessandro is an earnest kind of guy.

Still, I've gotta roll my eyes because they're not behind a black mask. "It's a bandana, not a mask, Alesso. And it's over my mouth. I'm a train robber."

He shakes his head, trying not to smile and failing, which makes his vampire teeth protrude over his lower lip. "You sure about that?"

"Sure I'm sure. Who are you—the Sesame Street guy?"

"I'm Count On It, cause I'm gonna get with something tonight, you can count on it."

I laugh, and Alesso gives me an abashed grin. He jerks his chin over his shoulder and says, "There's some *ribollita* that needs to go to the big table in the dining hall." He nods at the swinging double doors that separate the kitchen from the hall. "The table has tall green shit and a bunch of tissue-papery white flowers. Leo fucking disappeared after he brought the empty tray in here, and the sterno flame is kinda exposed. I'm worried someone's gonna catch their shirt on fire before we can drop another dish on top of that flame."

I nod, walking around the counter behind Alesso to grab the stain-

3

less steel tray, weighted with *ribollita*. I clutch the hot serving dish by its edges and start toward the doors. "I gotcha covered, Count."

He says, "Thank you" in what he must think is a Transylvania voice. It's not even a little bit convincing, which is why I laugh.

I'm still grinning as I start down the long hall that runs alongside the dining room, adjoining ballroom, and several big rooms labeled "parlors."

For this masquerade-themed *festa*, which runs from 9 p.m. to 1 in the morning, we're at one of the ritziest buildings in Tribeca. Alesso said it's owned by the Arnoldi family, and I'm sure he's right. This is the wedding reception for Clarice DeBourn, the younger sister of Roberto Arnoldi. Yeah, *that* Roberto Arnoldi. Which makes Clarice the daughter of the infamous Lamberto Arnoldi.

Rumor is he might be in the building at some point tonight. It was also rumored he might walk the bride down the aisle this afternoon at her second wedding.

I just got here, so I haven't really heard any of the new gossip. But even my mother had heard the news—and she was pissed. Lamberto, walking his *divorced* daughter to a priest *in a church*.

I try not to laugh at that as I make my way down the hall. I have to say "excuse me" half a dozen times as I move through a group of like nine women. I tip my head back when one catches my eye, giving her a smile. She looks good—but she's old enough to be my *nonna*.

The woman beside her pulls a feathery pink mask away from her face, waggling her white eyebrows, and I laugh as I pass them.

"Look at that train robber," I hear one of them say.

I move under an archway into the vast space of the dining hall, and my throat tightens a little. It's not nervousness so much as claustrophobia. The room is almost as big as a high school gymnasium, and it's packed with bodies wearing gowns, tuxes, and masquerade shit. The flowers smell, the perfume smells, the food smells...plus the talking, laughing, shrieking... I can hear music come from the ballroom. It's orchestra-style and loud as fuck, with all the whiny violins and trombones.

I look for the table Alesso described and spot it right away, beside a big ice carving of...a naked woman. I frown at the thing, but yeah, that's definitely a nude lady with pointy tits rising out of a crystal trough of…is that champagne? Why the hell didn't Alesso use her for a point of reference?

That gets me laughing again—so much that I almost drop the *ribollita*. I squeeze between a group of girls and guys around my age, keeping my head down in case I know someone; it's possible, given where I go to school now.

Finally, the fucking chafing dish is in its spot, covering the blue flame, and I take a second to look at the ice goddess.

I'm thinking of how I'll rib Alesso when I see him in a minute. So although my gaze is aimed at the arched doorway leading back into the hall, I'm not really looking. But then someone steps into my frame of vision who looks like…

What the fuck?

I stop in my tracks and watch as the tall guy in the hall turns fully away from me and then steps into the shadows.

I make a beeline for the next arch down. The dining room is lined by arches like this all the way down its left side. They open into the hallway so if I go through the next one down, I might be able to come up from behind him and—

Fuck! The hall is jammed with people again. I can see a group of men moving toward the ballroom, flanked by women and a waiter or two, but they're too far away now to make out faces.

I take another second to try to chill the fuck out before pushing through the kitchen's swinging doors. I tell myself I'm crazy. He wouldn't be here. Not in a million years—for so many reasons. The fact that I'm seeing him, that my brain has got him showing up where I am, even though I know that he's in Red Hook right now…

I don't want to think about what that shit means, so I shoulder through the kitchen doors, where I almost collide with a big dude—like, giant-sized. He frowns at me. I'm wearing black pants, a white dress shirt, and a black bowtie—the clothes Alesso's uncle makes us wear for these gigs—so even with the train robber bandana, I don't think it's hard to guess what I'm doing in the kitchen.

He gives me a nod, murmurs something into an earpiece, and passes through the doors.

As soon as he's gone, my friend Leo steps around a support column—done in gray tile, just like the rest of this space—and bugs his eyes out at me.

"Dude, he's *here*."

"Uhh, huh?"

Leo's eyes pop open wider—one is blue, and one is brown—and he waves his arms. "Roberto Arnoldi just got here and Lamberto is in here somewhere, too. That was Roberto's guy asking me to bring up dinner for him. He's in one of the libraries. He thought I was Luigi because—" Leo tugs on his jacket, which has Alesso's uncle Luigi's nametag. He laughs, sounding slightly deranged. "Do you want to take it up there?"

"What, you don't?"

"Shit, no!"

"You scared to go up there?"

"Nah, man, I'm not scared."

"Then what's the problem?"

Leo shrugs. "I don't know man."

I shake my head again and glance around for the plate. "Well, where is it?"

"I haven't made it yet."

I hesitate. If Roberto recognized me, that could be bad, but…I pull the bandana up over my face more.

"Would you recognize me, Leo, if you saw me around?"

"I'd think you were Zorro."

What is with these guys? "Zorrto wears an eye mask."

Leo shrugs, and I groan. "Make the plate. I'll take it up there."

I was probably a foot shorter when I had my run-in with Roberto. It'll be fine.

Leo spazzes as he fixes the plate—really more a platter—and I try to talk him down without laughing at him. By the time I'm headed out of the kitchen, Alesso is coming back in.

"He's taking food to Roberto Arnoldi," Leo tells Alesso.

"What?" His mouth lolls open. "We're sending *Luca*?"

"Only the best." I shove through the doors before Alesso's surprise makes me second guess my mission.

I'm supposed to take the staff elevator at the end of the hall to the twentieth floor, where, two doors down from the elevator, there's a large library. That's where Roberto and his posse are.

The platter I'm holding is covered and heated. I feel weird as I ride the staff elevator up with the thing. Like a caterer, I think with an eye roll at myself. I'm a weekend caterer, and so the fuck what? I've never minded before. I clench my jaw as I eye myself in the elevator's mirror wall.

Fuck Roberto Arnoldi. Even if he recognizes me, so what? I'm taking one for the team. Leo wasn't gonna do it. Alesso's brother Tony—who's become one of Arnoldi's minions—would lose his shit if he found out Alesso did it.

I can handle this shit. I've got on the bandana. It's true my eyes are what my mom calls "crystalline" blue and that's unusual in this circle, but a library like this might be dark. Anyway, I'm not the only person in Manhattan with pale blue eyes.

I steel myself as I step out of the elevator and blink around the twentieth floor hall. It's dark as shit in here, with crazy-high ceilings, open flame wall lamps, and décor that's almost goth looking: long, velvet curtains, a sculpture of a stallion on its hind legs, marble floors.

I catch the unmistakable scent of pricey cigars—the kind these people used to stand outside my dad's shoe store and smoke when I was a kid, before I knew who any of them were. For a second, that aroma takes me back. And now I've got a nervous feeling—like I'm a kid who's gone wandering where he shouldn't.

The hall feels still, but I hear men's voices from a little ways away. Something clinks, like a liquor bottle on the rim of a glass, like champagne flutes for a toast. And then I'm there, I'm standing in the library's doorway.

As I look in, Arnoldi himself looks up from his lap—he's sitting in a high-backed chair—and his gaze locks onto mine.

He says something I can't hear, followed by a boisterous, "If it isn't my meal!"

I walk toward him, doing this thing I'm pretty good at where I fake it. Just fake the shit out of whatever. No one ever knows its bullshit. Not even Alesso, I don't think. What I do is I summon this memory of Alesso's uncle, Zio Mark, in my head, serving the governor with a platter just like this one. It was my first day on the job, about a year ago.

I don't go all out for Arnoldi, because that'd be weird, but I serve his platter with some finesse.

I take the top off for him, and he peers down at the platter. I take the paper cover off his glass, and he looks up at me.

"Luca Galante," he says in a knowing tone.

Shit. My heart gives a slow throb, but I straighten up and stand before him like a soldier at attention.

"Catering for Regio's." He drags each word out, as if this fact is of interest to him. His eyes are so dark, they look black in the low light. I feel everyone looking at me now...as I look at him. The thick head of black hair, the high cheekbones, straight nose. He's short, but you can't tell when he's seated. And it hardly matters.

I nod once. "Luigi is my friend's uncle."

"And who is your friend?"

"Alesso," I say, trying to sound casual—and avoid his surname.

"Tony Diamond's brother." He nods and picks up his steak knife. "Good kids," he says. "Working hard. That's the key, you know." His eyes bore into mine as he picks up a fork, preparing to cut his ribeye. "Hard work takes you everywhere. It's what I tell my daughter. Have you met my daughter?"

"I don't think so, sir."

That makes him smile. He looks to his plate, and I watch while he cuts the steak.

"Just the way I like it. Good to taste the...elemental." He gives me a smile that's full of shit but looks almost charming.

"Would you like anything else, Mr. Arnoldi?"

"Oh, I would like a number of things. What can you give me, Mr. Galante?" He lifts his chin, smiling at someone across the room as if he's just told a good joke. His gaze moves back to me. "I'm fucking with you, son. *Padre*—" He sits slightly up in his chair, clearly looking toward one of the room's corners. *"Non vuoi cenare?"*

There's a low chuckle from someone I can't see. Then a booming voice says, *"Sto mangiando questo sigaro."*

The room rumbles with laughter. Polite or sincere?

Softly—so softly I think only I can hear—Roberto Arnoldi says, "My father won't eat, but send him up a plate. Give it an hour." He winks. "No one likes to feel forgotten."

I nod and turn to go. I manage to keep my head up and my gait steady—until I'm almost to the door, and Roberto says my name. I look over my shoulder. He raises his brows as his face twists in a look that's somehow critical and imploring at once.

"Be careful what you get involved with," he says in whisper-quiet Italian. "I would hate for you to close doors you wouldn't want closed."

He lifts an eyebrow, giving me a pointed look.

I nod again, because I can't find my tongue.

CHAPTER TWO

Luca

Be careful what you get involved with. What the fuck does that mean? How does he know that I speak Italian? Does he know what I do for Tony? Why would he object? It bothers me so much, I want to chew on it for a few minutes.

There's a stairwell in the corner, right beside the elevator. I pull its door open, finding not the standard rubber-lined cement floor but polished wood topped with thick, red carpet. The walls are papered deep gold, and the one across from me has windows punched into it.

The windows aren't made of glass. Or if they are, the glass is distorted, so you can't see the city outside. Just smears of yellow, green, blue, and red.

I look down into the space between the stairwell's railings, surprised that the glossy, wood rail seems to go all the way to the bottom floor. I'm looking up, to see how high the staircase goes, when I hear a rapping sound from just above my head.

Heels. It's gotta be.

Whoever's wearing them is moving quickly, maybe even frantically, if the staccato of the *clap clap clap clap* is any indication. I realize that if the sound just started, and I never heard a door open or shut, then someone froze when I stepped onto the stairs, remained silent for the ten or fifteen seconds I stared at the window, and now they're...running?

I strain my ears and catch some sort of sigh—it's sharp and breathy. The heel sounds stop, and a moment later, I hear a door creak open. Whatever she's doing, she isn't being quiet about it.

I take a deep breath, and realize I can smell her perfume. It's rich and clean, with a whiff of something that's a little like vanilla. I...like it. It's...familiar. It makes me feel good. Why?

I start up the stairs behind her. On the next landing, the smell is stronger, filling my whole head. My body responds, heartbeat coming fast and heavy.

This is weird shit, right? I'm following some woman because of her perfume? I should stop. I know I should.

But I've always been too curious for my own good. And I wanna know if this girl looks as good as she smells.

I pull the door open and find myself in a hall with blood-colored walls. It's lined with gold doors, like something from a film set. I don't see her anywhere, so maybe I lost her. I'm kind of surprised by how disappointed I am.

Wait! I hear something, on down the hall. There's an Oriental runner down the middle of the hallway. I stay on it, moving fast and silent.

I'm so hot on her heels, I catch a fresh whiff of that perfume. It stirs that something in me again—a familiarity almost like a memory. How do I know that damn smell?

The hall continues straight, but there's another one that intersects. I look right then left, and there she is up ahead—standing between the wall and a tall potted plant. *Hiding*, I think.

Then she's off again, her pale dress trailing behind her so she looks a bit like a ghost. I duck behind the same big, leafy plant and hold my breath, sure someone is chasing her—but no one appears. Instead, she morphs into a dark blot at the end of the hall. It's so dark, it looks like a black hole.

I can't shake the feeling she's fleeing, hiding from someone. It's a feeling I know myself—and I hate it. Coupled with the bizarre warning I just got from Roberto Arnoldi himself, I feel worked up enough to jog after her.

The darkness is an open door, a door into a pitch-black-dark room, which lights up as I enter. It's a coat closet—more like a coat room, really. And there are stairs in one corner.

I swallow, listening.

"Be careful what you get involved with. I would hate for you to close doors you wouldn't want closed."

Fuck Arnoldi and his fucking warnings. I follow the familiar smell to the stairs, where I find a partition rope and a sign that reads "Wet paint."

The paint is undisturbed. My throat feels knotted as I pace the room. Where the hell could she have gone? I'm walking back toward the stairs, thinking I should check if they're even wet, when I notice a door behind them. It's got a coat rack pushed in front of it.

That's sketchy.

I try to think of something this girl could be doing in this obviously out-of-the-way place that would be okay. I want an excuse to leave, but I can't find one.

The door is short and narrow; it opens into a narrow hallway with a low ceiling. I'm six-foot-one and my hair is brushing the top. Right away, I feel the walls trying to close in on me. I close my eyes and breathe deeply, and it's that scent that keeps me going. And the way she was creeping around.

Women are as strong as men. I think a lot of the time, stronger. But they're easy prey for cowards. I can't say how I know this girl, the one running, is young—but I do. Must be something about the way she moved. I take a few more steps in and am relieved to find the small space expands into to a regular-sized hallway.

The floors are deep red marble with gold veins; they're framed by tall walls papered pink and white and pocked on each side by gold doors, all closed. I shake my head at the flashy gold doors.

To my right, in an alcove between the second and third door, there is a painting of a man in a white gown, small amidst a nighttime forest. Someone in brown stands before him, more shadow than man, pricking his finger with a knife or needle. Overhead, a moon glows behind gray clouds so real-looking that I have to blink to reassure myself it's just a painting.

Fuck, I'm getting spooked like a kid.

I jerk my eyes away from the thing and glance on down the hall.

It's dimly lit.. I glance quickly behind me then take a few slow steps, being careful not to make sound with my dress shoes.

Just a little ways, and then I'll have to turn around if I don't see her. I don't care how good she smells, I don't want to get caught in here. Whatever this place is, it's not intended for me.

I close my eyes and listen with intention to the space around me, listen for her feet or her breathing or for some sound that indicates that she's in trouble. I don't hear a thing.

I tell myself she's fine, but I can't make myself turn back yet. I wait another two maybe three minutes. Could she be hiding behind one of the closed doors? What if she's waiting here for one of *them*?

The thought sickens me, and I shake my head to get rid of it. Then I hear a murmur, and my pulse surges.

I take a few steps. There's a sound like something hitting the floor. Holy shit, I can't breathe. I move toward a door where I think the sound came from. I stop outside it. I hear something else—someone moving around. Followed by another muttered curse. I'm sure of it. She's on the other side of this door.

I listen for another minute, and then I open the door quietly. Slowly. With such care, I feel almost incorporeal. Then the door is open wide enough for me to see the whole room.

Most of it is done in black. There's a big-ass painting on one of the walls. These people like their big-ass paintings (I get it, though; I like art, too).

That's the last thought that crosses my mind before my gaze lands on her.

The girl I pursued is standing at a wall of built-in bookshelves, her dark head down as she flips through some sort of album she's got propped against one of the shelves.

I'm fascinated by the profile view I have of her. Her slightly parted lips, the slight blush high on her cheek. The way her black hair falls down her slim back, over her flowing dress, which must be an angel costume because there are ribbons in the back shaped into angel wings. She looks like a porcelain doll, and with a silver mask over her eyes... A bolt of lust moves through me, and I draw a breath in, feeling strange about myself, at my reaction.

I don't want to fuck her, I tell myself. It's just...animal appreciation. We're complimentary opposites of the same species. She looks soft and small and regal. Maybe even familiar. As I watch her, her mouth tightens and she blows a breath out.

Then her head turns. She looks right at me. *Whoa.*

I'm gripped by a strange sensation. Like I'm frozen, kind of, but my heart is beating harder and my face and chest feel hot.

Holding my gaze with her wide, masked eyes, she turns fully around to face me, revealing her flowing white gown. It tightens at her waist and hugs her bust and ties around the back of her neck. Another bolt of heat prickles through me like some kind of fucking *drug.*

"Who are you?" she asks me, at the same moment I say, "You look like a princess."

I blink as the words leave my mouth, because I didn't plan to say them. And they were kind of stupid. Obviously she's an angel.

"I'm an angel." She holds out her wings. "But I'll take princess." She peers at me like a dark-haired angel queen. "And you're a robber prince." She says it like an edict, but her lips twitch at the corners. At the last second, when it looks like they'll tug into a frown, she gives me a shy smile.

"Do I know you?" Her tone sounds like she suspects she does.

"I don't know." I widen my eyes at her, waggling my brows. "What do you think?"

She stretches, casting her gaze around the room before her eyes land back on me. "I don't think I care," she says. She yawns likes she's tired, and I step back, away from her and away from the door— so I don't make her feel cornered.

"I think I'm too sleepy to care," she says softly. "But I hope you're a nice guy, because we're in here alone together."

❧

Elise

When my mother was ten, someone hurt her as she walked home from her elementary school. Because of that, I think, when I was eight, I began receiving instruction in Kalari.

So I'm really not scared of this boy, even though he's on the big side.

I *am* curious. I pretend I'm sleepy, but I'm making plans. He steps away—from the door and me—and I watch as the corners of his eyes tilt in what I think is a smile. I can't tell for sure because he's got a black bandana covering the lower half of his face.

"I am," he says, and his deep voice sends shockwaves over my skin. They erupt into goosebumps which I ignore as I straighten my spine. I look him over once more.

"You're a server."

His eyes squint again as he smiles behind the black bandana. "I'm a train robber."

"And I'm an angel," I say softly, stepping closer to him. I don't know why my feet move me. I watch as he rubs a hand back through his hair. Black hair, darker than mine. His eyes, I see after a few more steps, are ice blue.

"Are those your real eyes?"

I love how they squint and his cheeks curve, another smile under the bandana. "No. These are just for parties."

They're amazing, I almost say. But I have self-restraint. I say, "They're very blue."

"Are those your real lips?" His voice is so soft I strain to hear it.

"Lipstick." I smile.

"What's it called?"

"What?"

"They all have names, don't they? Like 'Cherry Bomb' or 'Lust Duck' or whatever."

"Lust Duck?" I barely manage to not burst out laughing.

He shrugs. "Slut Swan?"

I can't stop my lips from curving, but I can twist them into a smirk. "This one is called Scandal."

His eyes drink me in, brows notching as he seems to consider me. "I didn't know angels caused scandals."

I lift a shoulder. "Princesses do."

"Do they?" he asks, so low and quiet.

His gaze holds mine, and my chest goes tight and weird, like I can't get enough air. And it's because of him.

My heart is racing as our eyes stay locked, and then he shuts his, and I see him swallow. When he opens them again, he gives me a

16

little smile. I know it's a smile because I see his eyes squint at the corners.

The sharp rap of footsteps in the hall breaks our spell, and his eyes widen.

"Shit," he says, at the exact moment I say, "Let's go behind the wall!"

Seconds later, we're crouching behind a folding privacy wall to the right of the bed—one of the ones they sometimes have in tailors' alteration spaces, so you can duck behind and swap your clothes out. This one is made of dark wood; it's just large enough to hide us both. He's behind me, in the space between my back and the wall. As we freeze in our positions, one of his hands goes to my shoulder.

"In a second," he begins quietly—but I don't get to hear what will happen in a second.

The door opens, and he shushes. I hold my breath and try to listen to the footsteps. It's more than one person. I think two, but I'm too scared to peek through the gaps between the privacy wall's slats and confirm this. I can tell it's men—and that they're speaking Italian. My stomach slow rolls as their gruff, low voices rise. They're speaking quickly, forcefully. I don't know Italian, but *I know one of the voices...*

The blood drains from my cheeks when he speaks in English. *"Please."*

The other man grumbles something—in Italian. Then, as quickly as they stepped in, one of them leaves. Below the divider wall, I can see the shoes of the one who remains. I watch as he shuffles his feet, and when he sighs, it's unmistakably familiar.

Seconds later, he, too, leaves.

A moment passes. I can feel the boy behind me, feel his chest warming my back and feel the tension in his coiled muscles.

He lets out a deep breath, seeming as shaken as I feel—but I assume for different reasons.

"What were they saying?" I whisper, feeling nearly faint with my shock. "Do you know?"

He rises to his feet, holding out a hand for me, which I take.

"I do know," he says as he helps me up.

"Well, what was it?"

He looks at the door. "One of them was warning the other. Telling him to get in line."

"Which one was doing the warning?" I try not to sound too desperate. "Was it the one who left first, or the one who left the room last?"

He frowns at me. "The guy who left last."

I can feel my pulse throb at the base of my throat. "You mean... mafia stuff?" The words are whispers.

"I don't know." He looks down. When he glances back up, I can tell from his eyes that he's troubled. "I..." He shakes his head. "Let's get out of here."

I nod, and he takes my hand. He holds it carefully, and my whole body buzzes beside him as he peeks into the hall, then leads me out as if it's his job to protect me.

We walk in silence until we reach the door into the weird, small space. Then he disentangles his fingers from mine and moves in front of me. He has to crouch a little so his head won't brush the low ceiling. I watch the fabric of his dress shirt tighten over his shoulders as he listens at the door then cracks it open before nodding over his shoulder at me.

"We're good."

His voice is low and soft and rough. He steps through the little door and turns back toward me, holding his hand out. I don't know why I take it. I don't need help walking. But it feels good to move through the coat room with his big, warm hand around mine. Especially after what I just saw. *Who* I just saw.

My suspicions are confirmed...maybe. I don't know how I feel, but I feel better walking through the darkened hallways with this guy beside me. He gives me a look that I think is supposed to be reassuring. Maybe even a little smile, although of course I can't be sure because of the bandana. When we reach the polished wood stairwell that I think he stepped into after me a little while ago, he lets go of my hand.

"Thank you," I whisper.

"*Grazie, bella.*" He gives me a slight nod—like a greeting...like an agreement.

"Thank you," I whisper again. It feels so strangely inadequate.

"Be careful, okay?" he says. "You've got friends here?"

I nod.

"Don't be wandering around tonight without them." He wraps his hand around the door to the stairwell and then looks back, his piercing blue eyes widening. *"Sei bellissima e gli uomini sono mostri."*

I don't understand his words, but they feel like a warning.

I watch as he disappears into the stairwell, my mind rolling outward like a rug unfurling, vast and empty all in the same moment.

VOLUME 1

Every story is a story about death. But perhaps, if we are lucky, our story about death is also a story about love.

—Helen Humphreys, *The Lost Garden*

CHAPTER ONE

Elise
Two Months Later

There's a photo on a shelf in our home's library. It's a Polaroid, which may be why I've always liked it so much. Some Polaroids are bleary, but this one is strangely clear—like a window to another time.

In the snapshot, it's spring or summertime. I know because the grassy field we're standing in is brilliant green. There are lots of us—thirty-four, to be exact. Arranged in four rows. Everyone is wearing dressy-casual clothes: flowing dresses for women, trousers and button-ups for men.

On the front row, surely just a few feet from the photographer, are six women. Each one holds a baby, and all around their feet are young children

If you look closely and you know Liberty State Park, you can see the lower part of the Statue of Liberty behind us. If you look closely and you know my family, you can see my mother among the six women holding babies. There's a chunky monkey in her arms, a big-cheeked drool machine wearing a lacy bonnet and, for some reason, only a cloth diaper. My mom is eighties-tastic in a navy sundress, gold beads, hoop earrings, and point-toe espadrilles. Her hair has got to be permed. I've never seen it curly like that.

What I like most about this picture—and, I think, what I hate, too

—is the look on my mom's face. Her head is tilted slightly in a dreamy fashion, showing off her swan neck and her elegant collarbones. Her lips, as red as ever, are curled into a little smile, as if she has a secret. A good secret. I'm sitting up straight like a young meerkat, smiling, I think—though I can't tell for sure. Her arms are wrapped snugly around me.

The woman to my mom's left, Isa Arnoldi's mother, looks similarly pleased. Or maybe proud. It's a look that I don't understand, but she's smiling. She's wearing a pale pink dress, a cross necklace baby Isa is pulling on, and a straw hat with a dark ribbon around the juncture between crown and brim. I can't see her feet to know what vintage shoes she's wearing, because Isa's older brother Gabe is sitting on them. His face is parallel with the sky, as if he's looking at a bird or plane above us.

To my mom's right is a smaller woman, also dark-haired, though her hair is shorter. She's not looking at the camera, but at the baby in her arms, who is a boy. He's wearing a blue outfit, with the mother in a white dress. I don't know her name. When I asked my mom and dad, they said they didn't either.

"Someone at the charity picnic that day."

The other four babies are my friends Dani, Max, Loren, and Jace. We've all known each other since we were in diapers. Our parents have sat on the board of the Most Holy Redeemer Catholic charity since before we were born.

The charity is for bragging and one-upmanship, and also for tax breaks. Now there is no summer picnic, only Christmas dinner at The Beekman, and an Easter egg hunt, although everyone in this picture is too old to hunt for eggs now.

At the lunch and hunt this year, held indoors at Gotham Hall, Dani and Max got drunk and kissed in a bathroom, and Isa offered me a cigarette on one of the balconies. I hate the smell and taste, so I declined, but I stuck by her as she smoked.

I look at my mother's buoyant smile one last time before setting the frame back down and stepping over to the tall window behind my father's desk. Objectively, I know that it's a stunning view of the Hudson. It has a stunning price tag attached, and it's only one of the homes my parents own.

Despite myself, I step back to the picture and look again. This time, I find my father. He's near the back, standing beside Isa's dad. I look from his face to Mr. Arnoldi's a few times, searching both their features. Is there any resemblance? I can't see Roberto Arnoldi well enough to know. Does it matter if they actually resemble? My dad speaks Italian. My *Irish* father speaks fluent Italian and he...well, I think he threatened someone.

My eyes well as I smile at his smile in this photo. It looks so real. It's a smile I haven't seen in years, and I can't understand that even when I try. Which is why I keep coming back to this snapshot—and a few others, which are tucked into my baby book in my room. Years ago, my father used to spend time with Isa's regularly. The men in this photo were his friends. And now they aren't. Years ago, my father was an attorney for Isa's, and now he isn't.

A few years ago, something changed. And then that one time I asked about Mr. Arnoldi, my mother told me not to again.

"Ever?" I'd pressed, being a pest.

"Not around your father," she'd said.

Sometime shortly after, Becca started to decline, and Mom told me my father was dealing with "challenges at work." Over the months that followed, Dad was home less and less, until finally, we only saw him at dinner—if then.

It's still like that.

I don't understand. Maybe I don't need to, but the whole thing makes me sad. Both my parents seem to have their own lives, sans kids.

I look at the picture of Becca on my father's desk. It's a tiny snapshot—just her face—before I leave. I grab my backpack from the chair outside the library door and slip it on. Then I hurry down the hardwood hall, hating that I wasted even one second that I could have spent with Becca.

❦

Luca

I thought of fucking off today, but here I am—ass parked on the old, familiar F train. Jane in Pink has her usual falafel breakfast clutched against her pale pink blazer, so that's mostly what I smell as I pull out a paperback and shift against the hard plastic seat.

The train starts down the tracks, and Jane starts on her damn falafel. I don't know how she eats it standing up, but that's how she rolls. I'd put her at 50, maybe, with coppery red hair and sharp brown eyes. I admire the way she won't wear anything but pink, but I wish she'd start eating that goddamn falafel before she gets on. Every weekday, makes my stomach growl till we pull into Jay Street.

Red Hook people mostly work on this side of the bridge, but there's a few who get on C train with me at Jay and head toward Wall Street. Jane's not one of them, but still, I think she sort of knows me; I've been taking this train on school days since the start of last year.

When I slip my book into my backpack and stand up at Jay, Jane's eyes flicker to my face.

Yeah, yeah. I quirk a brow up for her, and her gaze plummets to the remains of her falafel.

Yep, that's what I thought. It's okay, Jane. Ugly ass black eye, but it'll be gone in no time.

The C is cleaner than the F train. They clean it with something that smells like lemons. The scent is strongest in the mornings and more muted when I get back on the C at Chambers after school.

I should probably stand up on the C, since it's a longer ride with more old people, but turns out I can't. I hardly ever rode a train till junior year, when I started at my new school, and I found out fast trains make me dizzy as shit.

If I sit still and focus on reading, it's a little better. Today, I've got a Stephen King book, and it does its job. I forget I'm on a train till we're approaching Fulton. Back into fiction land until Chambers, and that's my stop. I slip the book into a slot inside my backpack and keep my head down as I step off the train and start toward the street.

I can feel the looks I'm getting as I pass the crowd that's heading into the station. I tell myself it doesn't matter. A week or so, and the eye will fade from ugly purple black to greenish yellow, and it won't be such a flashing light.

I stop as soon as I get into the sunlight, set my backpack on a bench, and pull out a ball cap my pal Missanelli gave me. Dude wants me to go out for the baseball team, but I don't think that's gonna work. Not with what I've got going this summer.

Don't think about that shit right now.

I fit the ball cap onto my head. It's deep purple with twin interlocked "M"s in gold thread on the front. With the cap on and my chin tucked, I don't get as many looks. It's a sunny day, and the cap's bill casts a shadow over my eyes. Plus, shit's busy.

Chambers Street always is. Guys unloading frozen cuts of pork from delivery trucks, people hawking stuff from stuff stands, all the shop doors swinging, cool air wafting out onto the sidewalk. Lots of people walking to work, and a few people pedaling. It's early October and the leaves are just starting to turn, with streaks of gold near their tips and spots of brown creeping along rich green facades. It's a perfect fifty-seven degrees this morning, according to a digital sign above a store's awning.

I lengthen my strides as I pass a crew on scaffolding, eight arms reaching to smear putty on the outside of a brick building. A green-haired guy nods my way as he pedals by on a bike towing a portable espresso station. I've gotten my caffeine fix from him a few times, and I'm pretty sure he's around my age.

"Hey, man."

An older guy in front of me glances over his shoulder before returning to his cell phone conversation.

Most students at Manhattan Magnet aren't commuting from Brooklyn, much less Red Hook. As far as I know, it's just me making the march from Chambers Station toward Washington Market Park—which is to say I'm walking toward the Hudson.

Some days—including this one—there's a breeze off the river that blows through my shirt. I always think the sunshine streaming through these trees seems sunnier than the stuff in Red Hook. At this new school of mine, damn near anything seems possible. Even if it's not.

By the time I get to the gardens at Washington Market Park, I'm feeling all right. Beyond the thick green trees that line the sidewalk up ahead, there are some tennis courts. If I time it right as I approach them, I'll see what I've waited for all morning. It's a familiar scene now: a black Lincoln pulls up to the curb. She always hops out the back door, which is how I know she's being driven by a service.

Every day, I watch her rise to her full height…which isn't too high. I watch as she lifts her long hair over her purple leather backpack. It's long and wavy, dark but not exactly black. It has some red, I think. Not hair-dyed, but a sort of maroon shine, when the sun hits it, which it does some days as she walks toward Tribeca Bridge, some twenty feet in front of us. The covered bridge takes us over West Street and into the school.

Every day, I watch as she saunters toward the bridge, and then I watch her as she walks across it. I stay back far enough so she doesn't feel as if she's being followed and close enough so I can appreciate her ass as it bounces below the backpack, usually clad in colored jeans or leggings, sometimes hidden by an extra-long blouse.

I stay close enough that I can smell her. Not because I'm fucking weird and like to smell girls, but because she smells abnormally good. Like what I think gold would smell like if it were a scent: pure and clean, with a hint of something like vanilla. It's probably some Bergdorf Goodman bullshit, but damn, it smells so fucking good.

Even after the bridge leads us to the school's side door and we go opposite ways, I can still smell her.

Elise O'Hara—that's her name. Kind of awkward on the cadence there. *Elise O'Hara.* Might sound better with Galante at the end. Elise Galante.

I stop under one of the trees shading my stretch of sidewalk by the park's garden, frowning at the empty tennis court and then out at the traffic.

Did I miss her? Did she come early? Or is she late?

It's kind of creepy, okay? I know. But I crouch down so I can fuck with my shoe, for just a second. I'm only going to wait here for a minute. I hate being late, and today especially, that would suck. Everyone will stare at my busted up face even if I'm at my desk early.

I toy with my new Jordans. My dad owns a shoe store. Usually he sells more formal shit, but I can get pretty much whatever for the vendor's price. I'm messing with the laces when the black car parks beside the sidewalk.

Almost before the wheels stop rolling, the rear door opens and she's out. Damn, she's like a rocket today. Doesn't even stop to pull that waterfall of hair out of her backpack straps.

She walks like she's pissed or in a bigtime hurry. I check my watch, but we're not really late. Maybe on the later side of on-time.

Black pants today. From twenty feet behind her, I can't see the stitching well enough to know if they're leggings or this new girl pants thing—"jeggings"—but goddamn with that ass.

I cast my eyes down to the sidewalk, but it doesn't last. Just a second later, my gaze jumps back up her curvy form. This time, my eyes rest on her slim shoulders, the sway of her arms. I can tell she's clutching something half a second before it hits the ground and bounces toward me.

A stuffed animal?

I scoop it up, smiling at its big bear eyes and happy panda smile—and then she's on me. I get a whiff of her—the clean, rich smell—before she snatches the thing from my hand and whirls away, her long hair brushing my cheek as she spins.

She lowers her head, draws her shoulders in, and dashes toward the bridge that's just a little up ahead of us—the one that arches over West Street and connects to the side of our school building. As she runs, I hear a clacking sound I realize is her boots. She's in a fucking run to get away from me.

I wonder if she'll stop when she gets to the side door of the school, or at least slow down so I can ask if she's okay. It doesn't happen. By the time I make it into the school, she's lost in the crowd.

I wonder about her all damn morning. During homeroom when my dickhead teacher, Dr. Brown, asks what happened to my eye—like it's his business. My pal Loren Missanelli snickers and whisper-hisses, "Did you run into a fence, Galante?"

"Why a fence?" I throw him a *what-the-fuck* look.

He shrugs. "Why not?"

"Fucking random, man." I shake my head and slip into thinking about her while everyone around me works on homework.

In first period it's the same song, second verse. My buds Liam and Max give me shit about the black eye, and this girl we chill with, Maddie, tries to touch it. When I lean away, she sits on my lap, wraps her arms around my neck, and leans in so her tits are pressed against my chest. I wrap my arm around her back, prepared to move her off me, and that's the moment our calc instructor, Dr. Sweedish, steps into the room.

"Mr. Galante," she chirps. "Kindly relieve yourself of Miss Sinclair and come to my desk."

Fuck.

Sweedish is a young, blonde hottie, but she's strict as hell. Stricter than she has to be, just to let us know she has a PhD and means business. When I get to her desk, her gaze flies up and down me as her pink lips flatten.

"We need a new desk for LaShaun Kinsey, your classmate whose desk is squeaking in a way that I find *most* displeasing. I'll let you walk to the athletic wing and fetch one from the supply closet. Closet C. Whatever you do," she adds primly, "don't hit yourself again in the eye. That looks awful."

I let out a breath and nod. "Okay, Dr. Sweedish."

"Oh, and from this point forward," she calls after me, "keep your hands and your body to yourself, or you'll be written up."

I stop for a second in the hall and rub my temple. Fuck, my eye is throbbing. Hell of a time to get asked to haul a desk halfway across the school. But I know it's my fault, sort of. Last week, Sweedish passed me in the hall when Lana Greene had her arms around my neck. Maybe around my waist; I don't remember. Lana's always like that, and it doesn't mean a thing to her. But I guess Sweedish thinks I'm—what? Threatening the chastity of the student body? Like there is any.

I shake my head as I start walking. I'm probably the only guy in this school who isn't prowling for pussy. Not for lack of wanting. Just —there are reasons.

Of course, now that I'm thinking of pussy, those reasons seems less convincing. Especially when I start thinking of her again: Elise O'Hara. She was so damn fast this morning, I didn't really even get a chance to enjoy the view. Not even her face, which was turned toward me and away so quickly, I'm not even sure it happened.

I do remember the stuffed bear, though.

Maybe she was embarrassed? I haven't had a stuffed animal since like first grade.

I close my black eye about halfway to the athletic wing because the sunlight streaming through the horizontal windows hurts. Everything looks weird with only one eye.

Thinking about the black eye gets me thinking about last night, and that makes me feel weird and sort of drifty. I don't like the drifty feeling. And so, again, I try to think about Elise O'Hara. Elise and her stuffed bear.

I think about the first time I ever saw her, on my first day at MM—the first day of last year, my junior year. She was wearing a dress and some kind of strappy sandals, walking right in front of me as I headed to the office to check in. And I could smell her. It's so fucking weird. So *animal*. But that's what caught my attention, and then her body did, and later I found out her name when we had history together.

I didn't see her much in that class because as a "G," I was at the front of a row of desks, and as an "O," she was always behind me. But I could hear her when she answered questions.

Thinking of that sultry voice—something hits me. This summer, when I was catering a thing, I followed this girl up some stairs, into a bedroom—and it was her. Holy shit, that was Elise O'Hara. I stop mid-stride, stunned at the realization.

It makes sense, though. I rub my forehead, remembering how good this girl smelled at the wedding reception. She was beautiful and smart...like I remember I felt like I should protect her, but also, I could tell she wasn't weak. I close my eyes, imagining her mouth and cheeks as she stood by those bookshelves. It was *her*.

I was right behind her, kneeling behind a wooden board thing, when I heard some Mafioso give my dad a stern warning. My dad who shouldn't have been there at all.

I pack that part away and replay how I felt with her back pressed to my chest. Then I shake my head. All this shit is pretty weird. I've never thought about anybody this much, especially some girl I don't really know.

I try to push her out of my head, and to help, I look for colors, like my old school told us to do. Check if there is any blue, or green, or red, or gray around, and find all of that color. It helps calm you down.

I'm feeling better as I swing a left into the hall that leads to the athletic wing. I've still got Elise on my mind, but sort of in the background.

Until I hear her voice.

Sheesh. I must not be— No. There it is again. That *is* her voice.

I stop to figure out where it's coming from.

The hall is empty. I sweep my gaze down the dark purple tile, over the rows of gold athletic lockers. Mine's not on this hall because of when I transferred in, but I don't give a shit about what kind of locker I have.

"I said no, Bruce!"

Every atom in my body freezes as my eyes fix on the right side of the hall, where there's a girls' bathroom. I hear deep, male laughter. It's the jeering kind, I realize as I step a little closer. "Just offering to help, since you helped me."

"And me," another male voice says.

I double check the restroom's sign: *Girls.*

"I *didn't* help you, no I didn't. You two copied my test." There's a little breathless pause, and then her voice comes louder, harder. "Which, by the way, makes *no* sense because you'll have to learn calculus at some point, but it's also completely unfair to other people in the class who are struggling. Dr. Birkenmeyer scales our grades. You're making other people's grades worse when you get high scores like I do."

Someone chuckles. "So then you're part of the problem, too, Elise. Isn't that how it works?"

"Well, no. Because *I'm* not cheating."

"Not cheating, but sneaking around. What class are you skipping, O'Hara?"

"I don't have a class." She sighs, a little huff. "I'm an aide this period. For the assistant principal."

"Does she know you're in here?"

"No, but I'm sure she'd care much more that you two are."

"We've got track. Coach Burns doesn't give a shit."

"This is the ladies' room. You two should go."

I step closer to the door as one guy chuckles. "What, you don't like us in here? We both know you're wet for Rainer."

"Ewww, gross," she says. "You two need to leave. Like right now. Really." Her voice seems a pitch too high on that word.

"Or what?" I can fucking *hear* that asswipe leering.

And suddenly, I'm shoving through the bathroom door. I spot Elise between two porcelain sinks, holding that stuffed panda she dropped earlier this morning.

Bill Rainer and some prick I don't know are right up on her, blocking her exit. Elise's eyes are wide, her pretty mouth a small, alarmed "o." Her eyes flare wider when her gaze collides with mine.

"Elise..." I say her name like we're old friends as I stride toward her. I knock Rainer's shoulder with mine, and the fucker has the sense to step aside.

"Hey." My voice is soft—a cue. Our gazes lock again before I wrap a careful arm around her lower back. "Hey, E. Everything okay in here?"

I can see her puzzling things out. Then her eyes meet mine again, and her lips flatten. For just a second, she looks wounded, like a girl who's asking for help. Then her whole face hardens, and she throws a glare over my shoulder.

"Rainer and Friedrich were just leaving, weren't you?"

"Yeah," Rainer says, already stepping back—but his dumb fuck friend wants to glare.

"Maybe how about staying the fuck away from someone else's girl," I say as I move my arm from behind Elise and take a step toward the two asswipes. Neither is especially threatening, but there are two of them. "What do you think?"

I get a shot of perverse satisfaction as their faces twist in fear. Rainer takes two more steps back and wheels around to go. Dumb fuck sputters for a second and then beats feet. Their footsteps echo off the mustard yellow tile.

*

Elise

Luca Galante.

I don't know him, but I know his name. I have since last year, when I realized I see him every morning—or I *could*, if I were willing to look behind me after getting out of Mercer's car—which, as it happens, I'm not.

Still, I feel him on my heels, hear his heavy footsteps each day as we cross the covered bridge that stretches over West Street. I'm pretty sure he watches me. It's only fair. In one of my classes last year, he sat a few seats in front of me; I passed the time admiring his broad back and shoulders. Really all of him. Because he's beautiful.

Luca Galante. I've always thought it sounded like a villain's name. But he's the hero of my story today.

He's still standing close enough to make my heart pound. I don't want him knowing that, so I narrow my eyes as I look at him. "How did you know?"

"Those fucks were so loud I heard them out in the hall. Rainer is a piece of shit."

I nod. It's harsh, but it's accurate. Rainer and I went to the same elementary school. When we were in fourth grade, he found a nest of baby birds that fell out of a tree at recess. He stepped on it.

"He plays football, but I think he's quitting," Luca tells me. "Doesn't like to run." He gives a little shake of his head, as if football is all about running and Rainer is the biggest dumbass.

Maybe football does entail a lot of running. I don't really know.

I nod, since my voice seems to be gone.

"Elise O'Hara, right?" he asks.

"You should know if you're my boyfriend."

He gives me a smirky grin. "What's *my* name?"

"Luca Galante."

His thick, dark brows lift, making his gemstone blue eyes seem even bluer. Then he winces—probably because of that black eye he has.

"How do you know?" I can tell he's teasing, but I don't tease back. I guess my brain can't switch gears that fast.

"We had a class, you know." My voice is too high.

"Yeah?" A little smile twists his mouth. "Which one?"

"You know which one."

"What makes you think I do?" Again, the grinning. He has a radiant smile. I knew he was gorgeous, but up close, he's kind of stupid hot.

"I *know* you know." I give a calculated eyeroll. "You walk behind me every morning going into school. You must live around here."

I'm impressed when he shrugs off my accusation. "You think so?"

"Well, you're walking. And you don't look sweaty, like you've walked a thousand blocks." Crap—and now he knows I have, in fact, graced him with a few glances.

He smirks and tilts his head, like he's trying to read my face but he can't. I smirk back.

"So you're watching me, huh?" God, he's got a cocky smile.

"You must be joking," I scoff.

"Why?"

"You've been my shadow every morning for months now."

He shakes his head. "I can't help it we have the same route."

"Yeah right."

He shrugs. "All I know is, you check to see if I'm sweaty."

I narrow my eyes at him again. "Only when you grab my things."

His gaze falls to the bear in my hands, and his features soften. "Your beary best friend."

For some reason, that makes me laugh, even as I clutch my sister's dirty bear to my chest. But now I have tears welling in my eyes, and his face twists in alarm. "Fuck. I'm sorry. I didn't—I, uh, honestly don't know what I did, but I'm sorry."

I clutch Pandy and wipe my eyes with my free hand. Then I turn around and fiddle with the sink's knob, refusing to look at myself in the mirror, or at him as more tears drip down my cheeks.

"Hey…" His voice is soft and raspy. I can feel the heat of him beside me, which makes chills bloom on my skin. "What's the matter?" When I don't take the bait, he murmurs, "You can tell me."

I laugh. It's a hiccup sound, but there's a harsh edge to it. "Doesn't matter."

"Of course it does. I mean, what if a photographer from *The Talon* is outside? How am I going to play your boyfriend if I don't know the whole story?"

I want to say "you wouldn't understand," but it sounds cheesy— even though it's absolutely true. This guy would never understand my problems. Almost no one would.

Instead I say, "You're not my boyfriend."

"I'm not?" He feigns surprise. "What a way to tell me."

I try not to roll my eyes, but fail. He grins a bit. "Okay, so maybe I'm not your boyfriend. But…I could be your friend."

It's the last thing I expect him to say. For a long moment, I can't get my throat to work. But my tear ducts seem to be operating at max efficiency.

"Ahh, hell." His hand is on my back now, rubbing circles, and it's so gentle. "We don't have to be friends. Being friends can be…too much. We can just be bathroom buddies."

That almost makes me smile. I lift my head and our eyes lock in the mirror; his lips twitch at one corner.

"What do you think?" he asks.

"Do you have a girlfriend?" It's not what's supposed to come out of my mouth. I watch as a grin lights his face. Then I watch him shut it down.

"No."

By the time I turn away from the mirror to fully face him, his face is solemn. And he's taken a small step back. "Do you?"

"No." I sniff.

"A boyfriend?"

I wipe my eyes—mostly so I don't have to look at his face as I say, "Not right now."

"That's surprising."

"No it's not." I frown at him as my heartbeat quickens.

"It is."

"You don't know me. Maybe I'm a megabitch."

"A megabitch?" He almost smiles. "Hmmm... I dunno. I'm not getting megabitch vibes."

"Maybe you're bad at vibes."

"Oh, I'm not." He does smile this time. "I'm good at vibes."

I hold his gaze, somehow sure just from his eyes that this guy is, in fact, good at vibes. I arch my right eyebrow and try for a skeptical tone. "What makes you so sure?"

He holds his hands up. "Just trust me. I know people, and when I look at you, I don't see megabitch."

I want to ask what does he see, but I don't dare. He looks at Pandy. "Were you washing him—or her?"

"Him," I whisper. I swallow again and nod slowly. "Yes. It's my sister's."

"Is he on a field trip?"

I nod, smiling slightly. My smile falters because I know Becca's missing him. One of her caretakers tried to throw Pandy away this morning. Becca's been sick with a GI bug she can't shake—it's put her in the hospital two times in the last six weeks—and this morning, she threw up on him.

The nurse, one of the newer ones Mom hired a few months back, doesn't know my sister yet. She doesn't care about my sister. When I told her she wasn't allowed to get rid of Pandy, she called my mom, who told her she could do whatever she thought was best.

So I grabbed Pandy. I've gotta find some way to sanitize him so my mom won't make a big fuss when I bring him back.

"My sister is…sick," I offer in a voice that's just above a whisper. "Pandy is dirty. So I need to clean him."

I wait for the look of confusion on his face—or even worse, boredom. But he looks rapt, his eyes fixed on mine…so I keep going.

"One of her nurses tried to throw him out. But Bec's had Pandy since she was born. And she…is really attached to him."

Which matters a lot, because my sister is dying. I wipe more tears from my cheeks, and he holds out a hand—I guess for Pandy. He looks down at the bear: ragged from years of love and damp from my attempt to clean him.

"Have you thought about dry cleaning?"

"No," I whisper. I don't think my mom would even be willing to schedule a dry cleaning pickup. My mom doesn't care, I guess. She doesn't care about Bec anymore. I don't understand why, but then I've never understood my mother. No, that's not true, I correct myself. I *do* understand. Now that Bec is having more seizures, Mom is disconnecting one step at a time. And it's grotesque and awful. She keeps saying Bec was never meant to be with us this long, as if it's just… that time. As if it's fine to let her go.

I wipe more tears from my eyes and shake my head. "I don't think —" I manage.

"I could do it." He takes Pandy from me. "After school. He'd be first in line. After he's cleaned, I can take him home and freeze him. I know it sounds weird, but freezing things can kill germs. My mom… she has cancer. She's doing really well, but still takes maintenance chemo, and that means germs are bad dudes at our house."

He nods as if to reassure me that he knows about such things.

"Do you know someone? Who has a dry cleaner? Because if he gets lost…" More tears well. I wipe them quickly. "Not trying to be a beggar and a chooser—"

"My dad," he says quickly. "He's got a shoe store and a dry cleaners. Right next door to each other. I help at the dry cleaners after school. I help them close."

"Oh, which one is his?"

"It's in Red Hook." I can tell he's trying to act casual, but he's also watching me for a reaction.

I don't give him one. "So, do you like...do it yourself?"

He nods. "I could do it myself, and then take him home and drop him in the deep freeze. My dad's big on deli meat. We've got a pretty solid freezer."

"Could you...would you mind bringing him back to school tomorrow?"

"Yeah, for sure." He takes off his black hooded sweatshirt, revealing a ragged-looking Rolling Stones T-shirt. I watch as he wraps Pandy carefully in the hoodie.

"I'll be careful. I can give him back to you tomorrow morning at the tennis courts?"

I nod. "That would be great. Amazing, really." I smile, and then I'm beaming. I can't seem to help myself. "This really makes my day. Like...you have no idea."

He winks. "Not a problem, Elise."

I notice again that his eyes is swollen. I almost ask him about it, but he asks, "So you good now? You feel good walking back to your class?"

"Yes." I nod. "Thank you."

He gives me another strange look...like a smile, but with only his eyes. And he says, "You don't need to."

I watch him walk down the hall for a long time before I turn back toward the office. And I think about him for the rest of the day.

CHAPTER TWO

Luca

The part about the dry cleaners was a lie. I don't know why I told her that shit. Actually, I do: because I wanted to make her happy. I wanted her to let me take the bear. So I acted like my dad owns Diamond's place, like it's no big deal for me to take care of it.

When I get to Red Hook at 5:30, I swing by The Shoe Store, check in with Dad, then head toward Diamond's Dry Cleaners.

Diamond—Tony Diamond—is a prick. When I was a kid, I knew him as Alesso's big brother. Tony is ten years older than us, so at one point, we thought he hung the moon.

Incorrect.

Tony is an asshole *and* a loose cannon. Now that Tony does Roberto Arnoldi's bidding, every interaction with him carries some risk. Ever since things went bad between Roberto and my dad—and it was Dad's fault—we've been in a vulnerable position. With the store. With the debt. Tony knows all that shit, and sometimes he likes to try to play enforcer. I'm biting on the inside of my cheek as I approach the cleaners, one of dozens of storefronts along Van Brunt Street.

With any luck, Diamond will be playing Xbox above Matt Russo's pawn shop on the next block down, and I can get help from one of the assistant managers. They're all closer to my age than his, all from the neighborhood. Most of them are female, so that doesn't hurt.

ELLA JAMES

The red and white striped "Diamond's" awning looks dull in the afternoon light. It's cloudy today, probably going to rain later. I pass by Lisa Faye's, the pizza place, and wince at the smell. I'm starving. Then I catch a glimpse of Tony's fat ass through the glass door of Diamond's, and my stomach does a quick flip.

That's my luck, man. Tony's never here. It only takes me a second to decide to hoof it to the next dry cleaners down—it's pragmatic to avoid him, even if it's a walk. But just then Tony straightens up and looks right through the glass door at me like he heard my fucking thoughts.

He grins like a hyena, and before I can beat it, he's pushing the door open, and I'm hit with his weird, Diamond schtick.

"Howya doing, Bowsie Bow?" He lunges onto the sidewalk toward me, his big hand clasping my shoulder too hard, like we're long lost friends and he can't help himself. Except, of course, we're something very different and I'm sure he knows I fucking hate it.

"Diamond." I give him a nod, trying to keep from gritting my teeth at the sensation of his fingertips biting into my shoulder. "What's up?"

"You tell me," he says. "Still going to that rich boy school?"

I nod, my lips pressed flat. Tony likes to poke you where he thinks it hurts. When we were kids, he wasn't like this, but his father was. When old man Diamond kicked it, Alesso and I were in sixth grade; Tony was twenty-two and really into gaming. He wanted to get a job making the CG part of video games, but Mrs. Diamond pushed him to take over the store. That's how he got into what he's into these days.

"They treating you right?" he asks me. "You still got that Bowser T-shirt?"

He gives my shoulder another slight shake before letting me go.

"Grew out of it," I say calmly. Ever since this summer, he's been asking me about that Super Mario shirt. It's weird because the shirt is years and years old. I've grown a foot since I wore it, and I think Diamond knows that. I have to assume he's just making sure I know the pecking order.

"Too bad. That was a cool shirt."

"Yeah, love some Bowser."

He looks down at what I'm holding. "Whacha got there?"

There's a moment where I have a choice. I could try to extricate myself from this shit with him, but I don't—because I know Diamond. Dude is fucking weird now. If I try to keep the bear away from him, I think he'll grab it and look for himself. Better in the end to be direct.

"I've got a bear to dry clean."

I unwrap the shirt, show him the panda.

He laughs, but it's not a happy sound. "What the fuck?"

"My girlfriend's."

I'm shocked that I said it, but I keep my face on lockdown.

"That right?"

"Yeah."

He takes the bear from me, and I let him. "He does look dirty."

"I need it cleaned today. So I can get it back to her. It's actually her sister's, and her sister's sick."

"Oh, so like…a little kid."

"Yep." I don't know how old her sister actually is. I forgot to ask..

"So you expect some charity?"

"What?"

His bushy eyebrows waggle. "Gonna pay me?"

"I can pay."

"Nah, you're good for it." He smirks. "Or maybe I'll take it outta your old man this month, yeah? He's still got that debt."

"I think you'll do what you want to."

Our eyes catch, and his are hard. I make mine harder. For the longest moment, he holds my gaze. I know the script here: It's my role to back down. When I don't, he laughs. "You've got some weird eyes, Bowsie."

Yeah, yeah. Blue eyes. Super crazy shit. Clean the damn bear.

"I'll clean the bear for you." He pulls the glass door open and tosses the panda toward Zoe, one of the assistant managers. Then he turns to me with a hard grin. "I've got something you can do for me, too."

☙

Twelve and a half hours later, Tony's girlfriend LeighAnn slams the brakes on her Porsche so hard the tires squeal, and I swing the passenger door open and hop out.

Fuck!

I run like the wind and lunge into the train car just before the doors shut. Jane in Pink has her head bowed; she's chewing. She lifts her chin, and her eyes swing to my face. I swipe a hand back through my hair, realizing I don't have my backpack.

Fuck!

I give her falafel a long, hungry look, then exhale and sit down. What I do have is a clean bear wrapped in my sweatshirt from yesterday. I give the bear a stupid little grin and then I flex my legs. Same boxers, same jeans, same shoes from yesterday, but I've got on a fresh shirt.

Diamond's favor involved getting dye off stolen Benjis. I spent the entire night rubbing my hands raw on some chemical-soaked sponges and ended up back at the dry cleaners. I got Pandy back, plus some undershirt someone had left in their clothes. My shirt had been stained.

Without a book to read as we ride underneath Brooklyn, I think about my brother, Soren. He answered the phone when I called last night around eight. Told me Mom and Dad were sleeping.

"You mean Dad is passed out?" I asked.

"Well, yes."

Sometimes my younger brother's not so good at subtext, but he knew what I was thinking.

"Everything is fine here, Luca."

I look down at the bear again, sending up a prayer to the patron saint of misunderstood sixth graders. My little bro is super smart, but he's got what my mom calls *peculiarities*. He gets these mood swings sometimes. If he's pissed off enough, he'll just bolt from school. For some reason, Dad's been more tolerant of that stuff lately. He even lets Soren come to the shop and help him with stocking and sweeping.

I tell myself they had an okay night despite my absence, and everyone will have an okay day today. Diamond wouldn't approach my dad for money on behalf of the Arnoldis. Not now that he's hitting me up for these "favors"—and maybe not at all.

I didn't get a second of shut-eye last night, so I'm yawning by the time I have to transfer from the F to the C. There I fall asleep, waking with the train's vibrations and the mechanized voice over the speaker system as we pull into Chambers. I smirk, realizing I'm clutching Pandy to my chest like he's mine.

My girlfriend. I snort as I step off the train, but I head toward the tennis courts with a bounce in my stride. I end up arriving early, and I sit under one of the trees and watch the curb. But Elise never shows.

I'm ten minutes late to homeroom.

❧

Elise

I find him at the center of the track at lunchtime. I'm not sure how, but when I couldn't find him in the cafeteria, I knew he would be here.

I can tell before I'm even close—he's sleeping. He's got Pandy in the crook of one arm; his other rests palm up in the grass. His long legs, clad in black jeans, are relaxed, his dark sneakers tilted slightly outward in sleep. His cheek rests against his shoulder.

He looks like the patron saint of high school athletes. Something about his messy black hair and those gemstone blue eyes, the hard jawline and strong nose...that creamy skin. He's always stood out to me. His name sounds Italian, but I think he looks Irish.

I stand over him with my arms folded, wondering which of my besties squealed. Not that many people know I run at lunch on Thursdays.

I look from him to myself. I'm not wearing running clothes because today I'd planned to find him in the lunchroom. I've got on a comfy pair of skinny jeans, my favorite ankle boots, and a flowy, paisley scarf-necked blouse. I dressed carefully for him before the morning went to shit.

Wake up, I tell him—with the powers of my mind.

His lashes flutter, and I can't help grinning.

43

Sit up, Galante. Your eye still looks horrific, and it makes you even more attractive. That should be a crime.

He opens his eyes. A gentle smile flirts with the corners of his lips, and then he's doing what I asked. He pushes up on one elbow, clutching Pandy in the corner of his other arm.

I laugh. "You brought him."

He smiles. "I did."

I sink down into the grass beside him, sitting cross-legged, and he passes me the bear.

I thumb one of Pandy's ears. "Wow, this is crazy. He looks almost new again." His white spots look beige now instead of faintly brown.

My mother and I had an ugly fight this morning about Pandy and a lot more. But I won. I'm bringing Pandy home, and she said Becca could keep him.

I lay the bear on his back in the grass and trace my fingertip over his fine hairs. I feel Luca's eyes on me, can sense that he's still lying partway down, which feels too intimate. My neck and cheeks burn from the proximity.

As if he can hear my thoughts, he sits fully up, crossing his legs and leaning over a little, tracing Pandy's fur like I am.

"How old is your sister?"

My throat knots, so tight and painful that I don't know how I'll get words through. Somehow, I say, "Twelve."

"Yeah? I've got a brother who's twelve."

"Really?" I look up, and his gaze holds mine, his lips quirking in a small approximation of a smile. His eye today is shades of deep blue-purple, like petals of a poison flower. As we look at each other, I notice it's slightly squinted. "Does it hurt?" I whisper.

"Nah."

He tries to open the eye wider, but his mouth tightens, so I can tell he's lying. For a heartbeat, I think I'll run my fingers softly over his cheekbone… I don't know why, but I feel like this when I'm near him—this guy I hardly know.

"How'd it happen?" My throat tightens on those words, so they're soft and kind of raspy.

He smiles again, but this time it's a thin line. "It's not important."

"I think it's important."

"But it isn't."

I narrow my eyes slightly. "What if it's important to me?"

"It isn't."

I frown. "How do you know?"

"Because I know things." He's still smiling, only with the corners of his mouth. His eyes are somber.

"You don't know me."

"No?" he murmurs.

"Not even a little bit."

He lies back again, folding his arms behind his head. He's wearing a thin, white T-shirt, so I can see his biceps and his forearms in great detail. I can see the blueish veins beneath his soft skin. He looks like Michelangelo's carved marble.

If this were a snapshot, I would think he's beautiful—a study in ruined beauty, maybe, with his eye the way it is. But I'm living this moment. I can feel things swimming in the air between us. His eyes shut, and I think *he needs to sleep.*

"Are you a nice guy?" I ask him, impulsively. "Or an asshole?"

His lips curve—and this time, the smile is decadent.

"That's a game we play, my friends and I—nice guy or asshole. My friend Sheree thinks you're an asshole. I think it's too hard to tell." I smile, even though my heart is beating so wildly that I feel like I might die right here beside him.

He opens his eyes, peering at me with a notch between his brows. "You think I'll be honest?"

I look down at my nails. "People almost never are. One time I read about something called radical honesty. It was in a magazine of my dad's, and this man, he tried to tell everybody the whole truth, all the time."

"That sounds...terrible."

I nod. "And interaction is performative by nature, so I think it's never possible to be completely honest. There's always the echo of the other person influencing your 'truth.' Even if they're like you are right now—just lying there. Your face or mannerisms will give feedback to what I'm saying. And I'll feel compelled to bend my truth to you."

I stop to grab a quick breath, my face burning as I realize I'm rambling.

"Um, so anyway, I don't think you'll be honest," I manage. "But

I'm asking so I'll get a chance to try to read you. If you don't ask at all, then you can be sure you'll never know."

I'm so flummoxed, I'm sweating. Under my bra, along my hairline. If my skin were paler, I'd be sporting a bright red blush. But it isn't, and I'm grateful for that.

"Nice guy or asshole." He repeats it slowly, like he's tasting every word. "Lots of polarity there." And now he's smirking. *Smirking*, and he's so *right here* that it makes me feel ill.

"You could do percentages."

"Oh, like ninety percent asshole, ten percent good guy?" He grins, like it's the funniest thing he's ever heard.

I wonder if I'm blushing hard enough now for it to show. "Yes. So..." I blink quickly, urging him to answer.

He laughs. "I don't know. You said you don't expect me to be honest, but I feel some pressure to be at least sort of honest."

His eyes on my eyes, pulling my soul up into my throat, where it gets stuck so I can't breathe. I smile and grab a tiny breath. When I was little, my mom had a parakeet. One time I held it, and its little heart beat just like mine is beating right now. "Try to be as honest as you can."

He sits up again, biting the inside of his cheek and then his lower lip. He runs a hand back into his hair. Tired eyes, his dreamy smile—a snapshot that I save in my head.

"I'd say at least sixty percent asshole. Maybe more like seventy." His teeth on his lip again, that luscious lower lip. His brows are thoughtful. "Maybe sixty-five. No...that puts the good at thirty-five percent. But maybe thirty-five is right. I think thirty's not enough, maybe. I'm more like thirty-five percent good guy."

"I'd like it to be sixty-forty, at least," he tells me. "But I think it's really sixty-five bad guy/thirty-five good guy."

"Why is that?"

"Why...what?" He blinks, and I can feel his whole attention on me, like an anvil I'd love to be crushed by.

"Why are those your numbers?"

He smiles, fleeting. "I don't know. I'm not sure it's a choice. What do you think?"

"I say of course it's a choice."

"Is it, though?" He's frowning again.

"We do have free will. I mean, at least somewhat," I offer. "Or our illusion of free will is compelling enough that I think we're safe to call it that."

"Is it?"

"What?"

"Compelling?"

"I think so."

"So we choose who we are. Is that it?" He tilts his head, and now he's all professor—but a nice professor. One who cares about your answers, one who wants to understand you. There's this moment where he seems a thousand years older than me. Which makes no sense because if any one of us is so old, it's me...isn't it? Is he lying awake at night as I am, thinking of ways to tell his dying loved one to contact him from the stars? My sister probably won't be here by winter, and it's made me feel at least nine hundred years old. My heart weighs twelve tons all the time, and there is nothing I can do to change that.

"Maybe we don't choose. But...I think we do—somewhat." My voice wobbles. I swallow. "We don't get to decide everything. Maybe not even a lot of things. But the parts we get to decide, those are the parts that are important. And so if I get to choose, I want to be a certain kind of person."

"What kind?" His eyes tell me I can fall in if I want to.

"A good one. Someone who does the right thing, even if it's hard." I think of my mom pulling so far back from Becca. "Maybe especially if it's hard. I think it matters even more then."

There are tears in my eyes again, turning all this sunlight into prisms. I blink and a tear falls down my cheek, but I'm not really embarrassed. Maybe because none of this feels quite real.

"I don't need to talk about it," I say, swallowing again because my throat is aching.

I wipe my face as he says, "Okay." His face is gentle...like an angel.

He gets to his feet and holds out a hand, and I take it, letting him pull me up. For a heartbeat, he just looks at me—assessing. His hand squeezes mine.

Then he checks his watch and glances back at my face. "So you don't—need to. But I need to walk around. To wake up. I didn't get a lot of sleep last night, and I can't stay awake today. Why don't we walk, and you can hold my hand. I wear contacts, but I lost one. This one." He gestures to his black eye. "Fell out in first period. And now I'm dizzy." His smile is crooked, and *I'm* dizzy. "You don't need to talk. I need to walk. But you *could* talk, while we're walking."

I say nothing as we walk through the grassy field toward the orange-red track around it. I feel nothing. I'm a robot, not a human, my chest locked behind a plate of metal, every part of me attached with screws. I breathe deeply a few times, and his big hand shifts around mine, like he's giving me a hand hug.

"Did you really lose a contact?" I rasp.

"Yep."

"I don't need to talk." I blow a breath out. "I have therapists for that."

"Oh yeah?" Again, his fingers move around mine. I feel his thumb stroking my hand, and this time my heart stops and sinks a little.

"Yes," I rasp. "My family is…a mess. My dad is an attorney, and he's represented doctors over the years. So of course we see a therapist from his client's clinic. It's on Church Street. They have ginormous windows and fake plants. I consider that suspicious, don't you? All that sunlight and they chose fake plants? Which still have to be dusted—leaf by leaf, I would think, so they aren't *no* maintenance. Better to water something that's alive. So anyway…" My voice wobbles again. I look at our feet, walking in sync. As if we know each other.

"It's sort of weird to hold your hand," I whisper. I can feel my heartbeat in my temples, and my throat is so tight it feels raw. It's weird, and it feels dangerous.

"Bad weird? Or just…okay weird?"

"I don't know yet." I manage a laugh. "We might need to keep walking."

There it is—the easy smile from him. The blue eyes, pale but warm. They're on me so long my face burns. His arm bumps mine, and his long fingers stroke my shaky ones.

"I've been watching you since last year. You were right," he says. I would climb inside that husky voice if I could. Let it take me under.

"I could feel your stalking," I tease. "Did you feel mine in our class last year?"

He laughs. "No. Was it...there to be felt?"

"Well, you were in front of me. And I was always bored."

"Oh, so it's like that. When you're bored..."

His eyes close. His black hair is fanning slightly in a breeze that blows over the field between our track and the river.

"I was always bored."

"You shouldn't tell me that." He smiles slowly, and his eyes are on me—making me warm.

"Why not?"

"Because," he says. "I like it too much."

His face takes on a dreamy look, the angel look. It's a look that says the whole world hurts him, but he likes it.

Or maybe that's how I feel, holding hands with this strange boy as we march slowly around the school track, the river birds cawing and our blood whooshing through our veins, and we're alive—for who knows how long—but for this moment bound together by...confessions.

"Secrets are the currency of intimacy," I offer to him. "I read that once."

He gives me a somber, knowing sort of smile.

"My sister is dying," I say. It's like jumping off a bridge. My heart is caught behind my collar bones, my aching eyes half shut.

He lets a breath out, silent. Then he stops and pulls me into his arms, nearly crushing me against him.

I press my cheek against his shoulder, and my heart is beating hard and fast and taunting. "I'm sorry," he says, and I can tell he means it.

"It's okay." I'm on the verge of crying, so we both know I'm a liar. His hand comes to my back, and he starts rubbing. I close my eyes and take deep breaths, trying to get a grip. When I do, I notice he's pulled me close.

"You make a good boyfriend," I choke-laugh.

"You can rent me if you want to. If you need a stand-in."

I pull away, so I can see his face when I look up. I'm surprised at how somber it is.

"My sister always used to want to meet my boyfriend," I whisper.

He blinks, and I clarify. "I haven't had a serious one. Now that she's sicker, my dad went insane—like turbo controlling—and he won't let me date or go out really. Maybe I could take a picture of you for her. Would you mind that?" Now I'm pretty sure I might be blushing.

His hand on my shoulder feels heavy and warm.

"No." He blinks. "You can."

My stomach twists. He's got a poker face. Probably because he thinks I'm insane.

"Never mind." I try to laugh it off. "That's crazy."

"No, let's do it. You can take a picture of me. Do you have a camera?"

I assess his face, relieved to find he seems sincere. "I think you're at least sixty percent good guy, for what it's worth."

That brings a quick grin to his face. For once, he looks boyish.

"I don't have a camera, but I could bring one."

"Any time." Luca steps closer to me, reaches out and twirls a strand of my hair around his finger. "Too dangerous for me to stop by your place? I'll throw off as many good guy vibes for your sister as I can." He arches a brow and points to his eye. "Might want to wait another four or five days for this to fade, though."

I frown at it. "How'd it happen?"

He grabs my hand again and starts us walking. His hand in mine is looser now, not exactly slack but almost. And...I don't think he's going to answer.

"You don't have to," I say. "Tell me."

"My dad's elbow. He tripped and went backwards while I was helping him up the stairs. He's a drunk."

I blink at the track in front of us, blindsided.

"Listen, I'm just trading secrets. He started drinking when I was in sixth grade. He went to detox, and I think that's where he got introduced to tranquilizers. He's got a pill habit, but it's not like how it sounds. Most nights he just passes out. He's harmless. Old man is old and out of shape."

His mouth moves like maybe he's trying to smirk, but his lips flatline. "Anyway," he says after we walk a few more steps, "it doesn't matter."

Yes it does. My hand squeezes his. He squeezes back before his fingers disentwine from mine.

"Secrets, right?" He's asking—like he isn't sure I'll keep his.

"Secrets," I promise.

The bell peels from the loudspeakers at the corner of the school's roof, and we both jump.

And that's how it all starts.

CHAPTER THREE

Elise

"That's your boy right there. You see him, number thirty-two?" My friend Dani points toward the football field, where a bunch of guys in purple jerseys and tight gold pants are jogging onto the grass.

"Yeah," I murmur, which is pointless. There's no way Dani can hear me, as everyone in the bleachers is cheering. My friends and I follow suit. I let my gaze touch Luca; then it falls to my feet. And as we sit back down, it flits back to Dani. Her smiling brown eyes dance over the rim of her concession stand hot cocoa. She takes a swallow and lowers the paper cup, revealing a huge grin.

I roll my eyes, and she elbows me.

"Ow." I wrap my hands around my own warm drink and try to keep my features neutral as I trace the white lines on the grass with my eyes.

Dani leans toward me. "He's *tall*. I didn't really realize."

I nod, biting the corner of my lip as our other bestie, Sheree, leans around Dani, slapping my leg.

"Oh my God, he's stretching!" Dani half shouts. Now it's my turn to elbow her.

She's still flailing around like a cracked-out Muppet when I hiss near her ear, "Dani, you are *killing* me. That's his friend Leon in front of us." I nod at the guy with dyed green dreads, sitting with a bunch of skater guys and their girls two rows below. "And look, Max and Franco are right over there."

"Sorry," she hisses. "This is your first...thing."

"It is not my first thing," I hiss back—from behind my hand. "I've had other things."

She gives me side-eye. "Girl, you won't touch that funnel cake."

I look down at the greasy delight in my lap.

"I know you, I know you love your funnel cake," Dani continues. "I also know you can't eat before piano recitals or surgery or hospital procedures." She means procedures for Becca. "You're okay before a test, before confession, before those jazz dance recitals that we used to do in fifth and sixth grade. But he's not even here sitting with us, and you won't touch your favorite food of all time."

I give her side-eye as the "welcome to Friday night football" message starts over the loudspeaker. "That's not true."

I tear a piece of yellowish cake off, pop it into my mouth, and lick the confectioner's sugar off my lips. "I'm going to eat all of this."

Spoiler: *I'm not.* Naturally, Dani is right. We've been friends since third grade, after her parents decided to pull her out of private school and she became the new kid in Mrs. Moore's class. So, she knows me well.

She rests her head on my shoulder, and I feel her cheek round out as she grins. "Sorry, goldfish."

I sigh. "You are such a beta."

Our nicknames are from sixth grade, when everyone in our friend group was fighting all the time, so I ghosted on them for a few weeks. Ree called me a goldfish in a tank of bully betas, and it stuck.

She leans around Dani now. "What am I missing? I can't hear over all this..." She waves her hands in front of her.

Dani straightens, smiling. "This shit is what we're here for, Ree. The game stuff."

Game stuff. I shake my head at that. None of us knows the first thing about football. Our school has a winning team, but Dani, Ree, and I are more into arts and crafts and other geekery. We've been knitting booties and beanies for babies on Friday nights lately. My mom helps organize the Battery Park March of Dimes Gala, and our knitted goods are going to be auctioned there next month.

Dani's boyfriend Ty does online gaming tournaments on Friday nights, and Ree is perpetually single like me. Although in her case, it's because she likes "only melanated girls with round asses, small tits, big brains, good with a pan and a spatula, likes crime shows, and no one wanting to get married till we're at least thirty." Which, in Sheree-speak, means she's a total closed door. Her mom died suddenly we were all in fifth grade, and I think Ree hasn't moved past it. Very understandably.

"Ooh, look, he's on the sidelines warming up now," she says, leaning forward with her palms on her blanket-covered knees.

I squeeze my eyes shut. Suck air in through my nose.

"Goldie is losing it," Dani says—and she sounds amused.

I blow air out my mouth and glare at both of them. "Can we please just pretend we're here to watch the whole damn team?"

A man in front of us aims a glance over his shoulder at me, and I want to die. I want to explain to my girls again that it's not like Luca Galante is my *boyfriend*. We had some random encounters, and then yesterday on the track.

Yes, I went home and hugged a pillow thinking of him last night. And this morning I told my driver, Mercer, that I didn't need a ride and walked to school so I might bump into him earlier along his trek toward the building. But I didn't. I didn't see him at all before homeroom, which was highly disappointing. I couldn't find him in the cafeteria at lunch time, and he wasn't at the track, either—at least not at first.

I decided to run—since I had skipped my normal Thursday lunchtime run to talk to him. I was maybe halfway done when I heard someone on the track behind me. I didn't turn around—in case it *was* him. And then he was there beside me, jogging in his work-out gear and sneakers, his dark hair damp, so I figured he'd come from the football practice field.

He laughed and I laughed, and for a while we ran side-by-side, stealing glances at each other. Then the bell rang, and his gaze pinned mine down as we slowed our pace. "Football game tonight? Six o'clock?"

I laughed again. "You're saying you want me to go?"

His blue eyes widened. "If you want to."

"Do I?"

He gave a raspy laugh. "I don't know, do you?"

"I'll go."

His mouth curved in a small but satisfied smile. "Try to sit in the student section—so I can find you."

Then he turned around and jogged back toward the practice fields.

I told my parents Dani and I were going to hear a youth choir perform before spending the night at her house. And...here I am. At Luca Galante's game. To watch him play football. I'm sitting in the student section so he can "find me." After the game? I'm not even sure what he meant; that's how lame I am.

I chew the inside of my cheek and look down at the funnel cake. Finally, I get the nerve to look back up and find him as he stretches behind the player bleachers at the side of the field.

Luca. Even in the privacy of my mind, saying it feels like stepping out of the house naked. *Luca.*

Why do I react this way to him? Is it the way he looks? He's definitely gorgeous.

But now I've experienced him up close. The way he smiles. His voice. His hand rubbing my back when I was losing it in the bathroom.

It's the way he ran over to me on the track today and just jogged with me for a while in silence. The way his eyes widened slightly when I asked if he was inviting me to the game. How he swept Pandy away and cleaned him up for no good reason. That surprising hug the other day on the track.

He makes me feel like...like some part of me is falling open, and I can't even help it. It's a heavy, secret feeling—an unfurling. So it's terrible to watch him right now while my best friends tease me.

Every time he's on the field, I feel like I can't breathe. Near the end of the game, one of the opposing players slams into him, and he crumples to the grass and stays there for a second. My heart nosedives. Then he gets up, moving stiffly. A minute later, the set of plays they're doing wraps up, and he walks off the field and jerks his helmet off.

I hold my breath as someone in a purple Polo shirt sits beside him on the metal bleachers, offering him a water bottle and draping a white towel over his nape.

"Did he get hurt?"

"I don't think so." Dani shakes her head and squints down at the field. "I think it's a dramatic sport. And for real like tiring. After all these games, Teddy—" the team's quarterback, whom Dani dated briefly last year— "told me that he just goes home and crashes. He says it's exhausting and it makes him so sore he can barely move."

I watch Luca as he rubs the towel over his face and drapes it over his head. Then he's up again, standing with the rest of the team.

Not yours, I remind myself. *Might not even find you after the game.*

I get teased again about the funnel cake and force myself to eat more, so by the time the game is over—with a winning score for our team—I'm feeling buzzy from the loudness of the crowd combined with the fierce sugar rush.

I watch as the team huddles, shouts something in unison, and starts to trickle off the field toward the locker room.

"Why don't we wait here for a little while?" Dani says, her voice a pitch too cheery.

"There's no reason to wait." I pick at the funnel cake, and Ree says, "Goldfish, we are waiting. Mama Beta is deciding for you."

"I'm not going to just *wait* here for him," I mutter.

"Go to the concession stand, then," she orders, shooing me with her hand. "If he doesn't see you, he'll see us. You'll be right back."

I'm almost to the bottom of the cement bleachers when he moves into my frame of vision, leaning against a purple railing and peering intently in my direction. When our eyes meet, he gives me the biggest grin, and I dash over.

"Hi." My cheeks burst into flames as I step nearer to him. He's still wearing his football getup, including the big shoulder pads.

"Hi yourself." His voice is low and quiet, so casual, but after meeting my eyes for half a second, he can't stop his gaze from roving over my body as he runs a hand back through his damp hair. He shakes his head a little, snaps his blue eyes back to mine. "Sweaty."

Yes, he's sweaty. He looks like a big, male creature that's been tussling with the other males. Who knew that could be sexy? I swallow. "You played great. It was really cool to watch a game."

He gives me a teasing smile. "You've never been before?"

"Only one time, when I was a sophomore."

"To see your boyfriend?" One of his brows juts up, making him look rakish.

"My friend's boyfriend."

His eyes flicker toward my friends, which lets me know he must have spotted us before this moment. Then he looks back at me, brows narrowed in consternation. "You guys wanna come out? My friend Jace is having a thing at his family's...I don't know...some kind of river house or something."

"Jace Banetti?" I ask, nodding because I know exactly where that palace of a "river house" is. It's Jace's grandparents' second home, I almost tell Luca.

"You know him?" he asks.

"Since we were younger."

"Good." He gives me a big grin. "So you want to meet me there?"

"Yeah, sure."

"Oh, wait, the address." He squints, biting his lower lip. Then he looks at the back of his hand, where something's scrawled in faded marker script. "It's at Kings Point. Looks like...Nine Soundridge Lane. Banetti says it's near Kings Point Park?"

"Yeah, I think I know where that is."

His brows scrunch. "Wait a second. How long a drive is that?"

"Like...kind of long, I think. But I'm staying with Dani, and her parents are low key. Her driver's the one who's on tonight. He's super nice. He'll take us anywhere we want him to."

"I've got another idea. Do you want to come with me? With Jace? We're going in a helicopter." His eyes are slightly wide, as if he's concerned about my reaction. It makes me laugh. "Really?"

He nods. "If you're not good with that—"

"Oh no, I've been in helicopters. I mean, not since I was like thirteen. But they're fun. And at night..." I smile, thinking of it. "That would be amazing. If you're sure there's room for me?"

Luca nods, tugging on his jersey like he's hot under it. "He said nine of us can go, and so far it's just Jace, Loren, Max Romano, Franc Toliver, and me. There's some other people chartering two other ones, but our group's got some room. I think it's Jace's family's."

I nod. "I think his dad owns a fleet of them."

He shakes his head, like that's insane.

"It kind of *is* insane. If you really stop and think about it."

He laughs. "So you're in? You need a ride, or will your friend's... uh, person take you?"

"We'll meet you over there. Is it the Water Street heliport?"

58

He nods. "I think so."

"Perfect."

He reaches toward my shoulder like he's going to squeeze it, but at the last minute he touches his palm to the side of my arm instead. He gives me a funny little smile.

"See you over there, Elise."

And then he's off again.

CHAPTER FOUR

Elise

Dad flies all the time. There's a helipad on our building—not near our penthouse, but on the other side, on one of the lower roofs. I used to go with him, but that was years ago, I guess.

I'm trying to remember it now: how it feels to soar between the skyscrapers, the giddy rush that makes me feel a little sick as the helicopter teeters in the clouds before dipping quickly back to land.

I can't believe I'm getting into a helicopter with Luca. I think of myself sitting in his lap and close my eyes as I exhale.

You're going crazy, Elise.

When I open my eyes, I find Dani giving me a quizzical look. "What's up? Are you nervous?"

Dani's older sister, Maria, is a fashion model, and she takes Dani on her helicopter jaunts around Manhattan. Also—I forget this sometimes—Dani comes from a long line of jetsetters. Her family tree is home to senators and presidential cabinet members.

"I'm nervous," a wide-eyed Ree offers. Her father is an elementary school principal in the Bronx, so helicopters aren't a fixture in her day-to-day life. She grabs Dani's arm. "Remember that time we went with Maria to that weird warehouse in Brooklyn and there was all that fog when we were landing?"

"Oh, you mean the one with that neon paint set?"

Ree nods, and I ask for more details before realizing I wasn't there with them that time.

"It's going to be fine, you chickens," Dani tells us. "We'll only be up like fifteen minutes. And it's nighttime, so it's going to be super pretty." She adjusts the band around her high ponytail then flashes me a grin. "If you get scared, just jump in your football hero's lap."

"Or play footsie," Ree offers. "In that one we took, weren't the seats facing each other?"

Two rows of seats are often facing on other. I think about it eagerly, even as I roll my eyes at my friends. "You two are relentless."

For the next few minutes, I get coached on what to do at the party —as if I've never been anywhere—and then Dani goes over the emergency plan.

"I've got my Nokia in my purse." She pats the giant leather bag hanging from her shoulder, her palm covering the Hermes label. "If we get lost or separated, call me on yours."

"I don't have mine," Ree says.

"Me either."

"The house will have phones. Or you can borrow someone's mobile. *Or* you can find a payphone."

Then the car stops. It feels so abrupt that I glance out the window to confirm we're at the right place, and we are. Turns out, the ride just passed by quickly. Dani leans up to talk to Fil, letting him know we'd like to be picked up at the Banetti house in about four hours.

"I'll drive over now and wait," he says.

"If my mom calls, don't tell her?" Dani requests.

Fil looks reproachful, which makes me smile.

Dani rolls her eyes. "Whatever, then. It's not like Eileen will care."

All too soon, we're spilling out the car and onto a walkway. The heliport is all lit up and cool from a breeze that's blowing from the East River. We sign consents inside a small green booth, and then we're waved onto the spacious landing pad, where five large choppers await. One lifts off as we follow our escort toward the bird in slot five.

As we near, its long blades start to spin, tossing my hair into my face. Ree runs her hand over her tight braids and winks. I stick my tongue out at her. She gives me a goofy grin, then leans down to look under the chopper's belly. "I see your boy!"

The boys are sort of behind the helicopter, so I don't see him at first—not until we get closer and he starts waving.

Luca walks around the helicopter's tail, hands in his pockets till we're closer to him. Then he pulls them out and holds a hand out toward me, waving us around, where we greet Jace, Loren, Max, and Franco.

Everyone knows each other well, so there's lots of hugging and greeting while Luca and I stand awkwardly near each other but not overly close.

Someone opens the helicopter's door, and he takes my hand. We're the last two to climb in. I notice that the two remaining seats are beside one another. Luca motions for me to sit first, so I do. I sit by Max and across from Dani; Luca sits on the end, beside me and across from Ree.

As the chopper's blades thump faster, there's an upswell in the volume of our voices—and an uptick in my heart rate. My eyes bounce around the small space, clinging to the scenery outside the windows for a second before they snap like magnets onto Luca's face.

His smile is crooked, and I laugh, because he looks a little miserable. "Are you nervous?"

"Me? Nah." He laughs, and it's nervous laughter. I hold my hand out. He takes it. I can't breathe as he laces his fingers through mine. Something heavy settles in my body, like the feeling of exhaling. "Have you ever been in one?" I hear myself ask.

He's wince-smiling as he shakes his head.

"I've only done it twice," Ree tells him. "But never in one this big."

"Two virgins," Lorenzo chortles.

"How's it going, Elise?"

I turn to Max with warm cheeks; I'm still holding Luca's hand in full view of our friends.

"It's okay. What about you, Max?"

He gives me a dimpled smile, shaking his head. He pulls off his ball cap, rubbing a hand through his dark hair. "Just being tired. I'm gonna throw a sleepover for one in Jace's grandma's big ass bed."

"I don't think so, Max. Can't have your sweaty ass on Gran's good blankets."

Max snorts. "Better than what fucked up shit you'd do if you got on it."

I turn back to Luca as the thumping sound intensifies and the pilot's voice crackles over the speakers, letting us know we're about to depart.

His wide eyes meet mine, and I squeeze his hand. He squeezes back.

"You ready?" I ask.

He laughs. "What about you?"

I cover my face with my free hand, breathing through my gritted teeth. "It makes me feel a little sick at first."

The helicopter lurches off the landing pad, and Luca mutters, "Fuck."

We tighten our grip on each other, and he closes his eyes. I see his jaw tic when I look up at him. My stomach clenches as I shut my eyes again, as if I swallowed a pool ball and it's tugging me downward. Another roller coaster sensation and we're steadier. A *little* steadier.

The guys alternate between ribbing Luca and reassuring him. Dani hugs Ree, who keeps saying she's fine, just fine. And then we're really up—we're approaching the top of 4 New York Plaza, and all around are blinking lights and gleaming steel and glass. Luca's eyes flip open, meeting mine before he glances out the window. As soon as he gets a good look at things, he squeezes them shut again.

"I get sick from trains," he says, and gives this soft, embarrassed laugh.

I squeeze his hand then lean in closer—so my mouth is near his ear and nobody can hear me. "You're not really in a helicopter. You and I are at a carnival. It's just the two of us—we're on this ride that kind of makes you want to hurl but kind of feels like floating in an ocean. Do you know the one?"

He nods, and cracks open one eye so he can see me when he smiles. I smile back, and then I watch as he looks out the window again.

"This is better than the train, I think," he murmurs.

"It is?"

He nods, wiping his palm on his pantsleg as he blinks at the city through the window. "Better view."

The gang is still talking. Even Ree, who, thankfully, seems to be handling the helicopter almost as well as me. They're on the topic of who lives over on Kings Point, and Jace tells everyone that the author F. Scott Fitzgerald used to, which I knew already.

That's the flow, then there's an ebb where Luca and I wade out of the conversation...just enough so we have space to look at each other again. He's smiling, and I don't know what to do about it. I'm so hungry for him, I feel almost sick: dizzy and overheated. I look down at our clasped hands. His is curved around mine—large and protective.

"Ladies and gentlemen, we will now begin descending. Tighten your seatbelts and we'll be at our destination in another four or five minutes."

Luca lets a breath out, smiling when our eyes catch. I rub the tips of his fingers, and he rests his head against the seat's back.

"Thanks," he murmur-whispers, and I lean my cheek against his shoulder to tell him he's welcome.

❧

This house is a castle. Three levels of rose-beige stone with grand, arched windows and massive mahogany doors. It's shaped like a vertical rectangle, with four tall, cylindrical towers guarding each corner. The towers are topped with pointy, witch-hat-looking roofs and covered in crawling ivy.

The balconies on the west-facing towers hang over the Long Island Sound. Water sparkles below them, sloshing gently as boats slice through the inky water, their wake rippling outward.

I could stay out here all night, inhaling the river smell, letting the autumn air sink through my gray pants, through the fabric of my soft green sweater. It's cold, but I like that. I like that I hear people chatting above and below me—people out on other balconies—but I'm alone on this one.

I lost track of Luca. Maybe an hour after we arrived, he offered to get me a virgin daquiri. I saw him talking to Max by one of the coolers; then they disappeared into the crowd.

I tell myself I don't care. I think of Becca—what's she doing at home?—and I get the frozen feeling I have sometimes, knowing what will happen. It's like being on a train, and I can't get off. And I know it's going to crash. And I'm not sad. I'm only bracing.

I think of my dad calling home from the office before I left to go with Dani for the night.

"Be careful tonight—all nights, but especially right now. We don't need to split our focus." By which he meant he and my mom don't want to worry about me in addition to Becca.

Sometimes Dad will say, "We didn't know things would be like this," as if to imply that if they had known about Becca's disease, maybe they wouldn't have chosen to bring her into the world at all. I don't know why he says that. I never said I was upset or that I thought they should have known. Our family isn't normal, but I don't care. All I want is for them—my parents—to just...be around. And talk and stuff. But no one is, and no one does, and that, they *can* control. But they choose not to talk to me. Or Becca. Dad picks work and Mom picks her appointments.

"Hey, you."

I look up, finding Luca in the doorway between balcony and bedroom. He's wearing a crooked smile and looking like all kinds of hot with his dark hair sticking up from how it dried after his post-game shower. I tell myself to play it cool, but I can't help the way my gaze laps up and down him, taking in his slightly snug black tee and faded jeans and sneakers.

Why do guys look so good in plain clothes? Or maybe only the hot ones do. And he is definitely hot.

I swallow as he moves onto the deck, a panther stalking to where I am by the rail. He's so close, and he's smiling, clearly looking me over, and I'm having trouble breathing normally.

"Hi," he says again, and I realize I haven't spoken.

"Hi there."

He hands me my drink—in a red Solo cup. His sparkling eyes feel hot on mine. "You okay?"

I nod, and it's not untrue. I'm glad I came out tonight, and I'm even gladder that he's here beside me.

He casts his gaze over the sound, focusing on a light I see across the way—a boat or barge—before his eyes return to my face.

"Did you need some air?"

I smile. "Something like that." After I lost track of Luca, my friends went different ways. Dani bumped into her melodramatic cousin Maya, who pulled D into a bathroom to talk about some "crisis." Ree and I wandered into a big, stately library where someone had set up strobe lights, and she bumped into this girl she met at the skate park last summer. When someone turned on music, I left them and made my way upstairs.

"I like balconies," I say.

"Yeah?"

I nod, cringing inside. *I like balconies*. Who says that?

He laughs, leaning on the rail, his big body angled toward mine. "What about them do you like?" He's grinning, as if he can read my mind.

I cover my too-warm face. "I mean…I guess just the ivy…and the water. And—okay—sort of the lack of people."

"Not a people person?"

"No. I mean, I *am* a people person. I just…I sometimes need a break from all the people talking at once." Luca's face looks rapt, not bored, so I continue. "My friend Ree calls me a both-i-vert. Because I'm sort of extroverted, sort of introverted. What about you?"

"Both-i-vert." He smiles. "I like that." His tongue flits over his lower lip, and I think he bites the corner before meeting my eyes. "I don't know…I'm kind of both, too. I like doing shit with friends, but I can also kick it with a book."

"What kind of books do you like?"

His lips twist as he looks down at the iron railing. "Now we're talking secrets." He arches his eyebrows, and I laugh, wanting to die at my own utter lack of coolness.

"Oh, so this is really good then," I say. "Are we talking Artemis Fowl?"

He grins, shaking his head.

"Harry Potter?" He smiles. "Gossip Girl? Oh, I know!" I snap. "Anne Rice."

"I like Anne Rice," he says, so I guess that's not the secret.

"Manga?" I try.

"Eh."

"No?"

He gives me a crooked grin. "I might have read some with my brother."

"Psshh. You know you're watching all the anime."

He smirks. "Maybe."

"Well, I'm glad to hear that you're a reader."

He gives a loud, low laugh, his chin tipped up. "What, did you think maybe I can't read or something?"

"Can and do are different things."

"True is that." He says it in a Yoda voice, and it makes me laugh.

"You a *Star Wars* fan are."

He shrugs.

"You like sci-fi and super nerdy stuff. That's what you really like," I say, just fishing.

He gives me a brief grin, and I note that he didn't comment.

"Do you read on the trains?"

He nods, looking like I just made him confess something outlandish.

"Have you read *Merrick*?"

He grins.

Guess he really does read Anne Rice. "What about *Blood and Gold*?"

He nods once, eyes fixed on the water—as if he can't look at me while he's confessing.

"*Pandora* and *Vittorio the Vampire*?"

He laughs. Now he looks up at me, and he's definitely embarrassed.

I decide to push more, just because I'm feeling wicked. "*Sleeping Beauty*?"

His smile disappears. "Don't tell me you've read that," he says— and his voice is rough and low.

"You think I can't read it, too?" I feel heady as I lean beside him, propping my forearms on the cool, iron railing. I look at the water, wondering what spot his pale blue eyes are locked onto.

"Don't tell me about it," he says, and my heart begins to gallop.

"Do you think I'm...*bad* for reading it?" Now I feel embarrassed at my rash admission. I'm not sure there are any books more erotic than the Sleeping Beauty trilogy from Anne Rice.

Luca's hand reaches for mine, closes over it and squeezes. "Of course not." He lets go and straightens up, then turns toward the door.

My throat tightens as I feel him stepping right behind me. "It's not bad," he says quietly. "It's too much. For me."

"I don't get it," I whisper. But I'm lying…because maybe I do.

"I'm your fake boyfriend, remember?"

My cheeks burn with shame. *So I misunderstood this.*

"I'm not—" I feel him step back. "We're not…"

"Not what," I force myself to whisper as I straighten my spine.

"I'm not really…good for you."

"What do you mean?"

He laughs, but it's a cold sound. "You don't want me thinking about you. This way."

I turn around to face him. "What do you mean?"

Light from the bedroom door spills all around him, making him look like a shadow.

"Why would you say that?"

He shuts his eyes. His hand comes to his forehead, and he rubs his temple on the hurt side of his face.

"Because of that?" I whisper.

"No." It's almost groaned. "Because of other shit." He says that darkly, as if it should speak for itself.

"You don't like me?"

His jaw tics. "I like you."

"You don't…want me?"

"Oh, I want you."

I take a small step toward him.

"You're fucking beautiful, Elise. And you're all good. You have a good heart. That's what my Nonna would have said."

"And you don't?" I'm close enough so I can touch him, so I do. I wrap a hand around his wrist and pull his arm toward me. His hand balls loosely into a fist, and I press it just under my throat.

He shakes his head. My eyes fall to where his Adam's apple bobs, and so I almost miss the way his eyes gleam. "No."

I hug him. I don't know why. Maybe it's too much, but it feels right. He goes still, his body rigid as I press my forehead to his shirt. I can smell detergent…and him. "I don't think that's true at all," I tell him, with my eyes squeezed shut. "You're very good. Remember Pandy? That was the nicest thing someone has done for me in ages."

My throat aches as I listen to his heart pound underneath the cotton of his T-shirt. This is a boy who lives with misery, the same way I do. I can feel it. When he smiles, it's real and kind. I can tell he's good.

He starts to breathe a little faster. When he steps back, I let him.

"I'm sorry." His words are thick.

"For what?"

I can feel him moving toward the door a half second before he does. So I step closer.

"C'mon. Stay out here. We can talk about Anne Rice or Stephen King, or anything you want."

He blinks twice, as if he's waking up. "Do you want me to?"

"Yes, please."

He nods, staring past me. His jaw flexes.

"Come sit with me."

His eyes are somber, but he does as I ask. He sits beside me on the stone floor of the balcony. When I hold my hand out, he takes it, threading his warm fingers through mine. He looks at his lap, rubs at his knee.

"Did you hurt your knee at the game?"

"Last year."

"Playing football?"

He nods. He won't look at me, even as he presses our joined hands to his thigh.

"Do you like playing?"

"Yeah." He still looks slightly dazed, but this time, his gaze catches mine for just a second before dropping back to our hands. "I like the team."

I squeeze his hand. "I like your hands. They're big and a lot warmer than mine."

His fingers rub mine gently.

I close my eyes. "Like that."

CHAPTER FIVE

Luca

She's got her body leaned against mine, and I'm holding her hand.

I don't know why. I got freaked out and acted weird and tried to tell her. Tell her...how I am.

When she said she likes those *Sleeping Beauty* books, it got to me. To my dick specifically. And all I could think was what would happen if I let myself push things. If I let myself...have what I want.

Dirty books or not, it turns out Elise is pretty damn nice, which is good and bad for me. Good because she already seems to have forgotten that I was spazzing not five minutes ago. Bad for me because she's soft. And she smells good.

Elise. She likes balconies at night and naughty books. She's got nice friends and a nice house and parents who might be dicks but it's safe for her there, I bet. I think about that, and it makes me think of what I told her about my eye.

No, no, nope. I don't let myself go there. But part of me does. It's like a penny you throw in a fountain and it flutters near the top then sinks because sinking is what metal does in water. Part of me sinks. I can't get that part to come back up—even for her. I know I should walk away. It's a bad idea for me to get to know her.

But I don't.

I'm always thinking of myself in some way or another. Like right now. I love having her up against me. How her head feels on my shoulder. So I tell myself that she's enjoying it too. I'm rubbing her hand, and she likes it. So it's okay.

I take another deep breath, try to banish my darker thoughts.

"You know what I think sometimes?" she asks quietly.

I shake my head, avoiding her eyes.

"Probably at most, we're not even a fifth of the way through our lives right now. Isn't that weird to think of? Whatever or whoever we feel like we are right now, we've got a whole other four-fifths of life left. Even people our parents' age—no one's life is locked in."

My eyes throb...because I *want* to believe her—more than anything. But I know that's not how it works. Maybe for someone like Elise. But not for me.

I feel her eyes on me as I stare at the bedroom door in front of us. Then I look down at her and make myself say something normal. "That *is* weird to think about. One-fifth, though, wow."

"Do you think that's a lot?"

I shrug. "It seems like a lot."

"I guess so. But most of it is just totally unwritten. And I think this first fifth or so of our life is for scouting locations, you know?"

I think so, but I want to hear her explain it, so I shake my head.

"It's like—do you ever think how Paris is just sitting there, and you could walk around on those streets right now if you were there? But since you're not, it's just going on being Paris without you. Australia is just there with waves rolling in. And as big as New York City is, Tokyo is three times as big and half a world away. I think about London and San Francisco and all of these places, and they're out there just waiting. Even though I know they're not waiting for me specifically. But they could be. If I wanted them to be."

I feel her let a breath out. "All the options, all the possibilities make my brain feel tired. It seems crazy how we have this giant world, and we're in one single spot, having just this one experience." She sucks a deep breath in. I hear the smile in her voice as she says, "Do you think that sounds crazy?"

Crazy? "No way. I feel the same way sometimes." Except those aren't the places waiting for me.

"It's just like...narratives. I think about things like that, since English class last year. There are these...I don't know, like infinite possible narratives. For every person and then for all the other people. So many *options*. Life is nothing but a bunch of choices." She swallows and goes quiet. "I feel like I have none. But I'm not trapped. That's not true. I'm trapped but it's my own trap. Because we could do anything, at any time. That's what's true," she murmurs.

She heaves this big sigh, but it's quiet. I ask her, "What would you do if you could pick anything, Elise O'Hara? What's your number one choice?"

"Provence. France," she adds helpfully.

"That was fast."

"It's been my place for a while."

"Yeah?"

"I want to rent a little stone house with one or two rooms and exposed wood beams and no dishwasher. And then I want to read. I want to read one book per day. And eat fresh bread and drink grape juice and eat apples and walk in lavender fields."

"Maybe that's why you like balconies." I'm not really one for making assumptions. But she seems like someone who likes speculating; I can do that, too. So I push myself to say the thing in my head. "Maybe what you like isn't the balcony. It's the view." She looks up at me—I can feel her eyes, even though I don't have the nerve to look into them. "Maybe you like looking out and picturing the locations. Where the boats are going. Where they could go."

I don't really plan to press my face against her hair. I do because she's soft and small and smells so fucking good, and I think she seems sad.

Something shifts inside the house, like I guess someone changes the song, so I feel the base start bumping through the balcony's floor, reminding me of where we are. We're not alone, but it sure as shit feels like we are. Elise curls up a little more against me, and I shift us so her head and shoulders are on my lap, so I can wrap an arm around her back and run my fingers through her dark hair.

I know she likes the feel of that because she makes a little sound. And that's when things go sideways. Having her on my lap becomes a bad thing because now I'm hard. I take a deep breath, swallow. Try to think of something that'll get this to go down a little. But there's nothing. My heart starts beating harder—because my body wants to fuck her.

I rub my forehead with my free hand and brush her hair up off her nape. I rub at the base of her skull with two fingers, the same spot where my neck hurts sometimes. I'm rewarded with a little groan, and a sharp throb that sends a wash of good feels from my dick down to my knees.

Shit.

She giggles, and I keep rubbing. "Your hair is soft," I say in a voice that vibrates.

"Thank you."

I want to touch my dick so fucking bad. I shift my legs a little, hoping that a reposition might help. No. Fuck. That made it worse.

Elise is smart. She lifts her head up, and her cheeks are flushed. She's smiling like she's kind of sleepy, relaxed. But her eyes give her away, flitting down to my pants for a millisecond before latching back onto mine. "Thank you for that. It felt so good."

I reach out to push some hair out of her face, but once I've got my hand on her—even her hair—I can't seem to move it away.

"No boyfriend," I say, my voice an octave too low. "I wonder how long that's going to last."

Her lips twitch. "What?" She looks puzzled—and self-conscious.

"Just every guy you meet with a functioning brain must want you." The words come out so rough they're almost hoarse—and her eyes widen. Then a blush sweeps her cheeks.

"That's not true."

"Oh yes, it is true...*la mia rosa.*"

She looks down again, and I know she can see where my boner strains at my pants. I shift so it's not so fucking obvious and run my hands through my hair. "Sorry." I'm almost scared to look at her, but when I do, she's got this tiny smirk on her face.

"Sorry," she whispers. Her smile widens—along with her eyes.

"Are you laughing at me?"

"Of course not."

"I don't know," I say slowly. "I think you might be."

She turns redder. "I would never."

"I'm just kidding." I stand up and turn away from her, toward the water. I feel her hovering behind me, probably afraid to get close.

Jesus Christ, Galante.

I grit my teeth and inspect the railing. There's ivy curved around the iron; I trace a leaf with my finger, surprised to find it's kinda shaking from...I don't know what this feeling is.

"Sorry," I say quickly.

"Don't be sorry. I'm not upset."

My finger rubs something between the iron and ivy. I reach down and brush my fingertips against it. Rope. I pull on it.

"A rope ladder," I murmur.

I feel her stand up beside me. "Is it?"

I nod, drawing more of it out.

"I guess it's some fire code thing," she murmurs.

I drag it all the way out. The thing is long. "It'll probably reach to the ground." I stare at it while I work up the nerve to flash her a quick, palate-cleansing grin. "You think I can climb down?"

"Ummm...yes? But should you?"

"Might be fun." My heart is still beating too hard. My hands feel weird and hot as I toss the rope over the balcony's ledge.

"Are you really going to do that?"

I laugh, giving her a glance to be sure she doesn't seem too freaked out.

"You are," she laughs. "It's one of those guy things, isn't it? But let me tell you something, Galante. If you go, I go. You can go down first, but I'll be coming down right after." She smiles, as if I didn't make the last five minutes awkward as fuck.

"I don't know if that's good."

She puts a hand on her hip. "Are you saying you're more capable than I am?"

"I'm saying I care more about you falling."

"And I care more about *you* falling. So I guess that makes us even."

I look down again, at the wet grass below the last wrung of the ladder. There are people milling in the yard, but not too many, and they're not near us. I look at Elise again.

"If you get scared and decide you don't want to come down, I could climb back up to you," I offer.

She laughs, and it's a funny little laugh—sort of a giggle.

"Oh no, I'm going to do it. I'm athletic. I'm a runner. And—" she squares her shoulders— "I play tennis. I'm also lighter than you and probably more limber."

We share a smile, and I feel almost dizzy with it. "It sounds like the deal is sealed then, O'Hara."

She widens her eyes at me, incredulous.

"What?" I laugh.

"Are you *really* going to go over the side of the balcony on a rope ladder you just found tucked in some ivy?"

I do—moving slowly and carefully, clutching the top rungs of the ladder with both fists so I don't fall and scar Elise for life. Then I decide I want to scare her a little bit and flap one hand dramatically. "AHHHH—"

"Luca! You—" I laugh, and she scrunches her face angrily. "You jerk! I knew it was fake."

"Sure you did," I tease.

"I did!"

I start down the ladder, and once I'm seven or eight rungs down, I call up, "This is pretty easy. But you still shouldn't do it."

"Why not?" She sounds offended.

"I don't know. It's kind of wobbly."

"I can handle wobbly."

I laugh, and then I'm moving down more quickly, glancing at the dark expanse of grass below my shoes. Someone shouts, and I'm aware that people on a balcony above ours are peeking down at me.

I hear some dude shout, "Don't flick your cherry, man!"

"Yeah, please don't," I mutter.

Finally, I reach the ground. The grass squishes around my sneakers. I look up to find Elise already over the ledge.

"Sweet." I cup my hands around my mouth. "Keep coming. You got it…" She's moving pretty fast. Damn. I guess she knows her skillset. "Almost halfway now…"

The people on the balcony above ours start to chant. I hear Elise laugh. Her feet are just over my head now.

"There ya go," I murmur.

When she's close enough, I wrap my hands around her waist and pull her down into my arms. Everyone cheers. We both laugh like idiots. Elise beams up at me, and her eyes have this look. I smile back and then take off toward the long dock maybe fifty yards away.

She squeals like a little kid, and I jog till we're out of the lamplight and into shadows draped across the wet grass.

DARK HEART, VOLUME 1

"Oh my God, your shoes!"

"A little wet." I laugh again, and then we're on the dock, a single arm with two slots filled by a giant sailboat and what you might call a small yacht. I walk toward them, through circles of amber light from three black lamp posts. Then I hang a left, so we're at a narrow strip of dock between the two vessels. I lower Elise onto the slats and wink at her before I sink down cross-legged by her. She moves so she's facing me.

"Hi." She laughs.

"Hello yourself."

Her face is happy, and her eyes are on mine, making me feel so warm. That thing happens again, like it did up on the balcony. My heart starts beating harder, and my ears feel really, really hot.

CHAPTER SIX

Elise

I lean in first, and then he does—so we're close enough to kiss. But I can't kiss him, and he doesn't kiss me. He just looks at me…right in the eye, as if he's looking past the outside of me deep into the inside.

Softly, he says, "You know…you're beautiful."

My pulse roars in my ears, even as I try to roll my eyes. "Don't say that."

Luca's lips curve slightly. "Why not?"

"Because it scares me." I laugh.

"Why?" He tilts his head a little, his face gentle.

"I don't know." Emotion rises in my chest, a gentle swell of something I don't know the name of.

He leans in and kisses my cheek, so when one hot tear falls—a mortifying shock to me—his mouth is there, lovely and soft. And then it's natural to kiss him. We're kissing, and it's strange and wonderful, scary and soothing. Him and me. Me and him. We're like a puzzle snapping into place. My hands are on his hard shoulders. His fingers sift through my hair, careful. Then I'm moaning into his mouth. One of his hands cups my nape and he pulls me closer.

We kiss until we can't breathe. He wraps an arm around me, and the world constricts to just this moment, and it's vast and slow and quick and frantic and so tender I feel like my heart is being tugged outward. I'm the first to pull away, but we're both panting. His hands on my shoulders secure me up against him. His arm wraps around me like he never wants to let go.

For the longest time, we sit there with him holding me like I am so important to him. Like I matter. Really matter. He holds me like I'm cherished. Like I'm his.

Another tear drips down my cheek, and I think he can tell, but he doesn't ask. He just holds me as the water laps and the air hangs around us like a curtain. As our classmates' gleeful, laughing screams echo around the sailboat's mast and, sometime later, people stumble onto the dock.

We slip back into the house through a back door and make our way upstairs to that same bedroom with the balcony from before. No words are exchanged. We are simply drawn there, moved by our own gravity.

Inside the room, he drops my hand and sprawls out on his back on the bed. "Sorry." He shuts his eyes. "I'm so tired. You trust me?"

He peeks at me through his eyelashes, holds out his hand, and I climb onto the bed so I can take it.

"I don't think I could ever be scared of you."

I stroke his dark hair, loving the warmth of his forehead and the way his lips part slightly.

"That feels good," he says—and it's a soft, hoarse, sleepy voice.

I have the thought that my frantic pulse may never slow again. Not while I'm near him. Then the ether hears me, and the wheels of fate conspire to make that true. From outside the door, someone shouts, "Cops!"

It's shouted a few times before the word permeates my love-drunk brain. I jerk my hand from Luca's forehead.

"Oh shit, I think the *cops* are here!"

We scramble over the balcony's side just as the bedroom door bursts open. Somehow, we both make it down the rope ladder and through the yard—where everyone is running, screaming—and then to the sailboat. There's a hatch that's unlocked, so we drop into the inside of it.

I hear shrieking, and the smacking sound of shoe soles on grass quickens. Someone blows a shrill whistle.

"They have whistles?" I hiss.

Luca laughs quietly.

When we dropped in through the hatch, we landed in the front, on a hard, triangular bed. Or at least I think that it's a bed. Luca locks the hatch and then he wraps an arm around me. We hear a helicopter taking off from the pad near the boat.

"If cops get on here," Luca whispers near my ear, "I'll go out by myself, and you can hide."

He presses his cheek against the top of my hair, and I can feel his chest expand as he drags in a big breath. For a moment, we're just quiet. I can feel the boat rock slightly. He hugs me a little tighter, and I curl against him.

"I hope Ree and Dani are okay," I whisper.

"Pray to Saint Jude."

I lean back a little, giving me a view of his face, swathed in shadows "Why St. Jude?"

"You're not Catholic." His lips twitch.

"No, I am. Kind of. We go to a Catholic church on holidays. My mom's from Bangladesh, but she's an atheist."

I can tell from his face that he's not sure what to say to that.

"I'm not an atheist," I clarify. "I'm down with praying. What will St. Jude do for me?" I ask him in a teasing tone.

"Patron saint of lost causes." Luca's eyes dance as he flashes me a crooked smile.

"Hmm. You smell good," I whisper near his chin.

He kisses my temple. "You do." He gives me a little sniff. "What is that?"

"I don't know." I laugh at how insane this all is.

"I could always smell it when I walked behind you."

"What?" That makes us both laugh.

"Seriously. It's the best smell ever."

"I wear perfume," I whisper, "but I'm not telling you what kind it is."

He shakes his head. "That's evil, O'Hara."

His cheek presses against mine. We're partway lying down, looking into each other's eyes. He shifts a little, and I reach for the waistband of his pants.

"You are, with these blue jeans."

I trace a finger over his denim-clad thigh.

"Don't say that." His voice is husky.

I know I shouldn't. I shouldn't want a repeat of what happened on the balcony. Even as I'm thinking that, I can feel him breathing heavier.

"Why are you so nice to me, Luca Galante?"

When I look into his eyes, I notice they look almost shut. Like he's relaxed or falling asleep.

"I don't know, Elise O'Hara. I like you."

"You do?" I whisper.

His lips curve into a lazy-looking smile. "I've always liked you."

"Always. That sounds like a long time."

"Since my first day of school at MM," he says softly. He glances up at the hatch in the roof before he goes on. "I was walking to the office. You went in before me, and I heard you talking about your schedule. You were doing something, working with the special ed department. Sounded like maybe helping one of the other students. So I noticed that. Also, you were hot."

I nod, ducking my head so he doesn't see how giddy I am. "I'm a buddy for a younger girl. It's one of my classes."

We're facing one another, inhaling each other's breath, and his smells like peppermints. I hope mine smells like spearmint gum. His eyes gleam like gemstones as they hold mine, but they aren't hard. They're molten soft.

His lips brush mine, feather gentle. I kiss him back as best I can, which I'm scared isn't very good—but then I think it must be, because he kisses me back, hard and hungry.

I shiver when his tongue strokes mine, and when we break apart, he's breathing hard. I'm breathing harder. It's like a switch flipped, and now I just want more, more, more. His hand is cupping my head, his grip firm and warm. Our lips meet again and my hands start roving up and down him, soft palms on his hard chest, fingertips catching in his blue jean belt loop. I grip the waist of his jeans between two fingers, jolted when I feel the heat of his skin against my knuckles.

His mouth leaves mine as his body shudders and I freeze, worried I did something wrong. But then his lips find mine again, and his hand on my nape slides down to my lower back, and he seals me against him—just our upper bodies, though. And I want more.

Naughty fingers. They stroke his hot skin, the soft skin over his hard abs. Every time a fingertip skates around, he groans and kind of bucks against me. We try to swallow one another while my fingers delve a little deeper, down to where his skin is hotter, softer. I reach the juncture of his thigh, and when I stroke there, finally he snaps and moves his hips in my direction. As soon as he does, his mouth is off mine, and he leans back.

"*Elise.*"

"What?" I'm grinning, almost laughing. My blood whooshes in my ears as my whole body shimmers with lust.

He laughs, the sound strangled. He looks down, and so do I, and I'm kind of shocked to see how...visible he is. It's pushing at the denim of his jeans. My cheeks heat up because I made that happen.

He kisses me another time, long and warm and deep, before pulling away again.

"Elise..."

"Sorry." That's a lie, though. I feel taut and throbby, hungry and impulsive. So shocked and unlike myself, but I don't care, it doesn't matter. Nothing does except this very second.

His hand squeezes my arm lightly. "Don't be sorry."

"I'm not usually like this," I say in a voice that shakes.

"Like what?" He smiles, and the look in his eyes makes me dizzy.

When I don't answer, his hand rubs my arm and his lips brush my cheek. Then he scoots about a foot away from me.

His palm cups the bulge in his jeans, and I realize he's gritting his teeth.

"Sorry," I echo.

He laughs. "No." He gives a shake of his head. "I don't want to mess this up."

My gaze sweeps up and down him, lingering for longer than it should on where his hand is.

"See?" His voice is so low it vibrates.

"I like it."

My mouth falls open after I say that. But it's the truth. I love the sight of him with his legs spread and that lustful but wary look on his face. I love where his hand is, how he's holding himself—even as it makes my heart pound.

He mutters something—I think "fuck"—and then the boat shifts as he steps off the mattress and down into a space that I can't see.

CHAPTER SEVEN

Elise

"Luca?" I lean forward through the opening that leads into a lower section of the hull. For a second, it's so dark, I'm not sure where he is. Then he's throwing me over his shoulder, hauling me into a larger, stepped-down space where I glimpse a kitchen and a love seat. He lays me on the love seat and steps back. He's standing in front of a stove, shaking his head as he gives another choked laugh.

"*Elise.*"

"Luca." I turn onto my side, propping my cheek in my hand so I can look up at him.

He rubs his forehead, and I think I see him smiling in the dark. "I don't know what you want."

Maybe not. His voice is kind of achy. I say, "Me either," which is a lie. I summon all my courage, but I still can barely breathe as I say, "I want…you to kiss me again."

He's on me in a single stride, kneeling by the love seat, leaning over so his breath is warm on my cheek. His hands rove through my hair and his lips brush mine. Then he deepens the kiss—slowly.

I grip his shoulder and lick at the corner of his lips until he invades my mouth with his tongue. I shiver and wrap myself around him. My arm goes around his back, tugging so he rises up on his knees.

"Do you want me up there with you?"

"Yes."

He crawls atop me, one knee settling between my legs...and then he leans down, sliding his hand into my hair, cupping my nape before he kisses me again—soft at first, and then it's deep and hard and hungry. A moan slips from my lips and my back arches as all my cells riot with sensation.

"*Che cosa vuoi, la mia dolce rosa?*"

I find his mouth again with mine, kissing hard then breaking away. "Say it again."

"*Che cosa vuoi?*" he whispers.

"The whole thing."

"*La mia dolce rosa.* That means...my sweet rose." His words are groans; his body trembles just like mine does. I wrap my arm around his back, pulling his chest down on mine.

"Elise." He shudders.

"Sorry." My voice quivers. "I want to feel you. Do you think that's bad?"

"*Non lo so. Anche io voglio quello.*"

Then he presses his hips to my thigh. I can feel him, and he's long and hard and stiff and...perfect. My hips lift. I want to press myself against him. I do, and he moans.

"Luca." I hook a leg around his flank and shiver.

His eyes burn into mine. "Are you okay?"

I nod, thrusting my hips a little so I'm rocking against him. Oh my God, it feels incredible. My body flushes like a firework. I feel desperate...so, so hungry. Every time we rub together, he groans like it hurts.

He starts thrusting against me. I roll my hips, and the thrusts...I push up against him and he groans. His body tenses, and I feel him shudder. Then he's panting, moving off me. I'm shocked as he stands and turns away from me.

"Oh fuck." He's holding his head.

"Did I—did something hurt?"

He groans, "*No.*" He turns back around to face me, one hand on his forehead. "Elise...you made me—"

His hand spreads over his pants, fingertips smoothing the fabric down around the outline of his erection.

As understanding settles in me, my cheeks burn too hot, and I'm almost too flustered to speak.

"So you…" I swallow. "Um, was it okay?" My head feels dizzy, all of me still dizzy. My brain isn't working, but my body knows what it wants, and I long for him to climb back on the couch with me.

"Yes." His tone is flat, almost angry. He crouches beside me, close enough so I can see his wide eyes. "Are you okay?"

I thought he seemed mad, but I realize he's frustrated. With himself, I think. And worried about me. "Was it—it didn't bother you or anything, did it?"

"No. No. It was…it felt good. I felt…good." And now I feel embarrassed. By how shaky my voice is. By how my heart pounds, my body throbs and trembles. And because I'm too ashamed to tell him it feels like a flame I swallowed that's slipped down between my thighs.

He breaks our eye contact to settle on his knees beside the couch. He leans down over me, presses his lips to mine. I can feel him waiting for me. He wants me to deepen the kiss, and I do. Every time he exhales, every time his chest pumps on a deep breath— I'm addicted to him. I need more of him; I need him closer.

I sink a hand into his dark locks, tugging so he'll come closer. When he doesn't—he doesn't get up on the couch—I whisper, "Please. Get up here."

He complies with his head lowered, crawling over me with care. He gives a soft, shy sort of smile before kissing me again, this time with open mouths and hot tongues. I can feel him try to keep his hips away from mine, but I don't want that.

"I want to feel you," I whisper.

We kiss, hard and frenzied, till we have to stop to breathe. I feel molten on the inside, everything swollen and heavy. Some fire in me rages, and I have this need to feel him like I did before. I want to rub against him.

Both of us are breathing heavy. Suddenly I'm so ashamed. I cover my face, and he takes my hand.

"You okay, *la mia rosa*?"

I nod. "I've never felt like this before." I look up at him through my tears.

"Like what?"

"Like…" I can't say, so I squeeze my eyes shut.

"Don't be embarrassed. You're fucking beautiful and perfect, Elise. I just want to make you feel good."

I wrap my hands around his arms, rubbing gently up and down as he props himself over me. "Could you...rub on me like before?"

Understanding flickers through his features. Then he shuts his eyes and takes a deep breath.

"You don't have to."

"No." He lowers himself over me, his entire body. I can feel him right away—he's hard against my thigh. He's hard again.

I hug his head against my chest and lift my hips toward him. I groan—just a sound my body makes without me—and he lifts his head and kisses my jaw.

"Elise, never worry. With me...just don't be worried. Okay?"

I nod, and he kisses my mouth.

Everything feels different this time. Both of us are groaning, sweating, shaking as we press against each other. I rub and he thrusts and we tremble. He drags against me, and I moan.

"You okay?"

His hand cups the side of my face, his thumb rubbing as his eyes sear mine. I tip my head back and he kisses my throat. He rests his head beside mine, then lifts it to look at me again.

"Do you trust me?"

I nod.

"Close your eyes, *la mia rosa*. I want to try something I think you'll like..."

CHAPTER EIGHT

Luca

I look at her and try to sear the image of her into my memory. Elise with her hair in waves around her face. The cat-like smile, a little smug. The way her cheeks redden when I pull her underwear back up and fix her pants and snap the button on them. She curls over on her side. I run my hand lightly over her leg.

"That was...perfect," she whispers. Her hand reaches for me, fingers brushing my forearm as her eyes hold mine. She traces down to my wrist, running a gentle fingertip around the round bone that protrudes a little.

"I like your hands."

"Thanks." A sound comes from my throat that's kind of like a laugh, but raspy because I get awkward around her sometimes. "I like your everything."

She's peering up at me, a little owlish, but she's still in shy mode. I can tell. Something with her mouth. "Do you really?" she asks.

I lie behind her, wrapping one arm over her chest and pulling her against me. "Do you really need to ask?"

"How did we not know each other?"

"Before the last week?"

I feel her nod.

"I don't know." I trail my fingers over her shoulder, then pause. "We kind of did. Or, we met and talked and stuff, at least."

She frowns over her shoulder. "What? When?"

I grin. "Can you not think of any place you might have seen me?"

"No." She turns to face me, looking amused. I run my fingertip over her pretty lower lip. Her lashes lower like she's too shy to look at me.

"Think hard, *mio angelo*." She was dressed as an angel that night.

I watch as her face transforms in shock. "*What!* That was you?"

I chuckle, holding my finger over her mouth so she'll remember we should whisper.

"That was you?" she hisses.

"It was."

"The one in the bandana?"

I grin.

"Wow, so that was *you*. Of course it was."

"Why of course?" I'm holding her, and we're face to face. Something warm moves through me—something that feels sort of like satisfaction, but it's heavier and...better.

She shuts her eyes, smiling brightly. "Because I liked him."

I kiss her cheek. "What did you like about him?"

She closes her eyes again and I hug her closer. "I liked how you seemed non-threatening in the room. I liked your eyes. And I liked how you were when you were behind me, when we hid. You made me feel safe."

"Good."

"Did you know I was me?"

"I didn't. Not until we came back to school. It just hit me once, the other day. Probably because I smelled your perfume that morning."

"So it was my smell." She giggles.

"Yeah, I kinda scented you out or whatever."

"That's awfully animalistic, Galante."

I wink. "I'm an animal."

"I am too," she whispers, widening her eyes.

She bows her head in mock shame, and I thump her chin. "Think we know who couldn't even get through kissing without..." I can't say it, so I just shake my head, grinning into her hair.

"It's okay." Her hands smooth my hair back off my forehead. "I love that you liked it."

"*Liked* it." I almost blew again when I was going down on her. Not coming has me hurting right now. Nothing's ever felt as good as rubbing up against her softness, but I don't want to sound too intense, so I just say, "It was the best thing I've ever felt." Way better than anything I've done with anyone else—not that I'm going to say that.

"Really?" She looks amazed, which makes me laugh. The sound comes out choked. "Uhh…yeah."

"I felt that way, too." She tilts her head back, looking into my eyes. "Do you think I'm terrible?" she whispers.

"Because of what we did?"

She nods.

"Hell no." I kiss her forehead—because I can't keep my mouth and hands off her. Then I lean my head against hers. "You liked it, right?"

I'm worried. Maybe she regrets it.

"Of course," she says, and I let out a breath I didn't know I was holding.

We're both quiet, rocked by the boat, and I think *this is all someone can ask for*. It's times like this that make the other shit more worth it.

I'm rubbing her hair when her cheek brushes mine. "Let's never not know each other again," she says.

I smile, even as my chest and throat ache. "Again? When did it happen before?"

"Maybe in another life."

I wrap her closer up against me, and she sighs like she's content, and I feel so good. Really, really good.

Her lips brush the bruise around my eye, and for a second, I can't breathe.

"You're a good guy for sure." Her soft lips feather kisses over my temple. "You know that, don't you?"

I don't, but I'm too content to argue, so I shut my eyes, and she kisses them too.

"My sweet Luca."

I open my eyes and I kiss her mouth, a really hard kiss so she won't say that. A hard kiss that turns tender because I don't want to hurt her.

Afterward, when all the air is gone from my lungs and my head is spinning, her fingers stroke into my hair, and she laughs softly. "What time do you think it is?"

I open my eyes. "I don't know."

She bites her lip. "I bet my friends left and now no one can find me. Dani has a mobile phone, but I don't know how I would call her. I left mine at home tonight."

"I can help you find them." I kiss her lips lightly.

"Do you think we'll get caught if we climb out?"

"I bet we've been in here about an hour. They're probably gone."

"Hmmm. Maybe. I kind of don't want to leave." She smiles.

I don't either, but we need to, so I get up, and I help her up. I smooth her clothes down, and she kisses my chin.

We open the hatch above the bed, and I climb out, then pull Elise onto the deck. A cool breeze wraps around us as we stand there on the boat's front, looking at the dark, deserted lawn.

She giggles. "That's a lot of Solo cups."

I take her hand. "Yeah, I hope Jace has a cleaning crew."

She snorts. "I wouldn't bet on that."

We walk slowly around the house, onto the vast side lawn, where we can see the street through a grove of trees at the end of a long driveway.

"Where do you need to be right now, *la mia rosa*?"

"With you." She gives me a shy smile. "But I'm supposed to be spending the night at Dani's house…so I guess there?"

I squeeze her hand. "I'll get you to Dani's. We can walk to Kings Point Park and get a cab there, maybe."

"Thank you. If you're sure it's okay."

"Of course." Dad doesn't care when I come home. Not that he knows what time it is after five o'clock anyway.

We walk through the trees, over the damp grass, toward the lamp-lit road, which is a little two-lane lined with ostentatious houses, leading to a larger two-lane that leads to a parkway that would eventually lead to Throgs Neck Bridge. I looked it all up after school, from a café computer, just in case I couldn't get home on the chopper.

"I really like it here," I hear myself tell her. "It's quiet."

She nods. "We have a place upstate—a bigger kind of place that's on a lake, but it has these two little cabins on the property. One time my mom let my friends and me stay in one for a night. It was so quiet. I felt like you could hear the leaves falling."

"That sounds pretty cool."

I can feel her hesitate a moment as we near the curb that marks the lawn's edge. Her hand in mine tenses.

"What's the matter?"

I notice the car at the moment I ask. There's this dark car parked by the curb, with one door open. She stops walking, lets my hand go. My eyes focus, and I realize a man is standing by the car—someone tall, wearing dark clothes.

Elise makes a little gasp sound. "Oh shit. That's my dad."

CHAPTER NINE

Elise

"We're going to have a conversation, Elise. Sit down." My father pats a wing-backed chair in his study, and again when I don't immediately follow instructions.

I clamp my minty gum between my molars and sit, waiting while he steps behind his large oak desk and settles in his high-backed leather chair. He tugs the pull cord on a Tiffany lamp, splashing amber light over the papers on his desk and lighting his face. It looks pitted with shadows from the angle of the light.

"This won't take long," he says slowly. "But I need to make you understand."

I rub my tongue over the bumpy piece of gum. During the car ride home—which took around two hours—my dad didn't speak. Not one word about how he found out where I was or why he showed up. Or about who I was with. Zip, nada, zilch.

I nod now, fixing my gaze on his face because I know if I don't, he'll think I'm a liar. That's the way my father's mind works.

"Do you know why I came to get you?" There's a pause so I can guess. I don't, and he says, "Your sister had two severe seizures."

"What?"

"She's in the PICU. Your mother is there with her."

"Oh my God." Something cool slips through me—terror. "How is she?"

He shakes his head, pressing his lips flat. My eyes well and my throat aches awfully. *Please don't let this be the night...*

"First, we're going to talk about this insubordination." His eyes are hard on mine as he asks, "Why were you at the Banetti home?"

My stomach sinks like a stone in water. When your father is a cutthroat lawyer and the questions start, you know you're in trouble. I tell myself I'll keep it casual; don't act defensive.

"Everyone went there after the game." As soon as I say it, my jaw drops—because *I wasn't supposed to be at the game!* "We weren't going to go to the game," I add, "but we did at the last minute. Dani had to work concessions."

"Concessions," he says, frowning like the word is foreign to him. "Why is that?"

"Oh, I don't know. Some club she's involved in." My heart beats harder.

"So you were there with Dani, at the game. And the boy—what was his name?—was he playing?"

"No. I mean, well, *yes.* But that's not why we went."

"I didn't imply that it was, Elise. But maybe it was, since you offered that it wasn't." My father looks down at his hand, curled in a half fist on his desk. My throat aches again as I think about the times I used to sit in that chair, playing with his briefcase, calling myself Elise O'Hara, Esquire. Before Becca got worse and he...changed.

His flat, hard gaze returns to mine. "Did you go so you could watch him?"

"No way. Of course not. I don't even know him." *Liar.* "Not well."

"You were never a good liar, were you? That comes from your mother. She's not good at hiding her feelings, either."

She just disappears, I want to say—but I don't. Because my dad would never stand for that, no matter what a coward she is.

"I'm not lying. He's a really nice guy, but we aren't like...close or anything."

"So you are distantly friends."

"*No*, Dad." Tears gleam in my eyes, accompanied by a swell of dismay at myself for sounding so plaintive. If there's one thing my father hates, it's weakness. I blink quickly, willing my tears not to fall.

"Why are you having this reaction, Elise?"

"I'm upset about Becca!" My voice shakes with fury, and my father lifts his dark brows.

"Would you like to tell me how you ended up leaving this party more than an hour after police were summoned? And why you were in a dark yard with a boy you don't know well and aren't close to?"

I inhale slowly, knowing that what I say and how I say it really matters. Then I look into my dad's eyes, keeping my face as emotionless as possible.

"We weren't alone, Dad. There were other people all around."

"That's interesting news. I was up and down the driveway several times, and I saw no one."

"We were out back by the docks. Cleaning up the Solo cups the other kids left."

"Oh, so there were Solo cups."

"Well, yes, but not *mine*. You can smell me if you want to."

My dad lifts a brow again, and I feel stupid for suggesting it.

"What's his name? This nice boy…"

"Why does it matter? I already said he's not my boyfriend or someone I'm close to."

"It matters because I asked."

"Okay…well." My stomach twists. "His name is Luca."

"Luca. What's his last name?"

"Dad, it's weird to have you asking this. It doesn't matter. What are you going to do, like call his parents? Because you saw him in a yard with me?" I'm trying to keep my voice steady, but it keeps rising on key words.

"I don't know. I might. That's my prerogative as your parent. I can do as I choose—as long as you're under this roof." He says it grandly, like a tyrant's proclamation.

I wish I were anywhere else. But I nod—because I have to.

"What's his last name?"

"Dad, that guy is not my boyfriend." I swallow as tears blur my eyes and bite down on the gum again.

"What is Luca's surname, Elise O'Hara? You've gone from grounded for seven days to grounded for ten. And that includes extracurriculars like running, tennis, debate club, volunteer Saturday with that other club…"

I jump up, unplanned. *"What?!* You can't do that! You—"

His face hardens. "I can and I will, unless you tell me that boy's last name."

"I don't want you getting him in trouble, Dad!"

"What makes you think I would?"

"Because you're acting so crazy about it!"

"Now it's two weeks." He tilts his head slightly, looking at me curiously. "How much is this worth to you? For a boy you barely know?"

I can't explain it—not with words. I just have this feeling, like I have to protect Luca.

"I care because you're being mean."

That makes my dad chuckle, and it proves me right; it *is* a mean sound.

He picks up a frame on his desk. The framed item is a handkerchief, embroidered with vines twined into the shape of an "A"—for *amore*. My mother's father gave it to him on their wedding day, making my dad promise to take care of her forever.

"Mean." He looks up at me. "Now you've earned yourself a month."

My body flashes icy cold. "A *month*? Of being grounded? For not telling you some guy's last name?"

"For not telling me Luca *Galante*'s last name." He holds something up—and I realize it's the program from the football game.

"How did you get that?" My face burns. "Did you go there?"

"Of course not."

"Did you have me followed, Dad?"

His eyes narrow. "Someone left it on the lawn. I picked it up. Galante is a name I recognize." He gives a little shake of his head. "The Galantes are not good people, Elise. Not people I want you spending any time with."

"What? The *Galantes*. Like you really know them? He lives in Red Hook!"

"I thought you two weren't close." He quirks an eyebrow, giving me a look straight from the courtroom.

"I know *that* about him. You don't know shit!"

He presses his lips together, glancing briefly down at something on his desk then back up. "I know what I need to know. Don't ask how, because it doesn't matter. Nor do I feel inclined to answer you. But let me make this very clear, Elise O'Hara: If I find you are cavorting with the Galante boy in any way—be it at a football game after school or sitting with him at lunch or looking at him in the hall or in *any* way—there will be consequences that will shock you. The biggest one being, no Columbia."

My stomach hollows. My mouth falls open. I close it and try to make words. "No—" I can't find the words to express my dismay. "You're saying you won't help me...go to college?"

"Oh no. I'm saying that you won't go at all. Whether you need my 'help' or not. I'll decline your scholarship for you."

"What?! For seeing *Luca*?" My heart pounds like a drum. "Why, Dad?"

"There's a reason you have parents, Elise. And a good parent does what he can to protect his child."

"I don't need to be protected! Just from *you*!" Hot tears spill down my cheeks as I shake my head. "You wouldn't do that..."

"You have no idea what I would do—or why. That's why you're going to trust me. I'll do what I have to do to keep you safe, including clip your wings. Your sister is stable for now. Go to your room. We'll talk more about your poor choices tomorrow."

CHAPTER TEN

Luca

"Thanks for the ride, Diamond."

What I really mean is *fuck you*. But I don't think that's the smartest thing to say to a newly made guy.

"No problem kid."

I reach for the passenger's door handle, waiting for him to say more—but he doesn't.

I roll my eyes as I get out. "You're welcome—for the help."

Diamond gives a wheezy sounding laugh. "That ain't the way this works, Bowzie."

I clap my palm against the roof of his brand new Mercedes as he pulls away from the curb. For a second, I watch as he steers into a crowded lane.

Diamond thinks he's Tony fucking Soprano. Really, he's a small fry —a nobody. Which means he gets the worst jobs.

The night I gave him Elise's bear, he was stuck with a truck-load of stolen hundred dollar bills stained with thieves ink. We spent hours scrubbing it off—with Mr. Clean Magic Erasers and some other shit. Stung my hands and ruined my fucking shirt.

Last night was a lot worse.

I woke up to Alesso knocking on my window at one in the morning, asking if I could help with "something." He looked tired and pissed off, and I was feeling guilty that I hardly ever see him anymore, so I pulled on a jacket and snuck out.

"Tony's got a job. Nobody wants to help him." Alesso folded his arms and looked down at his Nikes. I socked him in the shoulder just to lighten the mood, and he laughed like I knew he would.

"What kind of bullshit is it this time, Aless?"

He scowled at me using his mom's nickname for him. "Fuck you, you magnet fucker. Tony said you got a girlfriend over there."

I snorted.

"What's she like?"

I waved him toward the alley's mouth. "Let's get farther from these windows, and I'll tell you."

Once we got on the sidewalk in front of the apartment complex, I told him about Elise, and he told me the address of the warehouse.

"I don't know what went down there, but Tony said there's a *mess*." Alesso's eyes were wide, so I could tell what he meant.

"Ahh shit, really?"

He nodded grimly. Turned out, there was plenty to be grim about. Alesso is squeamish—he puked twice, and I cleaned extra quick so Tony wouldn't bitch if his brother just watched.

It took so damn long, I had to call my house from a booth phone when dawn came, and then I missed the connector from Red Hook into Brooklyn. I told Diamond he would have to drive me all the way to school, and surprisingly, he did.

He didn't thank me for the help. That's not the way it works. I snicker—even though it isn't funny.

Alesso's got to get out of there. I've got to get out of there. Maybe I can find us a job in Manhattan this summer. If we made enough, we could throw a little Tony's way and he'd stop asking us to help at the docks...or worse.

I'm thinking about the worse—how the blood *gelled*—when I see the black car park along the curb ahead of me. The door opens, and Elise is out like a shot.

Shit, I must be later than I thought. My heart gives a jolt and I think if it's blood that gets to Alesso, it's this girl that gets to me, because I feel sick as I trail her. She doesn't slow, which means she doesn't hear my footsteps—or she doesn't care to hear them. Maybe she regrets the other night. Something dark and heavy presses on me as I consider that, but I can't just let myself assume.

I catch her at the far end of the bridge, as she's opening the school door. I don't want to grab her, so I say her name. She spins around. The second her eyes lock onto mine, tears fill them.

"What's the matter, *la mia rosa?*" For a second, her face shutters, and I hate myself for the endearment. Then she moves in closer, bowing her head. I wrap her up against my chest and step out of the doorway, so my back is leaned against the wall of the covered bridge, and that's when Elise starts sobbing.

Jesus, but her father is a bastard.

And her sister...

Elise is devastated—almost limp as I hold her against me. We're both late to homeroom, but I take her to the girls' bathroom and help her wipe her face. In that quiet, echo-y space, she tells me that her dad said she couldn't see me again.

"He's crazy, and obviously he doesn't want me to be happy—since he's not." She wipes her eyes and sniffs. "Don't worry, I know we're not dating for real."

"We're doing whatever you want, *la mia dolce rosa.*"

She dabs at her eyes with tissue. "What does that mean?" There's a ghost of a smile on her lips, which makes me feel so fucking good.

"Sweet rose."

"Why am I a rose?" Her lips curve.

"I don't know," I tell her. But that's not true. I think it's because she's so damn perfect. My mom always says there's nothing prettier than a rose. "Maybe because of how you looked the other night." I say it teasingly, but I'm sure she can see I mean it.

"Now I'm rose-*colored.*" She fans her face with her hand, rolling her eyes. I think about teasing her again, but decide to give her a break.

"You know, a lot of the thirty days you're grounded are school days."

She nods.

"And your dad won't know what happens here, right?"

She hesitates before saying, "I hope not." She wipes her eyes. "But I can never see you outside school." Another tear falls. "Not even on the sidewalk, when I get dropped off."

"I don't remember any interactions offered on the sidewalk."

She smiles, looking abashed, and I pull her up against me. "I'm just fucking with you. I don't give a shit about the sidewalk. We've got covered bridges, baby."

That makes her giggle. She steps closer to me, so I'm fully hugging her, and fuck, it feels so good having her against me. I smooth her hair back off her forehead. "You want to try something? Tomorrow, I'm bringing you my favorite cake. It's lemon cake. Every day, I'll bring you something. Food, or other stuff. Just something to give you a distraction."

More tears fill her eyes as she looks up at me, and I laugh, though it's part groan. "That's not what I was going for."

"Thank you," she says. She looks down at the boots she's wearing, shy again. I hug her. I can feel her exhale. Then she kisses my pec through my T-shirt. "You're my favorite fake boyfriend."

I could keep the joke up, but I don't. I kiss her hair instead. Just so she knows this isn't fake to me. She gives me another of her sweet smiles, and I kiss her one more time because I can't help myself.

Then I walk her quickly to her homeroom. I double back to the guys' bathroom before going to my own class. I've still got blood under my fingernails. I need to scrub it off before I hold her hand at lunch.

CHAPTER ELEVEN

Elise

I wait on the sidewalk beside the tennis court like one of Pavlov's dogs. It's day seven of my grounding, which means it's Friday. Which means tomorrow and Sunday, I won't get to see him.

I hate that, but I can do this. I can wait out my dad. So can Luca.

Despite Dad promising to talk to me about my transgressions, he sent Mom—the first night she and Bec were back home. She came into my room as I was tucking into bed, nearly giving me a heart attack because I assumed something was wrong with Becca. She sat on the edge of my bed in her floor-length, green silk robe and told me, "Don't defy your father, *shona*. Trust me, you will regret it if you do."

When I asked her why—why Dad cared so much about Luca, and how he knew the Galantes—she just shook her head and left the room.

Since then, a few strange things have happened. Mom had the housekeepers move the furniture in my room one day while I was at school, and when I asked about it, she said something about fresh starts and changed the subject. My cell phone got a clip-on protective cover one morning while I was in the shower. And then, a few days ago, the school counselor called me into her office. We talked about my scholarship and plans for next year. I guess that's not so weird, but something about the timing felt suspect.

So, as of the other day, I'm walking to school. I told Mercer, the elderly Englishman who's been on our household's payroll since I was a baby, that I didn't need rides home from school until it gets colder in a few weeks. Then this morning, I told him I didn't need a ride to school either. I let my mom know so no one can say I'm trying to be sneaky. I told her Dani's walking now, too—which isn't true, but she's not going to call Dani's mom. They're not even friends.

Now, here I am, having walked the three blocks to school on my own legs, smiling the whole way because I can tell Bec's new seizure meds are working—she's more alert by far. The air is crisp, the leaves are gorgeous gold and flaming orange and wine red. Luca should be here in minutes.

I take a step back toward the fence that frames the tennis court, so people driving by won't be able to spot me on the sidewalk. I figure I should do that every morning as I wait for Luca. Not because I think my dad would have me followed—because I *know* my dad would have me followed. I don't know what's behind this Luca stuff, but he's been cool toward me the handful of times he's been home for dinner since that night.

I rub my fingertip over a leaf, wondering again why Dad said what he said about the Galantes. What did it mean? And how does he know them? I feel like there's no way he could know Luca, so does he know Luca's dad? Was Mr. Galante a client of his? Or does he know the Galantes in some other way? And are Luca's Galantes even the ones Dad knows?

I hope I never find out, because I don't plan to ask. With any luck, I can keep my first real relationship a secret for winter, spring, and summer. Then I'm moving into an apartment near campus, and we'll be home free.

I look down at the pointer finger of my left hand, where there's a star-shaped pink gumball-machine ring. Luca brought it to me yesterday, along with orange Tic-Tacs.

In a makeup bag inside my backpack are the other things he's brought—the ones I didn't snarf down, anyway. There's been lemon cake and orange-flavored chocolate, a tiny, two-by-four-inch canvas with a painting of the Statue of Liberty, and a little lucky clover paperweight his grandma gave him, followed by a tin of lavender lip gloss he got at an Italian market in Red Hook. And then the ring. I smile at it again before I cast my gaze down the sidewalk.

And I see him. My heart catches at the sight: his long, familiar strides, the wide shoulders and slight swagger, the black hoodie and worn jeans. His backpack is red, and there's a patch sewn on it that his brother gave him. Pokémon. When I asked about it the other day, Luca said he sewed it onto the pack himself.

"What about your mom?" I'd asked him.

"You saying a dude can't sew?"

I laughed, feeling embarrassed by my assumption—especially since I can't even thread a needle.

I'm smiling at that memory as I step out from behind the trees.

His face lights up, and he speeds up. When he's close enough, I launch myself at him, and he hugs me to his chest, squeezing me a little before planting a quick kiss on my lips. He takes my hand, and we start walking quickly toward the bridge.

I'm ready. Enclosed in my fingers is my gift for him. It's small and silly, but I saw it in a store window on my walk home from school yesterday, and I couldn't resist buying it. Now I press it into his hand, watching his eyes widen as he looks down at me in burgeoning surprise.

"What is this?" he asks as we walk into the covered bridge.

"What does it feel like?"

"I don't know." He's smiling, his blue eyes doing their crinkle at the corners thing that I love.

I can feel his fingers rub over the trinket.

"It feels bumpy..."

"Mmm hmmm."

"And round." His eyebrows scrunch up. Then he holds it out in front of him, and I watch his mouth twist into a smile. "That's a little lemon."

I grin down at the thing.

"That's a little lemon with a smilie face," he marvels.

"It's a little lemon keychain. I saw it at—you will never guess this —a lemonade stand! Really it's more like a shop, but they have lemonade and cookies. In your case, though, this is about lemon *cake*. That there is a lemon who aspires to be cake."

Luca's smile is so big, it makes my heart ache. He hugs me against his side as we walk. "Thank you. I'll attach it to the house key. Or my backpack." He frowns like he's contemplating and then gives me a careful look. "How was your night? Did things go okay?"

"Yep. My mom's still being nice—suspiciously so. And she's been around more. Becca had a good day yesterday. And Dad is working a lot. I haven't seen him in four full days."

"Sweet."

"Yep, I think that's the winning combo."

I haven't told Luca what my dad said about the Galantes. I don't see how it would make anything better, and there's a good chance it could hurt his feelings or offend him. I told him my dad was mad I'd gone to a party rather than where I said I'd be, and was extra mad to have found me there with a guy.

Dad would never have known where I was had it not been for Bec's seizure. He called Dani's mom, who asked her driver, Fil, where we were, and *viola*!

"You want yours now," Luca asks, "or at lunch?"

He pushes the school door open, and I step inside in front of him. "You pick. Is it lunch-able?"

He laughs. "Do you want it to be?"

"I think my surprise is you." I kiss his throat, glancing behind me right after to see if anyone saw—and there's Ree, making faces from across the common area.

"Oh my gosh."

"What is it?"

I point, and Luca waves. Ree blows him a kiss.

"Let's do lunch. So I'll have something to look forward to."

Someone calls his name from across the way—one of the guys on the team, whom I don't know well—and his eyes widen.

"Track?" I ask.

He steps close to me and kisses my hair. "Yeah, I'll meet ya at the track." A few strides from me, he turns around. "Don't wear lipstick," he mouths, miming putting some on.

I hold onto that image all morning—and the lit-up look in his gorgeous eyes.

He likes me. He likes me. Luca Galante likes me. I really like him, too.

He gives me my favorite book at lunchtime as we picnic in the field.

"*Wuthering Heights.*" It's the perfect copy, leather-bound and lovingly worn. I laugh. "Who did you ask?"

"Hm?"

"Who told you, Ree or Dani?"

"Oh, I didn't ask."

"This is my favorite. Like, of all time. Why'd you get it?"

"I don't know." He smiles. "I just saw it and I thought of you."

"You've read it?"

"Last year. I had Carr for lit."

"Did you like it?"

"No." His lips curve slightly, the only clue he's teasing. "I hated it. That's why I bought it. I hoped you could hate it with me. I mean, *Catherine*," he shakes his head. "Such a megabitch."

I shove him, and he wraps me in a bear hug, lying back in the grass with me halfway on top of him.

"I liked it," he laughs, nuzzling my chin with his cheek. "*La mia rosa*, she's a skeptic."

"Why are you so perfect?" I give him a shoulder punch, and then we're kissing. I don't remember until Dani laughs at me in fifth period that I forgot to scrub my lipstick.

Elise
Two Weeks Later

"Time is very slow for those who wait," I murmur.

"Very fast for those who are scared."

"Very long for those who lament."

"Very short for those who celebrate."

"But for those who love," I murmur, "time is eternal."

We're lying in the grass out in the center of the track, reciting Shakespeare to a soft blue sky because my lit teacher, Dr. Cowles, is out for surgery, so right now we both have Mrs. Lynch for lit, and Literary Lynch is obsessed with Shakespeare. Rightly so, I have to admit. If there's any writer worth becoming obsessed with, it's Shakespeare.

"Was that right?" I ask Luca.

He opens a tattered, school-issue copy of *Great Shakespeare*, holding it over himself with one hand since his other arm is serving as my pillow. I look at his face, shadowed by the book. He's got the longest lashes and the most delicious cheekbones...and those pretty boy lips.

I watch them curve and part. "Yep. We got it."

"Oh yeah." I wiggle my butt against the grass, laughing at what a dork I am. He gives me this funny look he gives me sometimes, like he's not sure what planet I'm from. Then he kisses my cheek.

"Do you know the one you have to recite for your essay yet?" I ask.

His lips press into a small, mysterious smile. "Do you?"

"Of course."

"Say it for me."

"Ugh."

"Do it," he says.

"No."

"Yes."

"No." I'm pouting.

"*Yes*

"I sound so stupid doing stuff like this."

"No you don't," he says.

"It's going to be awful."

"It's gonna be fine. Say it. You never told me what you picked."

"It's from *Macbeth*. Act five, scene five."

He raises his dark brows. "That sounds fun."

"Oh yes."

He rolls onto his side, sliding his arm out from behind my neck and using it to prop his cheek up as he looks down at me. When I rub my eyes, he quirks a brow up, prompting.

"I might get it wrong," I hedge.

"You know what will happen if you do."

I sigh. "I'm only saying the end part. The whole thing is really too long." I clear my throat, and his face does the angel thing, where his eyes shine warm fuzzies at me and his smile says everything in life is golden. It gives me a little kick of bravery.

"Out, out brief candle! Life is but a walking shadow, a poor player that struts and frets his hour upon the stage and then is heard no more. It is a tale told by an idiot, full of sound and fury, signifying nothing."

His eyes shut as he lies back beside me, resting his cheek against the top of my head. Then he leans away again and peers at me.

I shrug, feeling my cheeks burn. "It seemed less trite than some of the other things."

He shakes his head, smiling slightly. "Shakespeare—trite."

"People have made it trite. Over the years."

It's been twenty days since I got grounded. It's a Thursday, and which means that after school tomorrow, I won't see him for two whole days.

"Sad things are more true anyway," I try.

"Yeah, but does that make them better?"

"Are you saying all the bullshit happy quotes are better?"

He shrugs. "Gotta take the happy stuff where you can get it."

"What happy stuff can you get?"

He gives me a small smile, his eyes looking tired. "You."

I snuggle closer to him. "I'm a pessimist, I think."

"Are you?" He runs a hand down my arm, leaning in like he might kiss me.

"Yes." I shut my eyes. "Are you an optimist?"

"Nah. I'm a realist."

"What did you pick to say in front of everyone?"

He smiles. "Sonnet 116."

"I remember that one from the slide she showed in class. Do you know it?"

He gives me a mysterious look, but he can't help smirking.

"I bet you know it by heart already. Ree is in your homeroom. She says you got in trouble at the start of school for not doing your homework in there, and the teacher made you show it. Turned out, you had nothing to do in homeroom because you do all your homework at home."

"Imagine that."

I laugh.

"Actually, I do it on the train."

"Oh."

"It's a good time to do homework."

"You're avoiding the question."

"What question?"

"If you've got it memorized."

He clears his throat and lowers the book, which was shading his face from the sun. He shuts his eyes against the light and begins.

"Let me not to the marriage of true minds admit impediments. Love is not love which alters when it alteration finds, or bends with the remover to remove: oh no, it is an ever-fixed mark that looks on tempests and is never shaken. It is the star to every wandering bark, whose worth's unknown, although his height be taken. Love's not time's fool, though rosy lips and cheeks within his bending sickle's compass come: love alters not with his brief hours and weeks, but bears it out even to the edge of doom. If this be error and upon me proved, I never writ, nor no man ever loved."

I lean in and kiss his cheek. Because I *can't* not. He laughs, and then sits up and looks down at me.

I smile. "That was a rebuttal to my lines."

"I would like for it to be seen that way."

He takes my hand and pulls me to my feet, and we walk around the track to the spot where we can see the river best. I'm playing with a little ball of Saran Wrap—from the lemon cake he brought me today. He takes it from me, stuffs it in his pocket, smiles like Cheshire Cat.

"I'll bring more cake tomorrow."

"Thank you," I say, feeling suddenly shy. He squeezes my hand as we walk toward the school door.

"I don't think it is," he says.

"You don't think what is what?"

"That life is meaningless, like your quote implied."

I let my breath out slowly, looking at the grassy path before our shoes press over it.

"I know you kind of do," he says. "It's okay. Sometimes I do too, but I think we're both wrong."

"Why?"

His face turns thoughtful. "I don't know. It's just this feeling I get. Like things'll turn out okay." He gives me one of his decadent smiles. "Mostly happens when I'm with you, but I trust it."

"I'm going to Columbia," I blurt.

Surprise flickers through his features. "Oh yeah?"

"Here in New York."

"You're kidding."

I elbow him.

But I can't help the way my heart pounds as I look up at him. "Will you be…around here?" I manage. "In Brooklyn or somewhere nearby?"

"I think so." He gives me a small, strained smile. "Don't know where else I would be."

"I want to see each other," I breathe. Blood whooshes in my head as I wait for him to process and answer. His lips twitch into something, but I wouldn't call it a smile.

"We can see each other whenever you want."

We're at the door. He goes to push it open but I grab his arm and pull him up against the brick wall with me.

I look up at his face, trying to find words to explain. "No, Luca. I want to *see* you next year. I want to see you. As much as we can. Unless you don't."

His eyes shut. A breath moves through him. Then he leans down, kissing me so deep and hard it hurts. We kiss until my heart races, and then he hugs me to him like he's hoping we'll merge into one.

"I love you," he says, quiet and low.

"I love you more than lemon cake," I whisper.

That's the first time we say it.

CHAPTER TWELVE

Luca

For the rest of the school day, I carry her with me like something tangible. Elise O'Hara. *Mine.*

I know it's dangerous. I can't make the kinds of promises that other people could. And I have secrets. Not intentional ones, but lies of omission—like about the kinds of things I'm doing to keep Tony Diamond and the people above him from shaking down my dad. We can't go back to that. Not if we're going to be able to afford Mom's maintenance chemo pills.

Dad's been in debt to the Arnoldis for about ten years, since the store flooded and Roberto, one of his customers, loaned him some money. I don't know exactly what happened, but I can guess it involves a bottle—either plastic or glass. Dad fell behind on his repayment plan, so Roberto would stop by sometimes and try to make him pay up. One day when I was fifteen, I was feeling pissed off. I stepped in front of him when he came toward the door and told him not to come by anymore.

I said something like, "Quit kicking someone who's already down."

At the time I didn't really know who Roberto Arnoldi was. When I told Leo and Alesso, they figured I'd probably wind up sleeping with the fishes, but the opposite happened. Roberto just stopped coming.

A year or so later, Tony started stopping by. I told him to fuck off, too, and that's how I got into this shit with him.

Elise can never, ever know. Of everybody in my life, she's the one who really believes I'm a good person. And when I'm with her, I feel good. Like I could be good—good enough to justify continuing. And I have to justify it, because I can't stop. Even though I know I've got nothing to offer her.

When she told me about Columbia today, I couldn't bring myself to tell her I got a scholarship offer there, too. I don't think I'll ever make it there. Someone's got to watch out for my mom and Soren—and keep Tony off our backs.

I tell myself I'm okay with temporary. She'll move out of her parents' place and start college, and she'll find someone better for her. And until then...

I'm on the train, holding the new book I checked out from the library—*A Storm of Swords*, by George R.R. Martin—when the full weight of all this shit hits me. I really am in love with her. And she said she loves me.

It feels so fucking good...but I feel off the rest of the ride back to Brooklyn.

I grab a bag of donut holes on my walk from the station, and find the shoe store quiet when I arrive. For a second, I stop just inside the door. It looks the same, feels the same, smells the same—leather and dust. I find my father behind the counter; he can't stand up, so I organize shelves and dust for two hours till he can, and then we walk to the house in silence.

My little brother Soren has cooked dinner—spaghetti with my Tati's special sauce. My mom's quiet at the table, maybe upset.

Dad pours himself a glass of sambuca and beckons me into his room. He's had his own room for years now, right beside mine. Mom sleeps in the master—if you can call it that—and my brother in what really is a closet under the stairs.

When we step into Dad's room, he leans against his dresser and just looks at me. Up and down, and up and down, and then his face crumples like he might cry. "Luca," he says, heavy, "there's something that I've gotta tell you..."

He looks mournful, maybe even sorry. His brown eyes are watery. His bushy brows are drawn down. It takes work to keep a cringe off my face. But it doesn't matter. A second later, he totters toward his bed and face-plants on the mattress.

A minute later, I hear him snoring. "Good talk."

I wait another minute, but he doesn't stir. Do I want him to?

I think, as I look down at him, about the conversation I overheard at the wedding reception. Someone warning him—in Italian—about whatever he's been doing. Probably something to do with his fix.

Part of me still wants to ask him about it, to confront him about his presence at the reception to begin with, but I don't see the point. It's an easy guess: for some reason or another, Roberto Arnoldi expected him there, so he went. Even though Roberto has treated my dad like shit.

Before that, he was a longtime customer. I think he was Dad's friend.

In the kitchen, Mom is slicing homemade cheesecake onto painted clay plates. I make her sit down, then drizzle Hershey's syrup over the three slices. Mom and Soren and I eat together on the couch, scraping every smidgen off the plates with our forks, watching *American Idol*.

"Too bad neither one of you is good at singing," she says.

"Hey, I'm good," Soren says—at the same time I agree, "Too bad."

"Well you're both good, but not devoted," my mom clarifies.

"There are other things to do," I tell her.

"I'll stick to piano," Soren says.

He goes to his room to read comics after the show, but I stay out on the couch with Mom. She likes falling asleep in the blue light of the TV and then walking to her bedroom half asleep—something I like to give her shit for. She wraps an afghan around her shoulders and looks like a zombie walking down the hall.

Tonight, she nods off, but she doesn't get up for a long time. I look at her for a few minutes as she sleeps, taking in her short, brown-gray hair, the grooves in her face, the lines around her lips from smoking cigarettes when I was little. I think of the pictures of her at my age—mostly arm in arm with Dad, her head tipped back as she laughed at something he said. My dad used to be funny...or so I'm told. I've told Elise some sentimental shit about how he used to be a good guy before his problems started, but the truth is I don't remember any of that.

Mom's really out. I wait a while longer, and when she doesn't get up to zombie stagger to her room, I go to mine, leaving the door cracked so I can listen out for trouble. I lie on my back and look up at the light fixture, a brass thing from the '80s that's hanging crooked, like it's thinking about falling.

Then I close my eyes and think of *her*.

*

Elise

"Are you sure about this?" he asks.

I squeeze his hand. "I'm so sure. They're at a thing in Westport, and they're staying the night." I don't mention that they have a weekend flat there. Luca's always such a good sport, but sometimes I think he feels self-conscious about the difference in our family's incomes. Things like that couldn't be less relevant to me, so it's better to avoid the topic.

He looks up at the elevator's mirrored ceiling, and I use my hip to bump his. Then I bump him more and more, laughing as I pin him in the corner, where I wrap myself around him like an octopus.

And then he's laughing with me. That's my favorite part of any good day—hearing his low, slightly hoarse laugh. He always sounds a little rusty, like it's been a hundred years since he laughed. But when I look up at his face, his smile is radiant and satisfied, and I know he's really happy.

"Trust me on this," I say again, as the elevator jolts to a gentle stop on floor twenty. "Maura is my favorite nurse. She's been with Bec for almost six years. I told her you were going to come by, and she swore not to tell my parents." We step off the elevator, and I grip his hand as we walk down the sleek, echoey hall.

"There are cameras—like security—but they're for the staff quarters and the living areas. We'll go in the family door and meet Bec in the laundry room. Don't worry, it has a couch. And then we'll go up to the rooftop garden and part ways, and on Monday, I'll be free from being grounded. We can sneak around while I pretend to be with my friends. It will be the best thing *ever*."

I press my pointer finger into the keypad by the family door, and it clicks open. I glance up, and Luca's smiling—that good, satisfied, amused smile that's one of my faves. I nudge the door open with my fingers, and we walk through together.

"Here we are. Home not-so-sweet home," I mutter, making a face.

I watch as his gaze sweeps the foyer, with its glossy hardwood, thick crown molding, crystal chandelier, and marble-topped antique table.

"It's great."

"Mm. Let's go this way." I drag him down the hallway, past one of the things I do like in the house—a haunting Alyssa Monks painting —and then I open the door to the laundry room and come grin-to-grin with Maura.

"Hello there." She steps closer to my sister's wheelchair, wrapping her hand around the handle bar as she nods at Luca.

For a split second, my stomach does a hard roll as two worlds collide. What if Luca can't see Bec the way I—

And then my sister laughs

Her face is lit up in a way I haven't seen in months, and she's just...laughing. It's such a shock that Maura starts to laugh, and then Luca is laughing. He's crouching by her chair, and I'm trying to smile as tears of shock fill my eyes.

"Becca, this is Luca." She's grinning so hugely that I know she knows exactly who he is. My sister isn't mentally disabled. She has a rare disorder that's been ravaging her body for the last few years—it causes seizures and destroys her muscles—and some of the medicines she's taking make her a little out of it at times. But she knows what "my boyfriend" means.

"Luca, this is my younger sister Becca."

"Hi, Becca. It's nice to meet you."

Becca flaps her right hand—the only one she can control—and I'm surprised when Luca reaches for it, closing his big hand around her smaller one and giving it a light shake.

Becca laughs again, and Maura wipes her mouth, and Luca doesn't even flinch. I think *of course he doesn't*. Why did I doubt him?

Still, I watch in shock as he tells Becca a long, one-sided story about the time he and his brother decided to make an obstacle course in their house with their mom's magazines, couch pillows, and two pitchers of red Kool-Aid.

"Our mom was *rabbioso*." He says the word dramatically, making Bec smile again. "Do you know what that means?"

Maura smiles knowingly, and after a brief pause, Luca says, "Furious. She was so mad at us, we had to clean the bathrooms for the rest of the year."

"*Bambini cattivi*," Maura murmurs, and Luca looks up at her.

"*La tua famiglia viene dal vecchio paese.*"

"*Sì.*"

"Maura knows what's up, huh?" Luca says to Becca. "I bet Maura is your buddy."

I nod. "Maura and Bec make all kinds of craft projects. They dance and they do hammock time and therapy. Maura and I both read a lot to Bec. Bec is a good reader, but her eyes have been giving her some trouble, and I don't think she minds too much if we read to her."

"Elise has told me a lot of stuff about both of you. Good stuff," he says to Becca, who smiles again.

"What are you guys doing next?" I ask Maura.

"I think we'll watch a bit of TV and go for an early bed time."

"Luca and I are going to walk up to the garden for a minute. Then he's going home. So I'll join you for that TV. Sound good?"

Becca smiles, and I can tell she's tired. It's a lot of effort for her, asking her muscles to coordinate for a smile.

"Thanks for letting me come over," Luca says to Bec. "Maybe some other time I'll drop back by?"

She blinks a few times, big brown eyes trained on his face for just a second before swinging back down to her strap-crossed lap. Luca's hand moves over her head, the motion so gentle I think his palm barely touches her hair. Then he gets to his feet, looking so tall in the small space of our laundry room. He turns to me, and he's uncomfortable, not sure how to depart—even though I told him we would have to be quick.

"We're going to go, you guys." I brush my fingers over Becca's forehead. "See you soon, sweetheart."

"Nice to meet you both." He gives a little crooked smile to Maura. "*Prenditi cura delle mie ragazze.*"

I can barely look at him as we walk to the elevator...even as I feel the tension rolling off him. We step in, and he steps closer to me. I can feel him looking down at me, can feel him wondering what to say as tears fill my eyes.

He murmurs a curse, and then I hear him blow a breath out. I'm crying. I'm covering my eyes. He moves in closer. I can feel him wanting to touch me and trying not to.

"Elise...did I—"

I shake my head and just keep shaking it as I try to pull myself together. "No." I look up at him, laughing. "You were perfect." That's the problem. He's so perfect it makes me scared. I don't know why; maybe I'm afraid I'll lose him.

His arms twine around me as the elevator opens on the rooftop level. He leads me out into the garden—cold and humid with the nighttime. There's a breeze that cuts me to the bone. I'm shivering and he is leaning in the corner of the terrace, wrapping me in his arms, then unzipping his black hoodie...helping me into it.

I'm between his legs and in his arms, my cheek pressed to his chest so I can hear his heartbeat.

"I'm sorry," I whisper after a long time has passed.

"Why?"

"For freaking out when it went so well. You were really perfect with her. It was beautiful."

He takes in a breath and lets it out. More time passes, with the breeze in my hair. My tears are cold on my cheeks. His body is so warm. Finally my Luca says, "It was really easy. You know...because she's sort of like a part of you."

CHAPTER THIRTEEN

Luca

Everything is different after I meet her sister. More is given—gladly. More is taken—greedily. All things are assumed, and it feels right for us to be that way. It feels better than right.

And it's a good thing, because it's the only thing that does. In every other way, the next three months are a wash of bullshit. Dad started sleeping somewhere else most nights. It breaks my mother's heart, but not a damn thing anyone can do. And when he is home, he's got more piss in him then he used to.

I can feel him being miserable, hating himself and hating us because of it. One night when I'm lying awake, thinking of the feeling of her arms around me, I realize that's how this goes with people like my dad. It's sort of like he's falling from the hundredth floor of a building, and he's flailing with his arms grasping the air and legs all kicking, and he's fucked. He knows he's fucked, but he'll grab at anything to slow that fall. He needs something to hold him. Most of all, I think he needs someone to blame, and so we give that to him. Doesn't matter if we want to. He's not asking. When it comes to me, especially, he's gotten good at twisting me into the enemy he needs.

Christmas Eve is ruined when he comes home drunk after midnight mass, sits down to dinner Soren and I made for Mom, and spoons some of our seafood risotto into his mouth. He spits it out and stands so fast he nearly upends our small table.

"Cold," he bellows. "Couldn't even keep the food warm for your father!" He shoves the table before stomping off to his room.

That sends Soren to his own room, where he's locked himself inside. I can hear him screaming into the pillow. Mom, who was in the bathroom when it happened, helps me coax him out. Normally on Christmas Eve, we watch a movie, but no one trusts Dad not to make trouble, so we finish our dinner and retreat to our own rooms.

I'm nearly asleep—hugging a pillow, thinking of Elise in a way I only let myself when I'm half conscious—when someone knocks on my window.

What the fuck?

It's Leo.

For a second, I have sort of a flashback to when he used to live in the apartment next door—before his parents divorced and he and his mom moved in with his grandma over on Mill Street. With Alesso on the next block, we used to roam the neighborhood and call ourselves the Three Ninjas.

I frown at him through the window now. I shove it up a few inches. "What the—"

"Get out here."

Leo's got one blue eye and one brown one. Right now, they're both fucking huge. I hold up one finger, shut the window, scrawl a quick note for my mom in case she comes into my room, pull on my coat, and then swing out the window. My sneakers crunch dirt in the narrow alley. Maybe ice, too.

"Fucking shit, Luca. Alesso's with Tony, and he called my house from Tony's mobile. They were doing something with some truck— unloading some shit over by the pier—and Tony ran his fucking duck- bill, I don't even know—" Leo waves his arms around as he walks toward the alley's mouth— "He got his ass kicked. Alesso stepped in. He's got a bad cut on his head that he said's bleeding everywhere, and he and Tony ran off to some alley. They're pretty fucked up, but Tony's talking about going to kill those guys."

Leo hangs a right onto the sidewalk that runs in front of the apart- ment complex. He starts walking faster. Then he's jogging, and I'm jogging with him.

"Hotwired *zio*'s Cutlass so we can go to the pier faster. Clacking all around when I drive because he's got catering shit in the back." He waves at the red car that's parked like shit along the curb.

"Ah, shit. Luigi—" Alesso's uncle— "will fucking kill us if he finds out."

He shakes his head as he unlocks the door. "Fucking Tony. Alesso's been doing shit like almost every night."

We drive to the pier with Queen singing "Bohemian Rhapsody" from the dashboard speakers. Makes sense, because Luigi sings in a Queen cover band sometimes on weekends. When we get near the pier, there's a cop car with its lights on but no sirens.

Turns out Tony busted some dude's face up and then he and Alesso bounced. Leo can't find anywhere to turn around, and has to do a ten-point turn right near the cop, who pulls him over and writes him a ticket for driving without an ID.

I get home at two-thirty, after going with Leo to see Alesso. Aless needs stitches near his temple, but he won't go for them, so Leo and I tape his shit up with some Band-Aids. Alesso looks like ass. He's grown inches since I last saw him, but he looks skinny and scared, more like a kid than someone who turns eighteen in a few weeks.

I give him one of those back clap kind of hugs and feel damn sorry when we have to leave. Leo thanks me, like I need to be told thank you. I tell him to fuck himself, and he laughs, and it feels more normal—more like we were before I started going to Manhattan Magnet. We promise to get together soon, and I'm back up through the alley window with no further drama.

A quick trip through the house reveals that everyone is sleeping, which is good since I forgot to wrap my presents.

I fish the items out of the back of my closet and sit on the scarred floor, surrounded by gifts, tape, and wrapping paper. As I unroll some paper, I think of Elise. I wonder if she's sleeping, if her house is all dressed up for Christmas. Would it be the kind of place that has a twenty-foot tree? I bet it is.

I think about her sister Becca, and I hope their parents pull their shit together and make it a good time for them. I lean my back against the foot of my bed. Fuck, I really miss her...the way she feels all wrapped around me, and her good smell. We still have to sneak around, so we don't see each other all that much. But we meet up at parties, school sports shit, and sometimes at the public library near her house. I'm used to seeing Elise pretty often. So it sucks not to.

I wish I felt like I could call her—but her dad check's her cellular phone log. I've emailed her from the library that's near me, but it's not the same.

There's this feeling inside my chest like something clawing. Doesn't matter, I tell myself. School will start again in nine more days. I'll be okay until then. She said she might call sometime tomorrow—if she can find a safe time to try it from the house phone.

I get up, slip off my shirt, and pull on the sweater she gave me this past Friday night—at the MM Athletics Christmas party. It was the only way that we could swap gifts. I gave her a small gold ring I got one night I rode along with Tony on some sketchy jewelry store shit, and she gave me this sweater and a leather-bound edition of *Lord of the Rings*. I glance up at my bed, where the book hides in the covers.

Then I reach into the pocket of my jacket, where I've been holding onto something I was going to give her but didn't. It's a gold necklace with an amulet of St. Jude. I got it that same night with Tony, but when I arrived at the school gym for the athletics party Friday, I unwrapped the thing and stashed it in my pocket.

I thread the necklace through my fingers now and wish that I had given it to her. Maybe I will after New Year's. I can tell her it's Saint Christopher—for protection. One day, she'll figure out it's Jude. Or maybe she won't. Maybe it gets lost before she even moves to college.

I fasten the necklace around my neck, quietly wrap my gifts, and steal into the living room to see what Santa Lucia left for Soren and me. Our stockings each contain a few small oranges, the same honey biscuits "Santa Lucia" always brings, cannoli in those plastic boxes my Zia Eva always puts her homemade stuff in, gold coin chocolates, several handfuls each of Double Bubble gum, ten dollars for each of us, playing cards for each, Pokémon cards for Soren, and at the very bottom of my stocking, my grandfather's pearl cufflinks.

Seeing those makes me smile. My mom's dad was a high school math teacher. Everyone says I look just like him.

I wear Saint Jude to sleep that night, despite the tightness of the chain around my throat, and open my eyes Christmas morning dreaming of Elise and me. She's got on a fancy gown, and I'm wearing a tux with Nonno's cufflinks. We're going somewhere, but I can't see our surroundings. It's too dark out.

☙

Elise
Four Months Later

"So I don't get it…"

"Every reflection Ref of its own inverse."

I slap my textbook shut. "*Arggh*. This is tedious!" Calculus. "And boring, and not intuitive. It's like learning to speak another language."

Luca laughs. "Because that's what it is."

I drop my forehead down onto my notebook, letting out a sigh that seems to echo in the closet-sized library study. "I'm perfectly satisfied with plain ole English."

"But you can speak a few other ones too, right?"

I lift my head and then shift so I'm sitting cross-legged, facing him on our shared bench. "Some Bengali and a lot of French, which was my chosen language in middle school and ninth and tenth grade. I did Spanish in eleventh grade and this year." I smile softly. "And now I know a little bit of your language."

He gives me a silly grin. "Arubesh?"

I lean in closer. *"L'italiano."*

"Sei pronto per stasera, la mia rosa?"

It's a question, so I just assume that it might be about… "Tonight?"

"Anything you want to do?" He smiles softly. "Or do you trust me to come up with something?"

"I trust you. But there's that afterparty, too, remember?"

He looks blank.

"It's at my friend Isa's. We can go if you want, or not if you don't want to."

"Do you want to?"

"Sure. It sounds fun."

It's April 12, which means tonight is prom. I'm officially going alone, with Dani's driver, Fil, picking me up. I'll meet Luca at the dance. There's an afterparty at Isa Arnoldi's home that's supposed to last till 3 a.m. My parents won't let me spend the night with Dani, not after what happened the night of Luca's game. Like six months ago.

So Mercer will pick me up from Isa's house at 2:50.

Luca scoots closer to me. He cups his palms over my shoulders, runs his hands slowly down my arms. His fingers encircle my wrists as he leans in closer.

"Missed you yesterday…"

"I missed you more." Our mingling breath smells minty from the gum I brought to our calc study sesh. I brush his lips with mine…a little feather kiss. Luca can't hold back, and pretty soon I'm on his lap with his arm locked around my back, his free hand threaded in my hair, tugging as his mouth ravishes mine.

We kiss until my lips feel bruised and swollen. Then he tucks me against his chest—the place I most love to be. I hug him hard in return.

"Is everything okay at your house?" I murmur. He missed school yesterday, and his only explanation was that he had "something to deal with."

"Yeah," he says now. "Better today."

I can feel him take a long breath, though, as if he's tired. I hug him more tightly.

"Your family's lucky to have you, you know."

He sucks another big breath back and leans away.

"What's wrong?" I murmur.

He lets go of me, putting space between us.

"Nothing." It's a rough whisper. He gives me a strained smile.

"You don't feel that way…like they're lucky?"

He laughs. I know him well enough by now to hear how forced it sounds.

"Seriously though. How can you not see this?"

"I didn't say I couldn't see it," he says, sounding defensive.

"But you can't. I can tell it makes you feel weird when I say it."

"What, that they're lucky to have me?" His face hardens. "They're not lucky. And how do they have me? I come here for school. I want to go to college somewhere, and I would if I could."

"Do you really plan to *not* go?"

He shuts his eyes, then opens them again and looks down at the bench. "I could do a two-year school." His jaw ticks.

"Luca. Robert Malone told me that you're ahead of *him*, and he's been top of our class since freshman year."

He blinks, blank-faced. "Yeah, so what." He swallows, and I can see how hard he's fighting to keep feelings off his face.

"So you deserve to have a life. A really above-average life."

"People who do two-year school only ever have average lives?"

"Of course not—that's not what I'm saying at all, you know it's not. But Robert said you got a scholarship to Columbia." My voice cracks on the words I'm not supposed to say.

Luca's eyes narrow. "He told you that?"

"He told me his guidance counselor told him. Or like...implied that it was you. He...said you got a full ride, Luca." I'm surprised at the tears that fill my eyes when I say it aloud. I'm even more surprised by Luca's face, which softens instantly.

"Hey, it's okay." He's moving closer to me, touching my hair, then pulling me up against him. "Don't be sad, *la mia rosa*. I'm sorry, and I'm sorry that I didn't tell you." He sighs, a soft sound, and drops his face down to my shoulder. I can feel his warm breath on my throat. Then he lifts his head back up and looks into my eyes. "I love you, *la mia rosa*."

"I love you *il mio cuore*."

His eyes shut.

I called him 'my heart.' "I looked that up on our computer so I could say something back to you."

My cheeks burn. He kisses my lips gently.

"We'll figure something out," I hear him whisper. My heart's racing, and I'm warm all over. In that moment, I believe we will.

CHAPTER FOURTEEN

Elise

It's going to be a good night. I can tell as soon as I get home from school. Dad is home from work already, set up in his office drinking gin and tonic. When I poke my head into the room to say hi, he gives me a big smile.

"Are you ready for your special night?"

I nod, and he surprises me by standing up and walking around his desk to hug me.

"Safety first," he tells me. "Don't drink from a Solo cup." He quirks one of his dark brows, and I laugh even as I pray *that* topic doesn't come up.

A few weeks after my grounding ended, Dad said sorry. He even said that maybe he had been "too much a lawyer and not enough father" that night he found me at the party.

But I haven't let my guard down, and for good reason. I found a camera in my bedroom back in January, its lens hidden in my antique chifforobe. I assume my phone calls are recorded, too. There's a little symbol on the phone that wasn't always there; it appeared after my mom snapped on the phone's protective case.

"I won't," I promise.

"Make the boys treat you like a princess."

I laugh as he lets me out of the liquor-scented hug. "Dad, I think you're drunk."

"I'm not. I'm happy for my oldest daughter as she rounds out her senior year and gets ready for Columbia."

"You're just happy that I didn't want to go to Harvard."

"That too. Harvard is too far away."

It thrills me to hear my dad say that. For months, he's been checked out. Half the time, he doesn't seem to notice me at all. It's nice to know he still cares.

"I think you warmed on Columbia when Mom said you didn't have to live here with us," he says. "Unless…mistakes are made."

I snort, forcing a smile as I look down at my boots. "That's not true."

Dad ruffles my hair. "Sure it isn't, *cara*."

I stick my tongue out, and the intercom on his wall crackles. "Franc, will you send *shona* to my dressing room?"

"I will." He winks at me. "I think your mother's got the beauty army ready."

I stick a hand up in an awkward little wave, feeling weird but kind of happy about all the attention aimed my way tonight. "Bye, Daddy."

"I'll be there to see you off, *cara*."

Cara. I think about the pet name as I walk down the long hall past our home theater, Mom's Pilates room, and the art studio and therapy space my parents made for Bec when she was younger.

Why does my dad call me *cara*? I have some memory of him telling me it means dear little one…or something like that. Daddy calls me *cara* and Mom calls me *shona*. I know *shona* is a Bengali endearment. But Cara?

I feel like maybe *cara* is Italian. How weird would that be? If my dad knows Italian—and he clearly does—I figure he would have to have learned it sometime in the last few years, for whatever "work" he's doing with…whoever. But it's weird because I've never heard him speak the language once except that night at the wedding.

The night I met Luca, although I didn't know it at the time.

I shake my head as I approach the staircases. There are two of them—hanging staircases like frozen ribbons that curl down toward the first floor.

I smile to myself as I ascend the right-hand staircase. Both are made of glossy hardwood and covered with red carpet, such that I have always felt a little like a princess or celebrity as I climb them.

It's too bad my bedroom isn't upstairs, or I'd get to do this every night. But only the master suite is upstairs, with its prima views of the river. My room, Bec's, the suite my parents started using after Bec started using a wheelchair, and all the guestrooms are on the first floor, along with an additional 2,000 square feet for staff. Raya, the chef; Jazmine, the household manager; and Darryl, our security person, live under our roof, and one of the nurses sleeps over almost every night—in a room that adjoins Bec's—since Mom stopped.

That thought sours my mood, but I try to lift myself out of it. I can hear Ana, one of the newer nurses, singing to Bec as I walk past her room.

I try not to think about the difference between our lives—Becca's and mine. She can't even speak, can barely lift her head, and someone that she barely knows is singing to her—music that maybe she doesn't even want to hear right now. While I'm walking toward my parents' room to get dressed up for a ball.

Luca can't pick me up, but I'll be with him all night. I'm loved by him. Even if he doesn't come to Columbia with me—and I'm going to make *sure* he comes to Columbia with me—it's not as if I'm going to lose him. He's amazing, and he's mine. Sometimes I feel like I have the whole world, and sweet Becca has nothing.

And now *I'm thinking about it,* and I can't think about it right before I have my makeup done!

Does this make me just like Mom: so willing to move on and live my life?

But wouldn't Bec want me to do that?

Stop stop stop stop stop! Stop.

I step into a guest bathroom to dab at my eyes. There is nothing I can do about the way things are. Not one thing that I'm not doing. I spent an hour with Bec after I got home from school today, and I'll go by and see her again after I'm dolled up. Despite my guilt, I know she'll love to see me in a gorgeous gown—just like she loved seeing my Luca.

Everything will be okay. Becca is okay right now. There is nothing wrong with having fun. These are things my therapist, Yvette, tells me weekly.

My parents' rooms are on the west side of the building. Their bedroom door is passcode protected. Each of us has our own pass-word, and the door won't let anybody through unless one of my parents has pre-authorized the entry. Now the door is propped open.

Laughter bounces out into the wide hall. Perfume wafts into the warm, heavy air. My parents' suite has always smelled amazing, and has always looked rich and textured. My mother was only two years old when her parents moved to New York, but she visited Bangladesh many times, and the style and décor made a strong impression on her.

I see the gorgeous gold and burgundy tapestry that dominates the room's right-hand wall before I spot my mother and the women standing with her. Actually, it's two women and a man. I recognize Tito, my mom's longtime hair stylist, but the two women are strangers. When I walk through the door, they all greet me at once.

The next two hours are amazing. My mom is one of lower Manhat-tan's queens, and never has that fact been more apparent than as I recline on a chaise longue in her dressing room and she directs the masseuse to work me over and the aesthetician to glam me up.

Cindy slathers me in fragrant oil, works the tension out of every muscle in my body, and wipes me down so I won't glisten too much but my skin is still incredibly soft. Farah smooths gel on my face and uses a heat gun to "plump" my collagen. Then she gives me a makeover that's to die for. She presents me with a bag of new prod-ucts, and then she and Cindy leave, asking my mom to send a picture when I'm in my gown.

Mom and Tito talk like old friends as he trims my hair, washes it, and sweeps it into an updo. When he hands me a mirror and twirls my chair around, I see it's melded into the shape of a conch shell.

"Wow. How did you do that?"

"I could do hair with my eyes closed." He makes a few adjust-ments, instructs me to "take advantage of your glorious night," and then walks out with my mom, leaving me to stare into the mirror. I'm wearing a silk slip with my bra under because I'm shy around so many strangers. With my hair and makeup done, I feel like a different person—someone beautiful and adult.

It's so weird to realize that I kind of am one. Next year I'll be at college, geographically close—so I can see Bec lots—but a whole world away. I feel buoyant thinking of what my life will be like. I'll have someone sweep my apartment for cameras and recording devices, and then I'll invite Luca over. Maybe he could even live with me. Who would know?

My mother drifts back into the dressing room, smiling in approval at my new, grown-up reflection.

"You look stunning, *shona*. You will be the belle of the ball."

"Thanks, Mom."

She stands behind me, giving my left shoulder a brief squeeze as she looks at her reflection in the mirror, then at mine. "They did everything I paid them to and more." She gives a knowing smile. It's what I think of as her Disney villain smile, because she seems to save it for moments when she's feeling superior.

"Thanks for having them come over for this," I say in the polite tone my mother prefers.

"Oh, of course, my darling."

I frown at my own reflection. "Mom, why does Daddy call me *cara*? What does it mean?"

Her eyes lift to mine in the mirror, meeting my gaze for a moment before picking at a bobby pin in my hair. "It's an endearment. Like my *shona*—what your Nani called me as a young girl. She would have so loved to see you like this. Nani loved all things beautiful. I'm not sure you remember how lovely she always looked."

"I do," I lie. My mother's mom died when I was seven. I remember mostly that she always gave me dates and little ground nuts.

"Mom, is *cara* an Irish endearment?"

The smooth, Botox'd place between her eyebrows twitches very slightly. "No, of course not." She laughs. "It's Italian."

She turns around, raising her arms to lift my gown's hanger from the high rack where it's hanging.

"Why would Daddy call me something Italian?"

She runs the wand of her steamer over the gown, tossing a glance over her shoulder. "I hope this is not about that *boy*."

"What? No. Because of a question about a nickname?" I roll my eyes.

Mom gives me a warning look as she removes the red silk gown from its black velvet hanger.

"You'll have to ask your father about this."

"*That* doesn't sound foreboding."

She gives a small shrug, and then curls her fingers, beckoning me to stand. "Everyone has secrets, *shona*."

"Secrets? Like…Dad is Italian?" I'm clearly joking.

When I notice my mom hasn't replied, my jaw drops. "Mom! *What?*"

She holds the gown open, and I step carefully into it, meeting her eyes as she moves around behind me to fasten me in.

"Elise, ask your father why he calls you *cara*. And get into this pretty ruby gown. For tonight, you get to be a princess, free of all responsibility. Enjoy it, *shona*," she says, smiling softly. "It will be one of the last times."

CHAPTER FIFTEEN

Luca

"Dude, this was a *big* mistake," Alesso says.

Leo grips the wheel of the Cutlass, and I watch his jaw tick before he glares at Alesso via rearview mirror.

"It's not so bad," I say. "We're going slow, and Leo knows what's what."

"I hate the tunnel," Alesso mutters.

"Everybody hates the fucking tunnel." Leo lets a breath out, braking as the car in front of us slows.

"I don't hate it that much," I offer. "It's like the subway, but at least you're going slower than those damn trains."

I've traveled from Brooklyn to lower Manhattan through the Battery Tunnel a handful of times, and it's never made me feel sick like a train or helicopter does. Alesso, however, feels differently.

Motherfucking Diamond. It's his fault we're piled into the Cutlass Alesso stole from his uncle—*again*. Earlier this afternoon, when I was trying to figure out the train schedule, Diamond called. He told me that before he loaned me the tux he promised, he needed a favor. If I did it, he'd get me to the prom on time—since doing this favor for him would make it impossible for me to catch the train.

"Fuck Tony," Alesso says, reading my mind. "Ten bucks says he thinks that since he loaned you the tux, he already thanked you for that shit you did this afternoon."

I shake my head. "Shit is right."

This time Diamond's favor was…different. He had me go over to some old rich guy's house and help him bake some fucking panettone. Dude was like half dead, and I was surprised he lived by himself.

"He kept blowing holes in his pants like he couldn't even help it."

Alesso groans. "That's disgusting."

"How old is he anyway?" Leo asks.

"Older than the world, dude," I say. "And obsessed with panettone. And loaded. After we finished baking the three loaves, he put his bony hand on my back and said thank you in this old-ass, wheezy voice, and then he gave me five one hundred dollar bills. Pulled them out of the pocket of his lounge pants like it was nothing!"

"What did you expect from old Lamberto?" Leo asks me.

For a moment, I can't speak. My eyes focus on the tunnel's dark walls, sliding by too quickly, and that makes me feel sick. "Old man— Arnoldi? That was *him*?"

"Yeah man," Alesso says. "How did you miss that?"

"Tony didn't fucking tell me is how! Why the fuck was I there?'"

"Tony said old man Lambo requested you by name, Luca."

"What the fuck?"

"You didn't know that was his house?"

"I thought he lived near Carnegie Hill."

"That's one of his places," Alesso tells me. "But he likes his place in old Red Hook. That's where they came from, after all."

"It was an apartment! And he called himself Bert!"

Leo looks at me aghast. "Focus on the road, man."

"Or we'll be deader than Arnoldi's Massacre," Alesso adds.

My stomach knots up. "What the fuck's Arnoldi's Massacre?"

"It happened right around the time Roberto Arnoldi was shaking down your dad. You remember that?"

"Not at all."

He rolls his eyes. "Old Lambo was getting up there. Tony said there was a lot of shit spewing, especially after he had a heart attack. Roberto had been ready to move up for years, but Lambo wouldn't give the crown up. People talked like he was getting frail. That pissed him off.

"So the Bellini family was run by the young guy, Noah Bellini—still is—but Noah's always been in bed with the Russians or some shit. That's what my brother says. So anyway, Lambo—your old fart—he figured out where they were meeting. It was in this very tunnel." Alesso's lips twitch. "I'm just fucking with you. It was over there somewhere in Bath Beach."

"Fuck you," Leo mutters.

"They were meeting sometime in the night, in a warehouse with garage doors. Our guys shot out the windows, and then the Russians opened up the doors already shooting—AKs, cause they're fucking crazy—but our people didn't give a shit. And...everyone died. I'm talking every single one of them. I think Tony said it was seventeen bodies in total.

"And the head of the Russians—I forgot his name, I think like Casper or something weird like that— He wanted revenge. Sick shit. So he set up a hit on Lambo's wife. Her name was Bella, and she was supposed to be some kind of angel lady, putting up with Lambo F.—for fucking—" he smirks— "Arnoldi for so long. Anyway—" Alesso shrugs. "They got her. She was at a hair salon. Do you remember someone getting offed at a hair place when we were like eleven?"

I inhale as I realize... "Yeah. It upset my mom. I remember hearing her talk about it."

"Bullet killed the stylist, too," Alesso tells me. He's still running his mouth when I turn around and sit squarely in my seat. I rub my closed eyes with my fingertips—hard, until I see gold spots.

Anyway, they got her.

I saw her today. Pictures of her. "Bert" Arnoldi had them everywhere. He had a fucking shrine to her.

I think about a bullet slicing through her torso. Maybe through one of those thin little sweaters first, the soft kind that Elise wears sometimes. Then a silk blouse. And out her back, between two of her ribs. Blood blooming. And then the other woman. In my head, I picture her as Dani. I imagine them both falling to the salon's floor, bodies clapping on those rubbery mats as the chair spins and dark blood mixes with the cut hairs.

I think of Lamberto Arnoldi's kitchen counter, sticky like it needed wiping.

"Why did he want me?" I manage, turning partway around, so I can see Alesso.

"Don't tell Tony—" his brows rise— "but he said the old man heard about you."

"Heard about me?" I'm cold now. All over. "What the fuck does that mean?"

Alesso's mouth flattens. "*You* know what it means."

"I thought Lamberto has been out of the picture for years."

"Tony told me Roberto is 'hung up' on you." I blink as Alesso's hands bend into air quotes. "Everybody knows," he adds. "You've got the biggest balls in Red Hook."

Something hot tingles through my body—like that feeling from the schoolyard when you're playing tag and someone's fingers come within an inch of your arm.

"*Leo.*" I gag hard behind my hand, and Leo hits the brakes, eliciting a cacophony of car horns from behind us.

"What the fuck?" Leo says, at the same time Alesso shouts, "Don't throw up!"

I don't. Throw up. I swallow a few times, feel a little sweaty for a second, and then the feeling passes. When it does, Alesso makes a heavy, sigh-like sound.

"Was that my fault?" he asks in a low, muffled sort of voice.

"What?" I turn around to face him, putting on my bullshit face. "Was it your fault I felt sick?"

He nods, wide-eyed, and for a second, we're in kindergarten— Alesso too scared to hide inside the tractor tires that formed our little crew's playground hideout.

"Nah, dude. It's this tunnel." I turn back toward the windshield. "Guess I was wrong about it. Being in here so long is making me dizzy as shit."

Alesso makes a crack about me and motion sickness, but it doesn't take him long to get back on topic. Especially with Leo asking him so many questions. I can see a different side of Alesso as he answers. He might hate his brother, but I think he loves knowing the answers.

I think about Lamberto and the hump in his thin back, the way the bread crumbs stuck in his white moustache. I think of his son, Roberto.

"I would like a number of things. What can you offer me, Mr. Galante?"

I remember Roberto's dark eyes from the shoe store that day years ago. They were unsure for a second, like he was either going to throw a punch at me or laugh his ass off.

"Tony told me Roberto is hung up on you. Everybody knows. You've got the biggest balls in Red Hook."

I think—with some dismay—about my riverside plans for tonight. I shut my eyes and see Elise bleeding. After that, I bar myself from thinking about the late Mrs. Arnoldi.

A few minutes later, I see light. We're in Manhattan.

❧

Elise

I twine my arms around Luca's neck and giggle as I kick my heel-clad foot back.

"What are you doing, woman?"

He grins down at me, and I reach up and poke his dimple.

"That's a dimple."

"No it isn't."

"That's what you always say."

"Because dimples are for baby butts and little kids."

"Then what is this?" I lean my head against his shoulder, closing my eyes. His chest vibrates beneath me as he chuckles.

"It's a *man indention.*"

I hear our friends laughing. It makes me laugh, too. The balmy breeze tosses my gown around my ankles as more of our classmates spill out the school's front doors.

Luca rubs my back as he holds me up against him. "I'm gonna have to talk to Ree."

"What? Why?"

"For getting my date drunk in the ladies' room."

I'm amused. "The 'ladies' room?"

He's amused. "I guess I shouldn't have mistaken you two for ladies."

I punch him lightly, then tip my head back so I can smile up at him. "It was just a little whiskey."

I feel his body move again as he laughs. "That's what they all say. That's what they all say."

"I'm so sleepy though! No one told me that would happen."

His hand cups the back of my head, fingers careful around my hairdo. "I think that's true sometimes. It can make you sleepy."

His tone sounds contemplative, like he doesn't know first hand—and something hits me. "Oh hell, your dad…" I say, and then I trail off, feeling terrible that I drank tonight.

When I dare to look up at him, he's looking gently down at me. "Did I ruin prom?"

"Of course not."

"No?"

He shakes his head. "I don't care. In fact, I think you're the prettiest drunk."

His lips curve into a funny little smile before he bends down a little, brushing a kiss over my cheek. Then our friends start cheering and I look over my shoulder to find the line of limousines is moving.

"How'd you set this up?" I murmur.

He takes my hand. *"L'ho fatto con soldi sporchi."*

"I can't believe you speak so much Italian."

"Not as well as my parents," he says, before Dani and her boyfriend and Ree and the girl from Jace's party head into their limousine together.

"I think you do," I murmur as we step back, so other friends of ours can get into their limo, which must have gotten here before ours.

He gives me a little smile.

"You're just modest," I tease.

"Better than the alternative."

I don't have time to agree because our limousine is next up. It's black and glossy, long and glamorous, and I feel like a princess as Luca sweeps me up and lifts me inside, settling me on his lap. I hear cheering behind us, and all that makes me feel a little flushed and dizzy as the door shuts and I look up at him.

He kisses my forehead as the driver pulls off and gives the guy an address. The divider wall goes back up. I lean up so I can kiss Luca. "Thank you for doing this."

"You deserve it."

"Do you really think that?"

"No." He smiles, a Cheshire Cat smile. "I know it."

I sleep on his shoulder during the ride to Isa's. I don't even know I'm sleeping until he jostles me awake and whispers, "We're here, *la mia rosa addormentata*."

"What does that mean?"

He chuckles as he helps me out. "The sleeping rose."

I blink up at the house—an ivory mansion made of some kind of flat, almost translucent-looking stone. It has a dark roof, narrow, dramatic windows topped by loopy, iron-looking accents and filled with long drapes. I glance toward the front doors. They're delicate and crystalline, framed by four columns and underlined by a gorgeous, bib-shaped staircase that has to be white marble. I can feel Luca looking at me as I take the place in for the first time since a slumber party when I was twelve.

"What do you see when you look at it?" he asks quietly.

"A castle from a fairy tale." I picture us as queen and king and smile at him. "What do you see?"

He swallows, looks away for a heartbeat, and then gives me an honest answer. "Another world." His lips twitch. "But not forever."

I want to say it's not another world. I want to reassure him that he belongs here. But I don't want to disregard how he feels.

I settle for taking his hand as we walk toward the door and asking, "What kind of life do you want?"

"One where I can buy you this."

CHAPTER SIXTEEN

Luca

I don't know how I didn't realize before. Elise told me the party was at Isa's house. I don't know an Isa and didn't care where we were going—but now that I think about it, Alesso told me last year that he thought Roberto's daughter went to school at "one of those magnet schools—maybe it could even be yours." At the time, I didn't figure anyone in that family would be at a public school.

I feel like I'm moving underwater as we're ushered through the front doors into an expansive foyer. It's got a huge hanging light fixture that looks like an explosion of rectangular black crystals. Out in front of us, there's a table that looks solid gold, topped by a mirror that's so tall it reaches nearly to the ceiling. On top of the table is the mother of all flower arrangements. It's got roses that are black and gold and red, and a bunch of vines that look like thorns arranged in different layers, so they're sort of reaching toward the ceiling.

I suck in a breath of rose scent as I blink down at the floor—black marble with little gold lines—and look to our right, where a woman in a black gown stands in a wide, arched doorway. She beckons us into a big-ass room that's centered on some stairs. And I get why. These stairs are motherfucking art. They twine together, curling every which way, looking almost like they're melting as they fall into this empty room from above.

"Dinner will be upstairs in the formal dining hall. Ascend the stairs and you'll meet another usher," she says softly.

I notice that she's pretty in a really made-up kind of way, with a dress that shows off a teardrop diamond necklace and huge tits.

Once Elise and I step fully into the stairs room, I look up and see how high the ceiling is. I'm looking at the way the stairs curl like the inside of a shell when I hear Elise's quiet gasp. I follow her gaze to the room's right wall, where, between two massive, red-curtained windows hangs a portrait that makes my heart sink.

There he is. Roberto Arnoldi.

I used to watch him read the *Wall Street Journal* while my father polished his shoes. I asked Dad once why he did it instead of Chris, the high school boy he'd hired to do such things. Dad said, "Respect, Luca. When a powerful man is your patron, respect is part of what you give him."

My dad talked about Roberto Arnoldi like he was some kind of legend. I sort of understood what he did, but when I was a kid, I thought of him more like a movie star—like Tom Cruise. He had a driver and wore crisp, clean suits that smelled like tobacco and money.

After the store flooded, it was Gabe Russo, an Arnoldi cousin, who became my father's point of contact for a year or so.

When Mom got sick and my dad defaulted on his monthly payment, Russo gave him six months off—with sixty-six percent interest. Six-six-six, I remember raging to Alesso when I found out. I was thirteen then, and sort of crazy from the shit with Mom. Then Dad just lost his hold on things. He kept saying how he'd have to close his doors, how we'd be moving to Mill Street. That was when he decided he didn't give a fuck if we knew he was still a drunk.

Now I stare at the painting of the mob don and his flawless family. I swallow, and for a second my eyes ache as I absorb that feeling I have sometimes—that I'm a traitor.

I didn't realize how right I was when I told Elise this place isn't for me. Yet, here I am—dressed up like a fraud, with Elise on my arm as if I've earned the right to her heart.

"Luca," she says, and I look at her.

"You okay?"

"Yeah. For sure," I lie.

We start slowly up the winding staircase. Elise looks up before I do and murmurs, "Look up, Luca."

The stairs, which go up far above us, make a swirling pattern that makes me feel a little like the stairs below my shoes are moving.

"What is this?" I half laugh.

"I think up there—" she points— "is the third floor. But these stairs keep on going to I guess maybe a fourth floor, and the design really does make you feel dizzy."

"Fuck. That's pretty crazy."

She nods, holding my hand. We step off the stairs at the second floor and are led down an long hallway to a cavernous room with dozens of candle-lit tables and a curtained stage. A band plays as servers mill around tables filled by about fifty of our school friends.

"He told me Roberto's 'hung up' on you."

We're led to a large, round table where we find Dani and her dude Ty, Ree and her girl, and Jace Banetti with some girl I don't know.

I pull Elise's chair out before I realize the server was trying to do the same thing at the same time.

❧

Elise

It's a delicious four-course dinner, but there's something wrong with Luca.

He's quiet, even when the band is replaced by a comedian. He doesn't really laugh—he barely smiles. We slip out when the band starts up again and the room is transformed into a dance floor. He holds my hand as we walk until we find an alcove, where he leans me against the wall, staring into my eyes before kissing my lips softly.

"What's the matter, sweetheart?"

"Just tired." He tries to smile, but it's a fail.

"Is it being here? Do you not like the party?"

"No, I like it." We kiss more, and he holds me against him—tight and close enough so I can feel him inhale deeply. I look up and see him shut his eyes.

"I'm never going to have a house like this," he says hoarsely.

"That's good, because it's kind of creepy. People could be living with you in here and you'd never even notice!"

He blows a breath out, and I nuzzle his chest.

"Let's go somewhere. Somewhere with just the two of us. My driver will be here in three hours and twenty minutes. That's plenty of time. Let's get fast food or...I don't know. Do something else. We could call a cab. I have my phone in my purse."

His mouth twists thoughtfully. "I know somewhere. It's not too far, and it's kind of a throwback to our first date."

"Take me away, Mr. Galante."

His driver, who apparently is waiting, takes us to a glittering marina that is so Manhattan, it makes my blood hum. The boats are yachts. The water gleams with city lights reflected on its choppy surface, and the river breeze kicks my dress up around my shins as we walk hand in hand toward the last slot.

"Whose boat is this?" I ask him.

"Just this old guy I help sometimes."

Luca speaks to someone on the dock, and the uniformed man leads us to a glorious, sleek, brown and white yacht. He swings a sort-of walkway out, so we can board the yacht, and Luca leads me up to the bow. There's a rounded door that clearly leads down in the hull. Luca punches in a passcode, and it swings open, revealing a door-shaped swatch of maritime opulence.

"Wowzers."

He gives me a teasing smile. "Do *you* have a yacht, Ms. O'Hara?"

"Oh no. My dad isn't into water. He learned to swim late...but shh, cause that's a family secret."

"I did too. Just took some summer lessons a few years ago. Did it with a buddy of mine." He gives me a grin, and I think he's kidding until I see the faint blush on his cheeks.

"That's the coolest. What was it like? Was it hard to learn?"

"Nah. A little unnatural at first, but we took to it like a boot in water." He mimes a drumroll.

I giggle, and I can't stop. Maybe because he looks so cute, half bashful and half proud. I press my body against his, feeling his warm chest and hard hips, and he groans.

"*La mia rosa.*" He throws me over his shoulder and climbs down the stairs into the body of the yacht, then sets me on my feet in the low light.

"What?" I slide my hand under the collar of his dress shirt. "Does this displease you, Mr. Galante?"

I rub myself against the hardness of his thigh, and he makes a soft, tortured sound.

"It pleases me too much," he whispers. His hand rubs up between my shoulder blades, until he's holding my nape. "Everything about you pleases me, Ms. O'Hara."

His head is tipped back, his eyelids half shut as his lips part and his face slackens. I'm still rubbing against him, just because I love that I can make him this way—drunk on me. It's the most amazing rush. In the past few months, I've become addicted to it. To the way he groans and pants when my hands touch him in certain places.

I run my hand down his chest, tracing the buttons of his shirt then toying with his belt buckle. I grin as I give up—only for show, of course—and rub my hand downward, my pulse racing when I'm touching him *there*, and he's groaning like it might do him in. I squeeze, and his knees nearly buckle.

He drags a huge breath into his lungs, and I move my hand lower, rubbing his shaft a few times before cupping his balls. He groans again and shudders. There's a leather couch a few feet away. He sweeps me off my feet and lays me out atop it, pushing my dress up so he can run a hand up my thigh and over my silk underwear.

His eyes shut and his head hangs as he gets a deep breath.

"Holy fuck, you're perfect." He lowers himself gently atop me. I can tell he's not resting his full weight on me—just enough so we can rub together as we so love doing.

He's breathing heavy as he uses his hand to rub himself against me. Through his pants and through my gown, he has me moaning and arching beneath him.

"Get rid of your pants," I whisper.

He sits back on his knees, rubbing himself as his lust-glazed eyes tilt and his lips pull into a grin. "Get rid of my pants?" He drapes his hand right where I want it, rubbing me gently with his thumb. "But rosa, this is someone else's yacht."

"Stolen boats are our thing," I moan.

He plays me like an instrument and I respond in kind, singing with groans and sighs until he lifts his hand off me and starts unbuckling his belt.

"What do you think will happen if we lose the clothes, *la mia rosa? Penso che non sarò in grado di trattenermi. Come ti piacerebbe?*"

I reach for him as he folds his pants down. His erection springs up and my fingers trace it gently through the fabric of his boxer briefs. I wrap my hand around him, and he laughs as he leans back, out of my reach.

"Not yet." His cheeks are flushed, his grin tender, and I can see his pulse thrum at the base of his throat. He's revved up, but he wants to tend to me first. When he pushes my dress up more and looks into my eyes for permission, I lift my hips, and his fingers loop beneath my silk panties. He hooks the small piece of fabric aside and leans down.

And it's all over for me. Conscious thought is over, all coherence gone. My body is a buffet and he's hungry; he feasts as my hands twist in his hair. He groans and it vibrates my flesh. His tongue laves me again and he groans, "I love you." And then his fingers press in.

I open my eyes a minute or a lifetime later to find Luca on his knees, smiling. Smiling like he's got a bouquet of roses behind his back and not his long erection pressed down by his palm.

"You okay?"

"No." I laugh, pushing up on one elbow. "And it's your fault. Come here…" I sit up more. "And let me help you with that heavy, heavy package."

His eyes twinkle as he stands instead. He laughs as he pulls his pants up, struggling to fasten them. He can barely fit himself in, and he's so hard that his erection has to bend to stay below the waistline of his trousers.

"There's a bedroom." He points to a narrow hall behind us. "I don't think anyone would come down into the boat, but…"

He helps me up, and we drift down a hallway, fingers laced. I can feel a dizzy echo of sensation as the yacht bobs on the water. Then we're in the bedroom and he's leading me to the bed. I reach for the zipper of my gown, and he unzips it for me, helps me out, and drapes it over an armchair. His eyes never leave mine as I sit on the edge of the mattress in my silk slip, crossing my ankles.

"You okay?" His hooded eyes squint at the corners.

His hand wraps around his erection, covered by black fabric.

"Are you?" I tease.

"I'm okay." His voice is low. He swallows, and I beckon him closer. "Come here, Luca Galante." He does, and I rub him through his pants until he grunts and sinks down on the mattress beside me.

"Lie down and undo your pants."

He does, and I climb atop him, hiking my slip up so I can straddle him. I take his hard erection in my hands and stroke it. He quakes under me. I feel his legs tense.

"Unbutton your shirt," I whisper. He can barely manage as I keep on stroking: firm grip at the base, then stroke upward and rub my palm around the head of him. He's slick up there. I rub my finger carefully around, and he lets out a loud groan.

"Oh God—Elise." His hands fist at his sides and then he's breathing in gulps.

"Is this okay?"

"So good." His hands stroke my thighs. His face is rapt, strained and exultant. "I feel like—I'm gonna—"

He swells under my fingers, and then his hand clamps over mine. He makes a hoarse sound, and I feel a burst of warmth. He moans and rolls his hips so he's pressed into my hand. Then he's sitting up and cursing, blinking at our hands.

"Oh shit. I'm sorry."

"You…"

"I'm so sorry. It felt so fucking good," he rasps. "I couldn't stop it."

My hand hovers over him. "I love it."

"What?" He laughs.

"Yeah, I love everything about it." I lean over, kiss his cheek, and then we're lying by each other, sticky, hugging. He looks half asleep, but satisfied.

"Well, I guess Anne Rice was right about the dark arts."

We both laugh at that, and he pulls a tissue from one of his pockets before he disappears into the bathroom, returning with a warm cloth for me. He's subdued and happy. After we're both clean, he pulls the covers over us and nudges his strong leg between mine, wraps both arms around my back, and brings my cheek to his throat. Then he kisses my hair.

"I love you," he says again.

"I love you more." I kiss his throat, a little flutter of my lips over his Adam's apple—and that's all it's meant to be. But our mouths act like magnets. Soon we're kissing harder, deeper. We're both groaning, panting, and his fingers find my sweet spot through the layers of my slip and start me rolling my hips, rubbing against his hand as my legs fall open and my hand starts rubbing his arm.

"*Ohh*, Luca."

"I can get you off again. Is that what you want, rosa?"

He leans down to use his mouth, but I can see the head of him is poking out of his pants. He's hard again.

"We're both...you know. And I want to..." I lick my lips, unable to confess I want to give him a blow job. "Let's do sixty-nine." My voice quivers. "I want to lick you."

Luca squeezes himself and says, "You don't have to." He swallows audibly. "It's not a trade." He offers me this little strained smile, trying to convince me that he doesn't care, I guess.

I wrap my hand around his nape, moving in to kiss his lips. "No one said I thought I had to, Galante."

His eyes are half shut as he runs his hands down my arms, kisses my cheek.

"Lie down," I whisper. I see chills on his skin as he does as I ask. I notice his cheeks look flushed. His eyes are glazed, and as I look down at him, he unfastens his pants and pushes those and his boxer-briefs down. His erection springs up, and he leans up so he can grab me, lifting me easily over his torso, so that I'm situated over his face.

I laugh at the awkwardness as I sit up above him, keeping myself off him out of shyness.

"Please," he groans.

"You're sure?" I whisper.

He pulls down my underwear, positions me so I'm—literally—sitting on his face. My gaze latches onto his length and the way his hand looks working the flanged tip of himself. And it's that sight that draws me forward. In between my legs, I'm warm and heavy. I shift down onto my hands and knees. I'm reaching for him as his tongue delves into my slit.

"*Ahhhhh, Luca.*"

Then his mouth clasps over my heat, and I'm taking his thick tip into my mouth. He starts to lick me and I wrap my lips around him, rolling my tongue all around and he is groaning...writhing...thrusting his tongue where it makes me crazy. I laugh with my mouth around him, and I feel his answering groan as it vibrates all through me.

We're both shaking, sweating. I'm so close. So...ready. God, I want to be consumed by this, to feel it all. On a whim, I take him out of my mouth, shift so I'm off of him.

I watch as his eyes blink open.

"Do you have a condom, Luca?"

"Fuck." He slides his hand down himself. "Rosa, don't ask me that."

I lie on my back, pull my slip up, and run a finger over myself where I'm throbbing. "I want to do it," I whisper. "Tonight. I'm so..." I can't say the words. "This is a good time for it. It might be the only time till college next fall."

He's on his knees beside me, looking shocked and alarmed. "You don't want me to do that."

I can't help a giggle. "Yes I do."

"It hurts for girls."

"There's no way you could hurt me."

His hand covers me, his fingers tracing as I lift my hips to urge him inside.

"Luca, *please*," I whisper. "I want it. And I feel...ready."

He slides a finger into me, then draws it slowly out. He pushes two inside, and I moan. "Yesss."

"I'm bigger."

"I want bigger."

He laughs, and it's a strangled sound. "Elise."

"I want to feel my love inside me. Right now."

He shuts his eyes, and I know I've won. I'm grinning like a fool as he peers down at me.

"You're sure?" He sounds hoarse.

I nod, and he blows a breath out, fishing something from his pocket.

"You did bring one. Can I help you put it on?"

He laughs and tears it open. "I don't know. I think I'll..." He trails off as he rolls it over his head. I watch as he smooths it down his thick length. He looks up at me with glassy eyes.

"You're sure?"

"Yeah, baby. I know it might hurt and I'm okay with that. It'll only hurt the first time."

He moves closer, kissing me until we're breathless. Then he lays me down and teases me with his mouth, pushing his tongue into me until I'm screaming and my legs are locked around him.

"Luca, please!"

He spreads my legs and moves between them.

"I love you, Elise O'Hara. Always." He rubs his tip through my slick heat till I'm groaning. Then he presses where I want him.

"Love you more."

"Close your eyes and take a few deep breaths."

I breathe once, and then twice. Then he moves in with a hard thrust. There's a burst of pain—a stinging ache—and then he's in me. A moan burbles from my throat. He thrusts again and I whimper. He's so...in me. I move my hips and... "Ahhh." It *hurts*...but it feels good, too. I shift my hips so my legs fall open wider, and he draws out slightly. I open my eyes, finding his face slack with pleasure.

He moves deeper and lets out a loud groan. "Ohhhh." His entire gorgeous body shudders. For a second, he looks almost stricken. Then he grabs my hips and thrusts so deep I see stars. I'm groaning as he draws out slowly.

"You okay?" he groans back.

"Oh yes."

He pushes in...and draws slowly back out. Then shoving in and pulling out...and in and out. Heat flushes through me, blooming mostly in between my legs, where pleasure ripples outward. I start breathing harder, tensing as I lift my hips toward him.

I can feel it coming. It's a balloon of sensation, swelling in between my legs until I'm screaming his name and it bursts, spreading through me and then fading into one spasming aftershock that spreads pure bliss through every cell.

I feel Luca's body jerk and hear his soft grunt. He murmurs a curse, and then he's pulling out—too quickly. He's lying beside me— collapsing, really and he's pulling me against him, whispering, "Are you okay?"

The last thing I remember before closing my eyes is my own voice, saying, "I've never been better."

CHAPTER SEVENTEEN

Luca

She falls asleep afterward, and I stare at her for a long time. I love her, and I love that she feels safe enough with me to fall asleep.

And do everything that made her so sleepy.

I don't know how to make any of this last, but I know I love her.

I cuddle up to her for a while, feeling almost tired enough to sleep —except I can't, because this vessel is the property of one Lamberto Arnoldi. What I know from Tony is that it's here until the morning and the passcode is Lambo's daughter's birthday, backwards. It was a risk to bring Elise here, but I think only for me. And it was worth it.

I let her sleep while I clean myself up. Then she starts to wake up, and I lie back down beside her, facing her, so I'm the first thing she sees when she opens her eyes.

"I'm not a virgin," she says.

I feign surprise. "Oh really?"

Her lips curl into a big grin. "I always hated that word: virgin. Like you're a *thing*. Somebody's ward or something, that they need to protect."

She is someone's ward—she's mine—and I'll always protect her.

I run my hand over her hair and then lean down to kiss her lips. "I love you. How do you feel?"

"Like a woman." She wiggles her brows and laughs as she sits up and smooths her silky dress thing down. Then she looks at me, more serious. "I feel good. It didn't hurt that much. Well, that's not true—it did—but it was fast, and then it felt amazing."

Her cheeks redden. I smile, and she fans them. "It takes a lot for me to turn this red, mister. This is your fault." She jabs my shirt, then scoots closer to me. "How about for you?" she whispers.

"How do you think?" I hug her close and rub my cheek against her hair. Then I swoop her up and carry her into the bathroom, kiss her cheek, and leave her to it. She comes out a few minutes later looking tired but happy.

I help her back into her dress, and then it's time to go. She laughs when I offer to carry her back to the limo.

"I'm sore," she whispers, "but I can still walk."

Still I help her into the car, shut the door behind us, and pull her close as she leans leans her head on my shoulder during the ride back to the Arnoldi mansion.

"I love you," she whispers.

"I love you."

"Come to Columbia with me. Please. We can live together. I'll have a place."

A sort of buzzing without sound starts in my throat and spreads into my chest.

"Working hard. That's the key, you know. Hard work takes you everywhere."

Elise is talking, but I can't hear her.

"You think you could go to college? Ha! You can have the shoe store. If it's good for your old man, it can be good enough for you."

"...We could watch TV between classes and cook together at night."

I stare at the window as she spills out all her dreams, the unrealistic things, her hopes—and hope for her is something she can hold onto. For me it's just a mirage. I can't leave my mom and Soren. I've been thinking on it, but I just can't see a way.

I look down at her. She's looking up at me.

She whispers, "What do you think?"

"About college?" I manage.

Elise nods.

I swallow, noticing how dry my throat is. I don't know what I can tell her. Honesty would crush her. I don't want to lie. Her eyes are wide and warm. I say, "I'd like that."

"You're lying."

"You want me to be honest?"

"I don't know. What would honest be like?"

I try hard to keep my shit together. This night is about her. It's not about my fucking anger.

"Tell me, Luca. I want to know."

"It would be like I can't go. I don't need college to run a shoe store, do I?"

I can see the restraint on her face as her lips tauten.

"Who will watch my mom and Soren if I'm not there? No one—is the answer. Everything would go to shit, and it would all be my fault. For being selfish...with you. Because that's what I want to do. I want to pick you, Elise, but I'm never, ever going to be able to." I gulp more air down. "You should break this shit off with me."

I put a hand over my face because my heart is racing and my eyes feel achy. This is what it all comes down to. This is what it always has. She's wasting her time with me.

I feel her hand on my back, then her body up against my side. Then her arm around me. She pulls me back, halfway atop her. I let her because I can't not.

She hugs me hard and strokes my back a few times. "You don't have to pick me. Ever. Pick your family, and I'll pick you."

My throat aches. "You shouldn't."

"I'm not asking. I'm not choosing because I chose already. I'm not scared of what challenges you have coming at you. I don't care. You're my heart. You are the only thing that keeps me going, Luca. I need you."

She kisses me, and I return it. *I'm sorry. I'm sorry. I'm so sorry.*

I don't know for what exactly. I don't need a reason.

I just know somehow, it's going to go wrong.

CHAPTER EIGHTEEN

Luca

The last week of senior year. There's so much shit to do. Turn in text-books and football shit. Get fitted for our caps and gowns. Go for one last meeting with the academic counselors.

I like it, though, because I get to do it all with her.

"How'd you do this to me anyway?" I'm looking at her through my half-shut eyelids. Elise's pretty face is blurred by my dark lashes.

"How'd I do what?" She smiles—upside down, because I've got my head in her lap.

"Make me start hiding out in closets."

Her fingers stroke through my hair. "Are you sure I'm to blame? It was you who orchestrated everything." Her face lights up. "Remember? The day I brought the bear and you saved me in the bathroom?"

I grin. "I remember." I told Diamond she was my girlfriend hours later.

Elise sighs. "I'm so glad Bec's doing better now. Like, *so* glad. Way fewer seizures. More alert. This medicine they've got her on now is a game changer."

I'm so fucking happy, too. Worry for her sister is a heavy weight for Elise. In my English class this year, we talked about how every-body has this one thing in their life that seems unsolvable. That makes them see life in a bad light. All E wants is for Becca to be well. So it's what I want, too. "Can I see her again sometime?"

She smiles brightly. "Do you want to?"

"Of course. This time I'm bringing something, though."

"Bringing something?"

"Yeah, you know, like something she would want. Or like. Some kind of toy or…I don't know, a trinket."

She starts blinking fast, and for a second, I don't get why. Then I do, and my stomach does a slow roll. I sit up. "Hey, don't cry. *La mia rosa…*" I hug her, and she hugs me tighter.

She sniffs and then draws back so she can peer up at me. "Why are you the best thing ever?"

It's so ludicrous, it makes me laugh. "I don't think so, *vita mia.*"

"What does that mean?"

I kiss her forehead as I pull her up against me again. "Look it up on your laptop, *mio caro tesoro.*"

Her eyes widen. "Caro!"

I smile. *"Tu sei il mio caro."*

"Caro! What does caro mean? Or cara. Does that mean something?"

"Somebody else calling you cara?" I tease.

"My dad did…when I was little."

Something catches in my throat. I swallow. "Your dad called you cara?"

"A long time ago." Her face looks startled. "What's it mean?"

"It means 'dear' or 'dear one.'"

She nods. "Strange. You know, we're Irish. Or I'm half."

"He knows *la lingua Italiana* is the prettiest. Just like his daughter."

She smiles, and then I help her up. "C'mon. Before that driver of yours gets suspicious."

"I swear I feel like he's reporting to my dad. Is that insane?" she asks as we walk down the hall toward the cafeteria, where she'll exit out a side door.

"I'd assume he is. Unless you really trust him."

"I don't know. He's always been nice to me." She's biting her lip, and I can feel my dick take notice.

"Don't do that." I grab her hand and squeeze it. She gives me a wicked grin.

"Really?" She's whispering, even though we're the only ones around; our graduation rehearsal ended an hour ago.

I arch my brows and try to adjust myself, smirking as I do. "Really."

We've only been able to *be together* twice since prom, and one time was here at school. Fucking crazy, but I guess we're fucking crazy now. I accepted the scholarship I got from Columbia and told Elise I'll find a way. I don't have to live on campus, even though the scholarship includes a dorm. I guess I could still commute each night.

"Don't do that," Elise murmurs. Her hand squeezes mine, and I blink.

"Sorry."

"No...not sorry. Just don't think right now. Look around. Stay with me." Her fingers rub mine, and I focus on that.

"Yeah. You're right." I'm trying to practice what Elise calls "mindfulness."

I stop her beside some lockers, leaning down to kiss her. She wraps her arms around my waist and grins up at me.

"I don't want tomorrow to be a half day and the next day to be graduation." She makes a pouty face.

"Don't worry. We're doing yoga, right?" At Rockefeller Park on Monday mornings. It's whoa expensive, but it's worth it to be in the same swatch of grass as her. "And remember, I think I can meet you Thursdays after your tennis lesson. We could maybe even play, if you aren't being driven."

She nods.

"Fridays after you and Dani do Italian lessons, we'll get lunch after. And Sundays when your parents go to meditation..."

"We'll meet on the roof." She smiles—because we've discussed this a million times.

"It's just a few months, and then college."

She nods slowly. "I guess."

Still, we stop in front of the school's doorway and hug like it's the last time we'll ever see each other. Then we kiss until we can't breathe, and I watch as she walks down some stairs. I go through the bridge and out beside our tennis courts, then start the old, familiar walk to Chambers Street.

❦

I haven't thought about the wedding reception in a long time, but I'm thinking about it now as I walk toward the shoe store. What was it he said to me? "Don't do things that might close doors that you want open?" What did it mean? Almost a year later and I still don't get it.

Was it a threat? If it was, would he really have sent me to help his father make panettone? And why take an interest in me at all? And what doors?

I walk past the donut shop, inhaling the sweet scent wafting through the screen on one of the half-open windows.

Roberto Arnoldi is the top guy. He runs lower Manhattan, Brooklyn, Queens, Long Beach, and Staten Island. Maybe even all of The Bronx.

Cross state lines into Jersey, and it's the Bellinis. Frank Bellini, but he's getting old, so I heard his son Vincent might take over. Except I also heard that Vincent is a sophomore at NYU, so that seems like a stretch. I don't know much about the Bellinis. I also don't know who's in charge of Yonkers, New Rochelle, or White Plains. New Haven and all that shit up there—it's make-believe land to me. I've never been there.

My research since the party at Isa Arnoldi's house has centered on her father's kingdom. And his army. Four lieutenants, one floater who doesn't really fall within the typical hierarchy; it's this guy that's in charge of Tony.

My dad told me once that the Arnoldis have a hand in everything in Red Hook. All the shops, including Dad's.

I've been trying to fit it all together into something that can buy Arnoldi that huge fucking house, make it possible for him to ensconce his daughter within the upper crust of Manhattan society.

Is it wrong, what he does? Or is it what Tony says it is: a system that exists parallel to Uncle Sam. The Arnoldi empire is like its own small country, policing its territory and providing for everyone all on its own.

I know for sure that's bullshit. But I want to chew it over. Mostly so I can decide whether I think my father was really "wronged"—or if maybe he made a shitty deal with the mob. I mean, it's not like he didn't know who Roberto was.

The more I think about it, the more I think he knew what he was getting into, and he chose to do it anyway. So when they came calling for their money, is that really evil, like I used to think? Maybe my dad is just a dumbass.

I look up at the shoe store's ragged awning, and the sight of it aims my thoughts elsewhere. Lately, Dad's been worse than ever. The other night, he came home smelling like another woman, and when my mom's eyes welled, he slapped her in the mouth.

When I tried to make him apologize, he said he didn't hit her, and when I called him a fucking liar, he shoved me. I didn't give a shit—I was getting ready to shove him back—but then Soren rushed into it, and my dad called him a dumb fuck, and that's when I lost my shit.

I'm not that kind of guy. I don't even have a temper like Leo and some of my other friends. But I can't let a bully live in my house, breaking my mom's heart and calling my brother names. This shit can't keep going how it is. I'm not sure what to change, though.

I hear the bell ding as the door to the shoe store swings open. Roberto Arnoldi steps out in a crisp white button-up and dark slacks. I'm so shocked I freeze in place, so it takes him a second to notice me.

When he does, he freezes too, but for just a second, and just his face. There's something in his eyes and mouth. Like he almost winced.

The next second he swings the shoe store bag he's holding, pulling my attention to his hand, where I notice a big, square gold ring.

He stops, nodding at me as his dark eyes hold mine. "Luca Galante," he says. "I understand we entertained you on prom night. Did you enjoy our party?"

I nod. "Yeah. The food was really good. Thanks."

"I hear you're attending Columbia University. On scholarship." He smiles, and although the smile is tight, I feel like his eyes are sincere.

"That's true," I hear myself say.

He gives me a shoulder clap. "No closing doors," he says, and it's a fatherly tone. "A young person's education is very important. My daughter's going to NYU, but I heard Elise O'Hara will be going to Columbia." He taps his forehead. "Smart girl. They're good people." He says it in passing, but there's a tenor to his voice as if he's trying to sell me.

"I agree."

He nods once more at me, his eyes holding mine a millisecond too long.

"Watch out for your mother," he says.

Then we're off, moving in opposite directions. I hear a car door slam a half second before I pull the store's door open and the bell tolls again.

I step inside. I'm pulling the scent of leather, rubber, polish into my nostrils, replaying Roberto Arnoldi's words. When someone jumps me from behind, I'm on the floor before I know what hit me.

CHAPTER NINETEEN

Elise

We're leaving for the Hamptons Monday. I'm not sure why I'm so surprised. We go every year after school lets out, and we pretty much always stay for at least two months. Dad stays the first few weeks, then only comes some weekends. Mom helps organize a charity speedboat race that happens on the Fourth of July.

A few months ago, Becca was so sick that I didn't think we'd do it this year, but she's a lot better now. We'll take some extra nurse staff, but besides that, I think it'll be the same as always. I'll spend time with Dani, Jace, Franco, Lorenzo, Isa, and Max. Dani's parents own a home a few doors down from ours, so she and I will be inseparable.

When Mom sprung it on me earlier this afternoon, she promised Ree could visit for a week—which means she'll be with me one week and Dani the next, so the three of us can be together two weeks.

I love Southampton more than almost anything, but I'm fighting tears as I slip into a hot bath. I don't want to be away from Luca. Not for a day, and definitely not for more than a month. I don't know how I'll do it. Maybe I should sign on for a camp or special lessons of some kind—to keep me in the city. I mentioned my plans for tennis and Italian to my mom, and she looked at me like I must have lost my mind.

"You'll do it when you get back," she said simply.

I could sign on for some summer classes at Columbia. Unless it's too late. Is it too late?

I lean back against my sunken tub's pillow and put a hand over my eyes. I'm so tired of sneaking around, tired of leaving Luca out of all my conversations with my parents. And it's unfair. I know life's not fair—boy, do I know that—but he is such a good guy. I wipe my eyes again and sit up, dumping more bath salts into the water.

I feel better when I realize that when I tell him I'll be in Southampton, he'll find a way to come and visit.

I'm aware of some sound then, and for a moment, I don't know what. Then I realize—it's my cellular phone. I hop out of the tub and dash into my bedroom wet and naked. Usually I don't lunge for it, but it's late, and all my friends call our home line…

I answer quickly with my damp fingers and bring the thing to my ear.

"Hello?"

"Elise?"

I know something's wrong because his voice is weird and off-key.

"Hey—what's the matter?"

There's a long pause, during which my poor heart starts to hammer so hard, I feel weak with fear. I don't know how I know, but I just know. Even before I hear him exhale and he rasps, "Can I come to the roof?"

"Of course." My pulse surges. "Where are you right now?"

"Payphone." I think the word sounds groaned, but he's too quiet for me to be sure.

"Can you come up now? I'll call the doorman."

"I don't want…to get you in trouble."

Something is *so* wrong. I can feel the blood drain from my cheeks as I say, "No, it's not going to be trouble. I'll meet you upstairs right now?"

There's another little pause, and then he says, "Okay."

My mind spins as I call the lobby, find my shoes, say "bye" to Becca and Maura, and sprint toward the elevator. My parents are out to dinner and a show.

I feel like I can't breathe by the time the elevator lets me out beside the rooftop garden. No Luca. I pace, hearing sirens, feeling the breeze, seeing the bleary flowers and cement walls and the city lights all around. And then he's walking out onto the rooftop.

His head is down. When he looks up, his eyes find me—they're a fraction too wide. Then he shuts them, and my heart sinks.

I feel like I'm floating as I move toward him. "Hey...what happened?"

He doesn't look up for a long second. Then he does, and I can see his face is strained. "Just wanted to see you." The words tremble from his lips. I realize he's holding his arm at the elbow.

"What happened?"

He shuts his eyes again. "Nothing," he says thickly.

A line of something dark is on the left side of his face. I move in closer, and I realize it can only be blood.

I start to put my arm around his back, to pull him to me, but he makes a groan-like sound before I get to that.

"No, don't. Sorry." He just stands there breathing in these shallow breaths, and tears fill my eyes.

I look him over, from the bleeding spot by his brow to the way he's holding his arm. His face is slack and tense at once, the way that people look when they're in pain, and I can tell he really is because of how he's panting.

"My parents aren't home. Let's go down to my room. Okay?"

He shuts his eyes again, wincing, almost groaning I think.

"It'll be fine. Come on." I rest my fingers lightly at his hip, urging him to turn around and come with me to the elevator. He's definitely shaken up. In the warm yellow glow of the elevator, I see sweat along his hairline. His face is pale, and there's a bleeding gash between his temple and his eyebrow on the left side.

When we step out of the elevator and move toward my door, a hoarse sound comes from him. I wait for his eyes to find mine, for him to tell me he's okay—the way he always tries to, even if he isn't —but he doesn't even look at me. I hurry with the door and hold it for him, and he steps inside.

"Come with me, *il mio cuore*."

His eyes lift up to mine and his lips twitch at the corners.

I put my hand lightly at his lower back again. I want to hug him so badly, but I don't know where he's hurt. My heart pounds as we walk toward my room.

I open the door and he steps inside, but just one step and then he stops.

"You want to lie on the bed?"

He nods. He looks at the bed and then at me, and I realize there's blood on his shirt.

"The sheets don't matter." When he doesn't move, just stands there with his eyes closed and his teeth clenched, holding his arm, I peel the duvet back and set a pillow under where his hurt arm might fall.

"Come here."

He stretches out on the bed without my help, panting as he gets onto his back.

"You want some more pillows?"

"No." His left arm is on the pillow I put down before. I think I'll get another one anyway, but he rasps, "Beside me."

I'm not sure at first, but then his eyes open and I can tell—he wants me to lie down beside him.

I do, and he leans his head toward me. His right arm goes behind my neck, and I ask, "Where can I touch?"

"Anywhere but the shoulder."

I run my fingers over his abs, and he nods once, so I wrap a light and careful arm around him.

He lets a breath out, and I can feel him relax. He sort of pants, "Please," and my stomach flip-flops. "Please what, sweetheart?"

"Don't let go."

Tears spill down his cheeks, and I'm so stunned, I feel like I've been kicked in the chest.

His bicep, behind my neck, flexes a little, and I feel him try to hug me with that arm. I turn myself toward him, wrap my arm around his lower abs, and press myself against his unhurt side.

There's a little tremor, followed by more deep breaths. I want desperately to know what happened, but I can tell he's trying to get a hold of himself. I hug him a little tighter and kiss his chest beside his pec.

"It's okay, sweet baby. I'll take care of you."

His body trembles and he's breathing harder for a second. Then he makes a noise that's half groan and rasps, "I think my shoulder's...

broken." He inhales. "Don't look at me." His voice is raw, and I can hear more tears there.

"I love you," I whisper.

He breathes in big gulps for a minute, then some longer, slower breaths. Finally he whispers, "I love you more, *la mia rosa*. *Ti amo più di tutte le stele nel cielo*."

"Can I kiss your cheek?" I whisper.

He inhales again and lets the breath out. "Okay."

I kiss his damp cheek, kiss his temple. When I see the cut up close, my eyes well, and he looks away. I kiss his hair and rub my fingers lightly over his head.

"What happened," I whisper.

He shuts his eyes. "Doesn't matter."

"It does matter," I say. "You know you can trust me."

"I don't have to tell you." His words are so soft, they're barely audible. "You already know."

"Does he...know?" If his dad hurt him this bad... I can't comprehend, except to think that maybe he was blackout drunk.

"He knows." His voice is soft but hard.

"So are you saying he—"

"He's an asshole and it doesn't matter." But I know it does because his voice cracks on the last word.

"Baby. I'm so sorry." I kiss his cool, damp forehead, press my cheek against his.

"Usually I'm ready but...I wasn't paying attention."

Tears spill down my cheeks as my chest aches so badly I can't breathe. "You shouldn't have to."

"I know."

I wait for him to say more. I want him to tell me everything, but he just lies there with his eyes closed, looking pale and hurt, not moving as I kiss his eyes and cheeks and jaw. Not one tear rolls down his temple.

"Where are you hurt, sweetness?"

His hand, wrapped loosely around my shoulder, moves a little, and I scoot away so he can move it without shifting his body. He brings his hand so that his palm hovers over his shoulder—or the spot between his chin and shoulder.

"Right there." His face tenses as he pulls on his shirt collar, revealing a swatch of bruised and swollen skin.

He inhales, blows the breath out. "Sorry I came." I think he's trying to keep that flat tone, but his words tremble again.

"Why would you be sorry? I'm your family now, and you're my family. Do you know how devastated I would be if you hadn't come to me?"

He sucks air in through his nose. Then he wipes his eyes with his free hand. "It's not a big deal."

"Everything about you is a big deal to me. And it always will be."

He reaches around with his good arm so he's got his hand behind me. Then he tugs on my shirt, urging me back down beside him. When we're snuggled up, our legs intertwined and his warm arm locked around me, I can feel him exhale.

I kiss his throat. "In a second, I can get a towel for your face. And then we'll figure out the rest. I think you should see a doctor."

I lift my head so I can see him, finding his eyes on me. Such sad eyes. Tears well in them, and I want to die from hurting for him.

"You're going to be okay. I promise. I will help you find a way to be okay. You and me, all right? Forever."

He nods, leaning his head toward mine.

"In a little while, I can sneak out with you to go to the doctor."

"I can go...by myself. I feel...bad for coming here." The words are forced through clenched teeth.

I kiss his cheek. "No, don't feel bad." I stroke his hair back, noticing it's damp. "How about I go grab you some Advil?"

He nods, closing his eyes again.

I kiss him one last time and gently disentangle my limbs from his. "I've got some in the medicine cabinet in the bathroom. I'll be right back."

I cast one last look at him, my heart bursting with love and sorrow at the sight of him on my bed. Then I grab the first aid kit. When I step back into the room, I find my father in the doorway.

CHAPTER TWENTY

Luca

Elise is all I care about, so the look of horror on her face as she sees her dad hits me right in the gut. I get a shot of adrenaline, which leaves me gritting my teeth. Elise is standing in front of me—like she's protecting me. I hear her voice, but I can't process. He says something, and she sits on the edge of the bed.

He murmurs something that's not louder than the whooshing sound in my head.

"No," she says.

"I'm not going to hurt him, Elise. What happened?"

"He got hurt, and he came here. Now he needs to see a doctor and I'm not throwing him out."

Elise's father puts his hand on her shoulder. He pulls her to her feet, and they step out of the room.

Fuck, I'm such a selfish, stupid asshole. I get up as fast as I can, blinking a few times before I pull open the door. They're standing just outside it. Both of them turn to me. Elise's eyes are wide; she's clearly upset. I can't read her father.

"Hey, it's okay. I'm gonna get going. I've got a few things I need to—"

"No," her father interrupts. "You're going to come into my office."

I'm too out of it to read his tone. I look at Elise, and she's biting her lip, looking on the verge of tears.

"I'm sorry. I think I should go." Before my legs give out, because they're feeling weird and shaky.

"Son, I want to check on you and make sure you're okay. That's all."

"I am." I try to steady my voice. "I just need to get home."

A big tear drips down Elise's cheek. Her father sees, too. He puts a hand on my unhurt shoulder and looks into my eyes.

"It won't take long," he says, and I can read what his brown eyes are saying: *right now, motherfucker.* I don't want to get Elise in trouble, so I nod.

"Bye, E. Thank you."

I feel weird and sweaty as I follow her dad down two long halls that I can't track, into a dark room that's not dark when he turns on a lamp. It's a library.

"Have a seat." He points to a leather chair.

I look at it, thinking about getting out of it with no hands. I think I can do it, so I sit.

"I'm sorry I came here," I say, and I try to keep my voice steady. Mr. O'Hara leans on his desk, crosses his arms, and frowns at me.

I'm kind of worried I'll puke on the nice rug, but I tilt my head back and make myself meet his eyes, and when he holds my gaze, I hold his back—because that's what men do.

Then he turns around and grabs another arm chair, pulling it closer to my chair, so when he sits in it, we're maybe three feet apart.

"I'm not good enough for her, but I love her." I say it in a rush, surprising myself.

Elise's father leans forward in his chair, his brows drawn together pensively. I feel nauseated as he looks me over, his gaze lingering on my face and shoulder.

Then he sighs. He sits back in his chair and says, "I'm the product of a married man's affair with his mistress. My mother was Elaine O'Hara. She was raised by her grandmother, who worked long hours in a clothing factory. So Elaine made her own way. She met my father, and he took care of her. Even part-time was enough to please her. She could have chosen to end her pregnancy. My father offered to pay. But she wanted to have me. By then, her grandmother had passed on, and she was lonely, I think. But I don't know, because she died while giving birth to me."

My stomach lurches.

"I went to foster families." His jaw tics as his eyes hold mine, but when he speaks again, his voice is smooth and easy. "There were twenty-seven. Homes," he clarifies. "Some families are good. They take kids because they want to help. I knew two families like that. One of them, I still keep up with." He smiles, but it's tense, like he's forcing it. "Most people took in an orphan because they wanted the extra income from the state of New York." He stands from the chair and holds a finger up. "I'm going to get you some water."

He walks to a marble-topped bar, giving me his back.

"Many of them had no problem hitting a child. I had never known a steady home or the same caretakers for longer than a few months. I was not a pleasant child. I met Elise's mother when I was eighteen and didn't speak to her until we both were twenty." He walks over to me, sits back down, and hands me a glass of water.

"I've got a flashlight," he says, half a second before he shines one in my eyes.

"Fuck."

"That hurts, doesn't it?" He does it again on my left eye, and I grit my teeth.

"Anyway—" The flashlight goes away. "Elise's mother was a beauty. Still is. She came from money, and she had brains, too. She was studying to be a chemist. I was a student of mere rhetoric." He smiles fondly. "I knew from day one I wasn't good enough for her. But I couldn't keep myself away." His mouth presses into a frown. "In the years since, it's been difficult for me to stay...available to her at times. Sometimes things happen, and I want to shut myself away. Sometimes I do that."

I swallow as my heart pounds harder again.

"When someone hits you, even someone you don't know well, something changes inside. It makes you a victim, even if you don't want to be. The way you see yourself changes—more so than the way you see them. I imagine it's a lot worse when it's someone close to you."

I inhale.

"Your father is a weak, pathetic excuse for a man. No self-control

181

or accountability. And somehow, you seem to have both. Some of both," he amends. "You stood outside for more than an hour before calling my daughter tonight."

My throat tightens. How does he know? "You came here because you wanted comfort and some kindness, but you almost backed out. Right?"

Tears well in my eyes, so unexpected that my inner recoil sends another wave of cold sweat through me.

"Luca, I think you need to see a doctor. Get some imaging done, to be sure nothing's wrong. I have someone who can take you there, and I can pick the bill up. For my daughter. I know she would want that."

I start taking bigger breaths, because my lungs feel too tight.

"Here's what I'm asking for in return." He hands me a bag of ice, and I grip the Ziploc bag as pain sears my shoulder. "I want you to go away from Red Hook. As soon as you can, you find yourself a place near the university and start the work of splitting from your family. I'll provide a stipend for your mom and brother. You cut your contact with Anthony Diamond and anyone who is in contact with him. Stop doing those things he asks you. Focus on your studies. Keep your honor, Luca. Get your degree, and if you love my daughter and she loves you, I'll pay for a big wedding and help you find a foothold."

I can't breathe. "Why?" I manage.

His hand clasps my unhurt shoulder. "I think you're a good kid, but I don't want my daughter near a man who's beholden to the Tony Diamonds of this world. If you can't look into your own eyes in the mirror, stay away from Elise. I've got ways of knowing. Do you understand?"

I nod.

"And treat her well. You don't have to be her boyfriend. I'll still pay your mother's rent and you'll pursue your education. But you have to treat her kindly at all times. Even if the nature of your relationship changes. Do we have an understanding?"

I nod as my eyes sting.

"You're going to go and say goodbye to her and I'll have someone drive you to an ER. Elise needs her sleep."

I nod again.

CHAPTER TWENTY-ONE

Elise

My dad has Mercer bring Luca back to our house when they finish at the ER. Unbeknownst to me, he sleeps in one of the guest rooms from four-thirty till a little after nine, when my dad's doctor checks on him and then my mother leads him to the kitchen to surprise me at the breakfast table.

He looks sleepy, with his hair mussed and his left arm in a black sling. As he comes closer, I see a thin strip of what looks like white tape to the left of his eye, ringed by a bruise.

"Hi…" I stand up, coming to stop right in front of him.

My mom leans around him. "We didn't want you sneaking in on him. He needed rest."

Last night, my dad came into my room after Mercer and Luca left, and we had a long talk—so I knew my parents had made a U-turn on my relationship, and this morning, Mom had told me he was out of the ER and doing well. But I didn't realize he was at our house.

"How do you feel?"

His eyes look slightly glassy. I see his Adam's apple bob before he murmurs, "Better."

"I'll leave you two to breakfast," my mom says.

"Thank you," Luca tells her.

She waves and smiles as she leaves.

I pull a chair out for him and watch as he sits carefully. About ten feet away, behind the counter, Raya is whipping up my favorite breakfast.

I run my socked foot up Luca's leg—which I notice is bare; he came into the kitchen wearing one of my dad's undershirts and a pair of his gym shorts—and his foot rubs mine in return.

"Are you really okay?" I ask softly.

He smiles. "Better than okay."

He looks tired, though, heavy-lidded.

"What did they tell you at the hospital?"

"Just the collar bone. It'll be fine."

"How long will it take to heal?"

"It should be fast."

"What about your—" I gesture to his head.

His fingertip traces the thin strip of tape. "Butterfly bandage." He gives me a little smirk.

"Does anything hurt?"

His free hand toys with the sling's strap, and I feel like he's avoiding my eyes as he says, "Your family's doctor made me take a pain pill."

"That's good. Really good."

His free hand reaches for mine, and I thread my fingers through his.

He squeezes my hand as Raya serves us homemade waffles topped by fruit and her special whipped cream, plus a heaping plate of vegan sausage. Every time Luca's eyes meet mine, his lips twist into this tentative smile, which makes my heart ache.

All these months, I doubted both my parents, but it turns out they both want me to be happy. My mom told me this morning she and Dad will let me see Luca some this summer, if he treats me well and stays away from "trouble"—which made me want to roll my eyes.

He's like the best guy. I can't even think of what kind of trouble he would get in.

I rub his foot with mine again, and he smiles. He doesn't eat a lot, and I can see some strain around his eyes, but after breakfast, before he goes to get a shower and put on some clean clothes my mom had delivered, he pulls me against him in the hall and kisses my hair.

"I love you."

"I love you more."

He kisses me again and leans his forehead against mine. I'm surprised when he asks to see my sister.

"Of course. If you're sure."

We spend almost an hour with Becca. Luca wants to play charades. For a long time, he mimes different animals, I make guesses, and Becca giggles. Finally I realize I should probably swap roles with him, so I jump in. Toward the end, even Bec's nurse takes a turn. When Luca leaves, he runs his hand over my little sister's hair again and gives her a big smile.

"See ya later, *stellina*."

"What does that mean?" I ask as we step out into the hallway.

He winks. "Look it up."

We go to my bedroom's balcony, where Luca sits in one of the wicker rocking chairs and beckons me into his lap. He wraps his unhurt arm around me and rests his head against the top of my hair.

"I love you," I whisper.

"Love you more."

He's so warm and solid.

"I love when you hug me."

He kisses my hair. A minute later, I feel his muscles twitch and realize he's nodding off. My stomach clenches thinking of the night he had.

I tell myself that starting with our graduation tonight, things are going to get better for him. I wish I knew what happened with his dad, but I know I can't pry. Still, I can't imagine how I'm going to feel if he—

"I need to go home."

I blink at him. Up just a few minutes after falling asleep. "You do?"

He nods, all blue eyes.

"Can I come with you?"

He laughs, looking beautiful and tired and like the whole world in one person. "I don't think that's a good idea."

I offer Mercer's services and he accepts, promising he'll go into his house quickly to get his robe and cap, and then Mercer will bring him to the stadium. I don't ask about his family attending, but I'm surprised he doesn't mention them. My heart aches thinking about it as I get ready myself.

Everything seems okay when I see him grinning at the football field, looking upbeat and relaxed as he chats with Arnie Gallway beside him. I see Arnie point toward the podium and watch with amusement at Luca's wide eyes as he processes the news that as salutatorian, he'll be sitting near the front.

He messed up his own grade in physics this semester so he wouldn't be the one to give a speech, but only I know that. In a weird way, it makes me love him more—how unassuming he can be, how modest. There's a part of me that wants him to just be *mine*, like a secret that I want to keep forever. But I'm happy he'll be everyone's one day. He's going to Columbia, and he's going to study economic policy and political science, and I know he's going to do amazing things.

I know it's probably crazy to think about marriage, but if we did get married, helping people would be our household's focus. I'm going to be a lawyer—yes, like Dad—but I think I might be more interested in advocacy and policy.

When Luca gets his diploma and I hear my dad's low hoot, I can barely hold back my tears.

After graduation, we have dinner at my house with Ree, Dani, and their dates. Then the six of us head to a party on Lorenzo's family yacht. It's supposed to be the party to end all parties. I've heard there are staterooms filled with liquor, but Luca and I don't drink. We find a nook on the deck and stay with each other all night.

When we can't keep our hands off one another, we find a stateroom. After, Luca falls asleep, I lie there beside him, kissing his cheek and breathing our shared air, and loving how hard his body is against mine. I love everything about him, and I don't care what people say about first love. Luca Galante is my forever. I can feel it in my bones.

✤

Luca

I wake up in darkness, confused until I feel her beside me. Her hand strokes my forehead, fingers careful for my little bandage, and it feels so good that my eyes slip back shut.

"Are we sleeping through the greatest party of all time?" I ask, smiling.

Her lips brush mine. "Yes. And one of us is only wearing underwear."

I laugh—or almost laugh before I realize that will hurt my shoulder.

"Left me naked," I murmur.

"Half naked. So I could enjoy you."

"Enjoy me?" I peek one eye open.

"Yes," she whispers.

We go for round two, and she blows my mind and makes me see stars—in a good way and also in a bad way.

"Did that hurt? I'm so sorry."

I laugh. "Worth it. I'd do anything to feel that hot mouth of yours." I fumble with my boxers, and she pulls them back up.

"Guess you men are all the same."

"How many men do you know about?" I murmur, teasing.

"Only one. Only ever one."

I pull her up against me, and I keep her there a long time. I know that I need to go home. This whole day has been me avoiding what I know is waiting for me. This fucking perfect day has been the calm before the storm. I know it in my gut—this shit with my dad is not going to end well. So I stay exactly where I am.

We lock the stateroom door and lock the bathroom door and get into the tub. Elise giggles the whole time and turns bright red when she steps into the bubbles.

"If someone comes in, I will die," she tells me.

"I'll distract them," I tell her, smirking down at myself.

"Hard to miss." She lifts her brows.

We don't stay in the water long, but it feels so damn good to have her arms around me. Then we're kissing again, we're back on the bed. I run my hand down her soft belly, but she moves it away.

"You're still infirm. You need to take it easy, mister. Maybe even one more nap."

I shake my head, kissing her before I get up. "Let's go to the deck. I think it's actually almost time to dock again."

I don't say it because it sounds stupid, but I want to stand up there with her in the warm breeze and look out at the lights. I need to hold her for a little longer. She's done so much for me, and I know what I have to do for her. I have to make it to Columbia. I have to stay the hell away from Tony—even though I've promised him I'll work for him all summer. Even as my family is at risk because Dad did something—he didn't bother to tell me what, before or after he jumped me.

I've got to find out what went wrong before I can extricate myself from Red Hook. Why did Roberto Arnoldi threaten Dad at his store? How is it my fault—as Dad claimed while he was kicking my ass. And what can I do to fix it?

Then I have to move Mom and Soren out. There's no ifs, ands, or buts. I simply have to. Then I leave.

"You're doing the thing again," Elise whispers.

I blink to find her dressed and standing by the stateroom's door.

"Sorry. My brain sucks."

She steps closer to me. "Your brain is perfect. Treat it nicely tonight if you go home. Are you going home?" I can hear the worry in her voice.

"I have to, but don't worry. I'll be careful."

"Careful for your father?"

I try not to answer questions like that. I don't want to make her worry. "He won't be around. Last night he told me he was leaving."

"Leaving? Like…forever?"

"I don't know. He was drunk and wasn't making any sense. I'm gonna find out."

Her eyes well as I close the space between us.

"Don't be worried, *la mia rosa*. Last time, I didn't know it was coming. He just…fucking jumped me."

She wraps her arms around me. "God, I'm so, so sorry. I don't know what to say to make it better."

I close my eyes and cup the back of her head. Her hair is soft and warm and I love every inch of her against me. "You don't need to say anything. You make everything better just by being here."

Her cheek presses against my chest. "Soon you'll be away from him."

I nod.

"I want you to be careful," she says. "Very careful. I've got a weird, bad feeling, Luca."

I look down into her pretty eyes. "Don't have a bad feeling. It'll be all right. I promise."

We go up to the deck, and I do just what I want, holding her against me as I lean against the yacht and we look at the water.

"Get a good night's sleep," she tells me as the vessel docks. "And if you can't, promise you'll call me and we'll pick you up."

"I don't deserve you." I kiss her forehead.

"You do." She rises on her toes and kisses my lips, soft and gentle. "You do." She smiles sadly. "We'll work on that part, okay? Until it sticks."

I feel uneasy as we walk the plank-like walkway bridging the boat and the dock. Like...it's all some kind of drug-induced dream. I'm playing a role that isn't meant for me. I think about that as I ride the subway home. I tell myself that I'm just tired. I need to sleep tonight. Maybe I can find out about my dad and all that stuff tomorrow.

I'm fighting to keep my eyes open when the train stops at Red Hook. Everything hurts when I stand up.

I step out into the warm, still air, and someone grabs my arm. My whole body reacts. I throw a punch before I see the person. There's a grunt and my own "fuck" as pain flares through my head and shoulder.

When I blink, I see Alesso holding his eye. "Shit!"

"Oh, fuck. Are you okay?"

His hand cups his eye. "Fuck." His face twists as he notices my sling. "Are *you* okay?"

"What are you doing here?" I ask, at the same moment as he asks, "What happened to your arm?"

I squeeze my eyes shut. I'm too fucking tired for this shit.

"Why are you here, Alessandro?"

"Dude..." He shakes his head. "You gotta come with me."

CHAPTER TWENTY-TWO

Luca

I lean over in the front seat of Zio Luigi's Cutlass, feeling like I might pass out.

"I'm sorry, man," Alesso says. "I've been looking for you for forever. I didn't know it was your graduation day."

I hold my throbbing head. "Say that again," I growl. "Tell me that fucking shit again."

Leo, sitting in the back, puts his hand on my shoulder. "Your dad's a rat. He's been squealing to the FBI."

I squeeze my eyes shut until I see stars. "He's a fucking drunk." I grit my teeth so hard my head throbs. "He's not working with the FBI!"

"Your dad's not a drunk," Alesso says darkly. "He's a liar."

"He might be a liar but he's not a rat."

"Tony has recordings."

"Of what? He's not in the fucking mob! What could he even be saying?"

"It's logistics shit," Alesso says as he reaches around me, buckling my seatbelt. "Like where they are and what they're doing. He listens for the FBI on some kind of device."

"That doesn't—"

"Tony said your dad was in deep with Roberto when we were kids. He was helping launder money through the store."

That makes me snicker even as my shoulder throbs. "Now I know *that's* a fucking lie."

My friends don't say anything.

So I ask, "Why would he even do that? What reason would he have to talk to the FBI?"

"Immunity," Alesso says, pulling away from the curb. "Tony said they promised him he'd get a new life."

"What kind of fucking life could he have? He's a fucking addict."

"Tony said he was promised help moving your family."

My throat tightens. "This is bullshit. Tony's a goddamn liar. I'm going to Columbia, so where are we moving?"

Leo whistles. *"Damn, dude."*

"I knew you were Einstein 2.0 or some shit, but fuck." Alesso gives a shake of his head. The car jolts, squeaking on its old shocks as he gasses it through a yellow light.

My stomach pitches. "My dad's not a narc, A."

"Listen, man, I know it's hard to buy. But *I* heard the recordings, man. He's a narc. He's a narc and someone from way up told Tony to fix it."

"Fix it?" My vision blurs a little. "What do you mean fix it?"

The car bumps over a pothole, sending a bolt of pain up my neck and down my left arm. Alesso's eyes slide to mine. "Luca." His voice cracks on my name.

Leo mutters, "Jesus, Aless."

"Fuck you," he shouts toward the back of the car. "What should I have said?"

"Look at him, he's fucked up!"

I turn around so I can glare at Leo. "No I'm not."

Then I glare at Alesso. "You better get your fucking stupid brother in line."

He laughs—but it's a helpless, strained sound. "How? Don't lie to yourself. I can't do shit, and you can't either. It's a done deal."

"Oh is that what goddamn stupid Tony said? That it's a done deal? It's a done deal, I know something else that's a done fucking deal."

Leo and Alesso both talk at once. Leo's hand grips my right shoulder, and I reach around to throw it off.

I hold my throbbing head and breathe till I don't feel like I'm going to hurl. Then I look at Alesso. "Where is Tony? What's going on right now?"

"Nobody knows." Alesso clenches his jaw. "Tony is out looking for him."

"So he's planning do it?" I laugh, and the sound is deranged. "This is crazy shit." I turn around toward Leo again. "You two aren't shitting me?"

"Your dad is a narc, dude," Alesso assures me.

"That's my fucking dad, motherfucker! Your brother kills him, you won't like what's coming."

"*Luca.*"

"You two shut the fuck up!" Leo slams his fist on the console between our front seats. "Both of you! Shut the fuck up."

"You shut up," Alesso snarls. "It's got nothing to do with you."

"He better fucking not do it," I yell. "You hear me, Alesso? You hear what I'm saying?"

"What choice does he have?"

"What choice does he have? Are you fucking serious? Stop the fucking car, Alesso."

"I came to get you so we can try to help! Tony won't kill *me*. Or you. Or Leo. Maybe we can help or something, I don't know!"

"I wanted to kill him," I murmur, picturing the way my shoulder slammed into the brick wall in the shoe store as my fucked-up father body-slammed me. My throat aches as I look at Alesso. "Go and tell your brother that."

"I'm really sorry, Luca. If Tony finds him, I don't think it's gonna come out good." Alesso's jaw works, and for a second, I feel sorry for him. Half a second.

"Tony is a fuck up and a lunatic. He is not killing my dad. Where are they? What do you know about it? Tell me everything you fucking know."

"I don't know," Alesso half moans. "I haven't seen him, and the last thing he said is that he has to do it, Luca."

"If he does it, he'll get caught. You don't think the FBI would *know*? Of course they will! That'll be the end of your brother."

"Just stop, Luca. Tony's got the orders. It's not his fault," Leo says.

I grit my teeth so I don't throttle him. "Who gave Tony the orders?"

"Some dude that's right up underneath Roberto. They call him *il diavolo*."

I roll my eyes. "The devil." How original. "And what about Roberto? He was —" My stomach does a slow roll, followed by a nose-dive. "Jesus! Roberto came by last night." Tears fill my eyes as the truth hits.

"Yeah, he gave your dad some notice. At least that's what I heard. Told him if he tries to run, he'll come take out your family. But that's a lie, don't worry. Tony wouldn't do that shit. Nobody's planning to."

Little stars dance in my eyes. I slam my fist on the door. "Fuck! Where's my mom and Soren!" I groan and rub my temple. "Fuck!"

"We took them to a hotel," Leo says. "They're safe."

I can't help the moan that comes from my throat. "Where's my dad?"

"I don't know," Alesso says. "I told Tony we were gonna help you, keep you out of it."

"I don't want to be out! Goddammit! How could my dad do this!" I slap the dash so hard Alesso swerves.

"Whoa Luca!"

"I want to talk to Tony. I can talk to— Maybe I can talk to Arnoldi myself. You said he likes me. Maybe I can promise him something. Anything."

I have maybe half a minute to consider what that might look like before Leo says, "I don't think that's how it works." His voice is soft. Regretful.

I shake my head. "I'm going to talk to him."

"You need to go to the hotel," Alesso says. Be with your mom and Soren. Leo and me will see if there's something we can do."

I laugh darkly. Not a goddamn chance. "I want to know where Tony is, and where my dad is. I know you two know!"

Alesso's eyes shift to the rearview mirror.

Leo leans forward again. "They're going to that old ship-building place that used to be a warehouse and then got turned into a theater and stores. You know where I mean? Near the stock yard? Boarded-up place? Sorta like a warehouse."

I nod, feeling dizzy.

"Luca, you can't go in there," Alesso says.

"Let us go and see what's up," Leo says. "We'll sneak around and try to see."

A thick swell of grief rises up from somewhere in my chest, but I shove it down.

"He can't kill my dad." My voice cracks, so I make it harder. "Tony is a stupid loser fuck. But I think that he wouldn't really do it." Fuck, my mind is racing. I feel sick.

"What did you tell my mom?" I ask no one in particular.

"Told her that your dad's involved in some messed up shit and they need to leave the house. She didn't say much. She was upset. I got them some food from the Wendy's," Leo tells me. "Since that's the only burger Soren will eat."

"Thank you," I say numbly. "I'll check on them, but I want you to come back and get me right after. I can sneak around, too. It's *my* dad. I deserve to know. And...be there," I add, making sure my voice sounds choked up.

"Whatever would help," Alesso says smoothly. "I can try to talk to Tony. There has to be another way."

I don't know if he's convincing himself, but he's not convincing me.

"Yeah, there's gotta be," Leo says.

"I can't believe I didn't know." I rub my temples, rub my forehead, hating myself, hating my dad more.

"You were graduating. Not your fault your dad's a dumb shit."

My throat aches as I start to tell Leo he's not. Then I look down at myself and shut my eyes as I take a long breath.

"How's your arm?" Alesso asks.

"It's okay."

"He's been doing this shit for the FBI for at least two years," he says quietly.

I want to scream at Aless, to jump out the door, rip my fucking hair out. Instead I close my eyes and lean my head against the head-rest, prop my right hand underneath my left arm so it doesn't hurt so much. I think of nothing. Just...nothing. Nothing's what I know, what I can do, what I am. Everything is fucked now.

Before I know it, Alesso's braking. We're at the hotel.

"You can't do shit about this," Leo tells me. "It's Arnoldi stuff.

Don't go crazy thinking you can do something to fix it, save the day. That's how you do, but it won't work this time."

Fuck you, I want to tell him. I nod.

Alesso's eyes hold mine. "I'll find out some more for you, try to talk to Tony." Something tightens in my chest—because I hear the bullshit in Alesso's tone.

"Give me a call, please."

He nods. "Try to stay chill, brother."

I get carefully out of the car, feeling a hundred years old as I walk toward the lobby. A few minutes later, the black car I called is waiting by the curb.

🐦

In the cab, I have a feeling like it's slipping through my fingers. All control. All...everything.

I'm heavy, fuzzy, floating... It's like my body is offline. I can't really move it. I'm stuck going where it goes.

I would never say it, not to anybody, but I know this feeling by its real name: *dissociation*.

I shift my arm around because that hurts. The pain, it helps me focus. Pain in my shoulder. Pain everywhere else. I focus on the window, framing the route to...whatever this is.

The idea that my father, a drunk who can barely put one foot in front of the other, who some days can't even walk home from the shoe store unescorted, is someone the FBI would want to work with is...impossible to believe.

And I don't. I can't believe it's true. Sometimes rumors get started, and Tony's crazy. Who knows if he even "got an order" at all. Maybe he only told Alesso he did.

I try to recall what Roberto said when he passed me outside the shoe store. How it began. It was just some offhanded comment about me being at his house. Then he congratulated me on Columbia. Then...he told me to take care of Mom. Could he really have dropped by the store because...

Right after Dad dropped me, in those first few seconds when the pain was so bad, he'd been furious. Raging. "I'm dead because of you!" He'd screamed. "Because you had to go catch his attention!"

His cheeks were red, his eyes were redder, but his face was pale and afraid.

It's not my fault, whatever he meant. None of this is my fault because Dad isn't working with the FBI. Tony is crazy. That's the only explanation. It's gotta be some rumor gone wild. Dad blames me for everything; it's his MO because he's got problems. It doesn't mean something is real. Fuck what Alesso said about my dad laundering money. I don't believe a word of that shit.

I run a finger over the thin piece of white tape on my forehead, thinking of Elise. What fucking luck that this shit goes down when I'm so sore I can barely move, when all I want is to climb into a soft bed with her.

The cab stops by a curb, and my heartbeat throbs through my head. Fuck, I must not have kept track of where we were.

"This is it," the guy says, drumming on the wheel.

I pay him and step onto the dark sidewalk. Everything looks old and busted, so I guess that makes it perfect for Tony's imagined drama—*if* anyone is even here. Two junked out cars line the curbside up ahead and garbage litters the sidewalk. The building to my right is covered in low-quality graffiti. The next one down is boarded shut.

This is a waste of time. Probably nobody's here and I'll be walking blocks and blocks to get another cab—if I even can. Maybe I walk all the way home. I run the fingers of my free hand underneath the sling, touching my sore arm. It's amazing how much the damn thing hurts and it's not even what's the problem. It's all pain from my collarbone.

Which one of these derelicts has the old theater inside? I haven't been down here in years, but I'm pretty sure it's the one up ahead that's made of dark-looking brick. I walk slowly, telling myself it's all okay. If I feel kinda panicky it's just because I'm so damn tired and those pain pills are long gone. They said at the ER that being hurt can make your heart beat faster.

You got this.

Quick look around, check it out, and I can go back to the hotel. Figure out what kind of weird shit Tony's doing. Probably a bad idea, but I decide to pull the sling off, stuff it in my pocket. Down this way, it's probably better if I don't look like an easy target.

I try to walk like my arm's not sore, keep an eye on what's in front of me and an ear on what's behind me. That's when I hear it: ghosts of words, like people murmuring somewhere nearby. I lengthen my strides, my heart pounding as I make it to the tall, dark brick building.

There are windows in its front wall, but they're not eye-level. They're five feet above my head, a row of squares. A few yards down, there's a dark, steel kind of door that's got a piece of plywood hanging off it. I think of pushing through, and something buzzy starts up in me.

Nothing's going down inside there. Even if it is, it's not what Alesso and Leo said. Tony's all bark, no bite. No way they'd tap *him* to kill Dad.

Still, I can't just wait this shit out. I need to know what's going on. Is my dad really in there? Probably not. I'm pretty damn sure... but I have to see.

I step closer to the front door, where there's some old wood signs half falling off where they were mounted by the building's entrance. I notice one is for a barber shop and feel like maybe I remember coming in here as a little kid. Beyond the brick façade, this place was like a really shitty, five-shop boutique mall. I think it smelled like dust and old stuff.

I step closer to the boarded-up door, try the handle. Despite the boards, when I tug, the thing swings right open.

Dust and old stuff. Fuck, and also mold and something smoky. I sniff. Squatters burning shit, I bet.

Something in my stomach coils. I tell myself I could go back to the hotel. Let these fools be fools. I've got a spot at Columbia. I told her dad I'd keep my nose clean.

There's a shout, though—at that second. It's not from right inside the door, but from deeper inside the building. Now I know there's no turning back. I duck the hanging board over the door and step into what looks like a hovel. There's a burned out mattress in one corner, a ripped up swivel chair beside it. Dark stains on the floor.... I note the small, peeling countertops and realize this is the old barber shop. I think of the old guy's murdered wife and cross myself. It didn't happen here, but something did.

I can feel it in the air, the way you feel a draft, as I walk out what I realize is the back door of the barber shop and into some kind of equally decrepit common area. There's a cracked fountain in the middle, surrounded by some old-ass benches and a couple of closed doors I think used to lead to little shops.

My eyes catch on a red door with peeling paint on the back side of the fountain. As I start toward it, voices rise and fall in a sharp burst of sound; I stop mid-stride as a louder, familiar voice rises over the rest.

Fuck.

That sounds like Tony.

CHAPTER TWENTY-THREE

Luca

I hold my breath as I move closer to the red door.

It's the door to the old movie theater. It's got a narrow, vertical window, and near the top there's a peeling sticker-poster that's shaped like a film reel.

I don't know what I'm planning. Maybe just to peek in. But when I look through the smudged glass, I see my dad.

He's down at the bottom of the room, on the theater stage, his torso duct-taped to a chair. All around him, guys in dark clothes— half a dozen of them. My blood runs cold as I see Tony up in front. I don't recognize the others, but I count five.

There's a moment that I think of running. It's self-preservation, like a reflex. But I'm not someone who runs. I keep looking through the window, trying to understand what's happening and why and how. Tony crouches by my dad, waving his arm as he says something I can't quite hear. Maybe my dad doesn't answer. I don't know, but Tony backhands him. My dad's head snaps back, and pure rage billows through me.

My mind feels blank and focused as I push the door open. All seven heads turn toward me. It's my father's face my eyes are fixed on. There's tape over his mouth; even from twenty or thirty yards away, I can see his face is bleeding.

"What the fuck?" Tony gives a throaty chuckle as he swaggers up the aisle, moving past folded red chairs toward me. His eyes widen as they meet mine and his face twists into a hard smile. "Look who it is," he says in a raised voice. "It's Bowser Junior. Come to see big Bowser one last time?"

I don't see a gun on him, so with a few long strides, I close the gap between us.

"What the fuck is this shit, Tony?"

"Diamond to you," he snaps, and my stomach feels like I got on a roller coaster.

I move slightly closer to him. "Why's my dad taped to a chair?"

I'm grabbed so fast, there's no time to struggle. Someone's hands are twisting both my arms behind my back, and my legs buckle from the pain. I'm blinking through tears, on the floor. I can't hold in a moan as I try to grab the hurt shoulder.

"Whoa! Someone's rocking the head wound. Careful with his melon, Bobby." Tony holds a hand out for me, but I'd rather die than take it, so I struggle up on my own.

He smirks. "We wanna let you go, my little dude. This is not the place for baby Bowsies. Your old man's one thing, but you're my brother's buddy. You need to get going. My man Bobby B. will help you get the fuck out."

My dad groans—or tries to speak; I can't tell because of the tape over his mouth. I look from him to Tony, and it's happening again. This feeling like I'm not inside my body. Like it's not really me that says, "I can't go until I know what this is about."

"Your old man's a rat," one of the guys down in the front says. He's some scruffy guy with a ponytail, who throws his hand up as he says it. I realize belatedly he's brandishing a handgun.

Everything slows down another big notch. The room feels farther away.

Someone else—some random thug type to the right, says, "We can't let him go, Di."

Tony shakes his head like that's just bullshit. "Bobby can watch him."

My eyes move to Bobby—a burly guy even for this crowd.

Someone snickers: Tony's friend Josh. "This the one on Roberto's dick?" He walks a few rows closer to me. "What, you come to save the day?"

"See him out," a loud voice from the front growls; I can't tell who it belongs to.

"You can't kill him," my voice says.

"He's a fucking rat, and we got no more time." The guy behind me pulls on my sore shoulder. I twist out of his grip, gasping as stars explode in my eyes.

"Let him go! He didn't do anything! Let him go!"

"Or what?" Tony swaggers down the aisle toward the curtain-framed stage, climbs inelegantly atop it, and yanks the strip of tape off Dad's mouth. My dad's eyes squeeze shut as a splotch of blood appears over his upper lip. He's panting, and I notice for the first time how beat up he really is.

"How'd you get that fucked up face, Galante? How you ever get that fucked up face?"

Tony's voice is easy, but I hear the latent threat—as well as his derision.

"Nobody with real balls tries to save someone who kicks their ass, eh?"

I grit my teeth. I can feel my body moving toward my dad, my legs walking like everything is okay. I stop right beside the stage.

"Dad, what'd you do?" My voice is raspy, barely whispered.

"Tell him, shoe guy," Tony sneers. "Tell him what you did."

Then he's got a gun. He's twirling a big ass revolver clumsily in his hand. Dad's quiet, and Tony laughs. "Well, Bowsie, I guess he'll take this one to the grave."

"*Dad.*"

"Unless you wanna take his place? What do you say, Bowsie? Wanna sit in for your dad?"

"*Dad, what did you fucking do?*"

His blood-shot eyes flicker to mine. His eyelids are half shut and I can tell he doesn't want to look at me—but for a second, he does. "Took some risks...and made some mistakes. I'm gonna be fine. Luca, go home to...your mother." When I don't move—because I can't; my eyes have filled with tears and my whole body feels like it's boiling—my dad jerks his chin up. "Go. Now," he says through gritted teeth.

"I tell you what, Bowzie, I've got a deal you can't turn down." Tony gives me a shit-eating grin. "Take his place, and I won't even off you outright. You can do roulette." He holds up his black revolver. "Just two rounds. Good odds for you."

Someone growls something dissenting. "Fuck you," Tony snaps.

For a second, I feel like I'm stuck under an ocean wave. My eyes fly up and down my father, taking in what this is. The whole room feels like it's tilting.

"Is that a real offer?" I manage.

"You want me to let him go?" Tony reaches out toward my dad, who yelps as Tony slashes through a piece of the tape with what I realize belatedly is a knife. Blood blooms on my dad's shoulder. My heart is beating a million miles a minute and I'm sort of worried I might pass out, but somehow I look Tony in the eye and make myself nod.

"Yeah, I want you to let him go, and I'll help figure out what happened."

Everyone guffaws at once—a jeering laugh track that makes me cold down to the bone.

"Fuck, you got some nerve kid," someone murmurs.

I latch my gaze onto my dad's and don't let go until his eyes flicker to mine. "Did you do it?"

Someone barks *"Sbrigati"*—telling Tony to get moving.

Tony shoves me. "Do or die, kid." He laughs. "And by that I mean *go* or die." He looks me over, his face turning serious. "Go now, Luca. Don't be fucking stupid."

Tears are streaming down my cheeks as I lock eyes with my dad. All I feel is love for him. I love him because he's my dad. He's fucked up, but he's my dad. I don't want to hurt him. I can't let someone else fuck with him either.

I look into his red eyes. *I forgive you. It'll be okay.*

Then I brace for pain and jump on Tony. There's a scuffle. I end up on top of Tony, braced on my unhurt arm. It takes every ounce of strength I have to wrestle him for the gun. Pain ignites all through me like a fucking fire. We roll on the stage and he's on top, then I'm on top, trying to reach between us to get to his fucking hand...

My fingertips brush metal.

Then things go black. When I blink, I'm being hauled off the stage. Up the aisle toward the room's back door. I hear fluent, hard Italian from behind me and I wrench around so I can see if—

Still alive. Oh fuck, my *head*. Hurts so bad I gag as my legs buckle.

"C'mon," someone hisses. They've each got an arm.

Someone smacks me in the mouth. I know it's gotta be the butt of a gun because it *pings* against one of my teeth, and pain explodes through my face.

"FUCK!"

I get a punch in, whirl, and see a gun pressed to my dad's cheek. I don't think. I just break free and run toward him.

I hear someone yell "Do it," and everything slows down.

Seconds pass while I'm trying to climb on stage with just the one arm. In those seconds, Tony kicks my dad's chair over. As I heft myself onto the stage, a deafening *BOOM!*

I feel like the world is folding inward as I sink to the floor. Blood spreads out around my father's body—thick, dark crimson, separating into slim vertical lines as it spreads across the smooth, wax-polished boards of the stage.

Two slow blinks cement it in my mind forever: the hunch of his back, the way his hands are purple—tied too tightly with a rope, the swollen fingers. He's got blue jeans on; I watch as the little denim fibers go red. Then my eyes shift to his ruined head.

The floor is hard under my shoe soles and the impact hurts somewhere far off. Distantly I know my legs are pumping, body's moving —I can feel the air around me.

Something slams into me—it's the peeling red door. I sling it open, unaware of anything until I'm outside of the building. I hear guttural screaming and I'm outside in the street. Someone is howling in the street. People shouting, tires are squealing. I smell burning rubber.

I can't go back inside.

I can't leave my dad like that.

Someone's screaming too loud. Someone's going to get killed.

I'm inside my house and something awful happened. Something awful happened. Something awful happened and I can't...

And so I get the baseball bat he kept at his bedside and swing it, swing it, swing it till there's black spots in my eyes and then it's all black. Everyone...brought down by something.

I curl over on my knees and let it take me.

CHAPTER TWENTY-FOUR

Elise

In the dream, we're on a boat. We're standing on the bow like in that movie *Titanic*. His arms are wrapped around me from behind, and I feel good. So it's strange that someone's screaming *"HELP!"*

I smile at him. Then the screams cut through the dream. I sit up, reeling in my dark room, gripped with knowing. This is real—and I know what the screams mean even as I jump out of my bed and fly toward my sister's room.

When I find Becca on the bed and Maura leaning over her, counting in a reedy voice as she does chest compressions, I'm not surprised. Only horrified as I move toward the bed, my eyes locked onto Becca's blue lips.

I hear a shout. My father nearly knocks me over rushing to the bed. He pushes Maura off Becca and grabs my sister's head—too rough. It makes my stomach lurch, the way her body's limp.

"Becca! C'mon baby!"

Then my mom's shrieking behind me. She's a rush of silk and braided hair. She doesn't get near my sister, instead grabs the bedside phone from Maura. The nurse moves away. My mother sobs as she holds the phone.

My sister is dying.

"Becca!" I dash over to the bed and lean down over her. "I love you."

"Get back, Elise!"

Maura scuffles with my dad. She's back in charge of CPR. My dad says, "Come back, Becca. You can do it!"

Her lips are so dark. What happened?

"Becca bear..." The word cracks as I reach for her, pushing dark locks off her forehead. "I love you." Her skin is cool and rubbery. I have the thought: *She's dead already.*

My eyes sweep her small form—lingering on her diaper, folded back the way she likes it. Something swells in my throat, something too big that I push out like a sob.

"I love you!"

I know that this time she won't be back. My mother's wailing rises to the ceiling, falls back down the walls. She pushes Maura off my sister.

"My angel!"

My father nudges my mom off Bec, resumes CPR.

My mother's sobbing. She shouts at me, telling me to back away, but no way. I'm talking to her—this will be the last time that I ever tell her anything—and Mom shoves at me again. I scream something at her and her fingernail catches my shoulder near my throat.

"Get out!" Her words are guttural. She means business, but I can't move. I just *can't,* and so my mom is leaning over me and Dad is shouting his counts, Maura weeping. Every time Dad pushes Becca's chest, her grayish head lolls back.

"Sweet one is gone," Maura says from somewhere that feels far away as Mom shrieks and my dad slaps Bec's cheek and growls her name.

None of this can be real.

I get closer so I can stoke her hair, so maybe that's what she'll remember as she passes on. She'll remember that I loved her...so much. "I love you, I love you Becca."

Her eyelids tremble. Only for a second, they flutter. Her lower lip twitches. I can feel her focus on me, see the parting smile she wants to give me. Then it's over and my mother must have seen because she's wailing. She runs into Maura's arms. My father stops the CPR but quickly starts again.

I can feel it—that she's gone. Something hot and cold and heavy passes through me. My knees almost buckle and I wonder if the planet might stop spinning.

I can see my mom's dark red nails as she slaps Becca's cheek. My sister *died!*

I hear hushed tones and the crackle of a radio as I flee, dashing to the laundry room for shoes I barely get on my feet. I rush out as paramedics reach the front door. I'm dying as I move. I'm going to die just like my sister.

In the hall, I'm by the elevator. Going down, and I should have some trinket with me. I should have her with me somehow. I put my hand over my throat and close my eyes and spots flare underneath my lids. I'm shorting out. Can people die from pain? I can't breathe.

You have got to breathe.

I walk out of the building, shaking like a leaf in the breeze. I see the ambulance and hate it, hate it. I rush down a little way and hail a cab and, with a strange and foreign voice, I give the driver an address in Red Hook.

❧

Down the dark and sparse streets, through the traffic lights—weak lights—and past the buildings that I know like home. I'm silent. The cab driver is a youngish guy—somewhere between my parents' age and mine. He's listening to NPR and wearing good cologne.

Underneath the tunnel, and it's very surreal. There are places in the burroughs where I've never been. Red Hook is one. I wait for it like a meteor or like a savior. Expectation. It looks black and white, broken and dingy. I don't mind the way it is. My sister's dead.

Industrial. Train tracks, docks, and narrow streets with buildings that are neither tall nor short but lean a bit, as if they're thinking of throwing themselves onto sidewalks. A red-light jolt, a squeal of brakes that need new brake pads or new rotors; I don't know. I don't know about cars.

My driver says, "You sure about this?"

"Yes."

He frowns at me in the mirror. I can feel concern, but I don't want that.

Garages, neighborhood stores with neon window signs, bars on broken windows, old cars parked on curbsides. Narrow streets. I wonder why they are so narrow.

Streetlights, pools of dim light, dirty sidewalks. I feel sad for Luca, but the feeling's distant. My sister is dead. Tonight she died. Obituaries, caskets. There will be no going back. A jump off of a ledge and falling. I wonder for how long.

Luca's street is drab and dark and quieter than some others. The cab pulls to the curb, the brakes squeak, and he asks again if I'm sure.

"Thank you. Yes."

I step out and tilt my head back to look at the building. Four stories. It's square and brick, with stairs and balconies and doors on the outside, like a horror movie motel. His unit is 104. I laugh; the sound is hollow.

Hi, Luca, my sister's dead.

His door is right there waiting for me. The zero between the one and four is missing. The door's wood is warped in one spot. I notice an ashtray in the dirt beside the door. I think of Luca going through that door and can't imagine.

I knock twice softly before realizing that I can't. I can't just show up. What time is it? I remember seeing a 3 on the clock inside the cab. Is it 3 a.m. or something:30?

I sit with my back against the door and draw my knees up to my chest. What if someone bothers me or...gets me? Do teen girls get gotten? *Yes, of course they do.* All the girls get gotten, isn't that the story? I'll be trafficked as a sex slave. I think of riding in a horse trailer and feeling wind come through the slits. Nothing clears the fog from my head. I know I should think of Becca but I can't. That's all a dream.

Why did I come here? I don't want to tell Luca.

There's an alley right beside his unit. I stand up and walk toward it, and that's when I hear the talking. Deep, male voices. I don't care —I almost want to see them—but then suddenly I do care. I don't want to die tonight. It's too much for my parents. I scoot myself behind a bush beside his door and hold my breath. As they walk past, tears well in my eyes.

They look...rougher than I'm used to. They sound angry, maybe drunk. *Or maybe you're just sheltered.*

But I'm not sheltered.

My sister is dead.

I blink and I'm dizzy. I decide to knock on the door.

I do knock. I knock a lot. There's no reason I know that they wouldn't be home, but I think no one is, because nobody answers. I'm too scared to yell his name or knock harder than normal knocking.

I walk into the alley by the building. All the windows I see on the left must be his unit. I look at each one of them—they all have plastic blinds—and then notice the back one is pushed open an inch.

My heart starts beating harder. I can't reach it, though. Too high. There's a rusted window unit on the ground. I shove it over on its side and stand atop it. Then I push the window upward with my fingertips. I listen. I'm afraid of Luca's dad—in theory. But in practice, I don't care. Maybe tonight, I want things to go really wrong.

I push the window open more and stick my head inside. I smell him, and it's like a bolt of lightning seeing the twin bed with a dark wood headboard and footboard. There's a threadbare rug that looks blue. I see his backpack on the bed. I blink around and feel my pulse beat in my eyes and push the window open more and slip inside and walk with care until I know for sure he isn't in here. I think no one is here.

I venture out into the hall which smells like bread and juice and carpet, maybe.

Oh my God...the house is trashed. Destroyed. No one is in it. There's no blood. I don't think I understand this. I start crying because everything good ends. That's what it all says—every thing that's not willing to lie will tell you everything will go, and all the good stuff first.

I sit on the lumpy couch and cry from wanting Luca. When the sun rises, I go out the front door and start walking.

CHAPTER TWENTY-FIVE

Luca

"Come on, big guy. Careful down the steps."

Someone's hand grabs my arm. I know it's not Elise...but I don't know...

"Luca? C'mon, man." There's Alesso. Hands on my back. "We've gotta get into the car."

She moves beside me. The wrong smell. Through the windshield... There's pink light on the dashboard. Neon light.

"You sure you have the cash?" she asks.

My eyelids shut.

"We're all good."

I jerk awake to that sound—

Gunfire.

It's ringing in my ears as I pat my body, searching for—but it wasn't—

I lie back...on something cold...and hard. I hear a whimper. My whimper. My shoulder.

I hold onto that arm with my good one, taking shallow, fast breaths till the pain ebbs and I can see all the blood, and know I'm gonna get sick from the smell. I swallow while I try to lean over the side of the tub. Then I can't control it.

So much...liquor? I can't move when it's over. So sick. What did I do last night?

I can smell the blood again. Blood on my fingers.

I go another round and rest my cheek against the cold tub, breathing hard as my heart gallops. When I get a breath, my shoulder hurts so bad I feel like crying out. But...*I don't know where I am.* I look around the dark room. *Where am I?*

Where's Elise?

I look down at myself. I'm in someone's tub, my hips wrapped in a rough towel.

Gotta use that to clean up.

My shoulder. Fuck. I've never hurt this bad before. I'm dizzy, and I feel sick again, when the door opens and someone steps into the dark room with me.

"Luca? You all right?"

My eyes shut.

Not Elise.

Leo.

Good it's not Elise. She can't. I promised her father...

❧

Elise

A few streets over from his building, there are several blocks where things are open. There's a corner store with metal bars over the windows and a strip club with a flashing neon pink sign. There's a parking lot with big, square chunks of asphalt scooped out, piled up inexplicably beside a big, yellow tractor type thing. Beside that are three cars, each one bumping loud music.

I don't walk by them. I turn around beside the strip club, and I run like I am running for a trophy—all the way to Luca's house, which is still empty.

I hide in the alley, and I wonder if whoever wrecked the house might hurt me, too—if they find me. How stupid was I to go inside and sit there crying?

I stand in the shadows for what feels like hours, watching pinprick stars behind gray clouds that move over the alley. Then, with my pulse thundering in my ears, I crawl back through his window, run to the phone, and call for a cab.

My cab driver is a woman. I'm so relieved by that fact that I almost fall asleep en route to Ree's house. Sometime later, I step out onto the sidewalk under fluffy gray clouds and a deep pink sky, and lift my hand at the pigtailed driver.

She pulls off, and Ree runs down the steps toward me.

"Goldfish..." Her voice breaks as she hugs me. "Your mom's assistant just called."

Ree cries, and I hug her, and she escorts me to her bedroom, where I sit on her bed trying not to cry until I do cry.

"I'm crying for Luca," I say as I hug her pillow. "I don't really believe Becca is gone."

Ree stretches out beside me and I close my eyes as I tell her about the night.

She sighs when I finish. "I'm glad you're okay. Not okay," she corrects. "But that you are here safe."

I nod, wiping my eyes. Staring at the pistachio green wall of her room, I feel feverish, off-kilter, like gravity has shifted and I don't know where to put my feet to walk. There's an awful, throbby ache that seems to've grabbed me by the soul and now is ripping at me. Knowing that I'll never see my sister again. Knowing that her beautiful, sweet body is on a cold table or zipped up in a bag...that I'll never feel her soft, wavy black hair again. That I'll never get to kiss the little freckle near her hairline. That I bolted from the house before the paramedics even took her.

I was right that night—on prom night. I have everything and Becca didn't even get to have a life.

I sob my heart out into Ree's pillow, and she rubs my back. When I think there's no more tears, I think of Luca playing charades for Bec on one of her last days and cry more.

"I want Luca," I tell Ree. She brings me her cell phone, and I call his house two times, but no one answers.

I wipe my face and feel pretty sure I'm going to cry a lot more, so I take a shower. Ree steps in to take my dirty clothes away and leave me some of hers.

"Thank you."

"Of course. Anything you need."

I stand there inhaling steam, trying to think of something that will ease the weight of my grief, but there's nothing. It's like living with a rock pressed on my chest and shoulders. I don't think I'll ever be the same again.

I sit underneath the spray, crying till I start to feel sick. Then the steam around me shifts as Ree steps back into the bathroom.

"Hey. Just checking in on ya."

I stick my head out. "I'm okay." Ree is holding her cellular phone.

"Is that Dani?"

She looks up. "I haven't told her. Have you?"

I shake my head.

"Max sent a text message."

"About Becca?"

She shakes her head. "He was asking if I could bring something later, but I said I don't think I'm going."

"Going where?" I rub my swollen, sore eyes.

"Oh, that party tonight."

There's a party tonight. I'd forgotten.

"Luca and I were going to meet there."

CHAPTER TWENTY-SIX

Luca

The sun is turning amber-orange between the slits of Leo's bedroom blinds. There's a note from Alesso on a little wooden table pushed beside the love seat.

You seem okay so we went out to get something. We'll be back around 5. Crackers, Ginger Ale if you can take it. I left a few pain pills that are mine from wisdom teeth. Careful if you wake up. -Alesso

I look at the pills, the crackers, and the little plastic cup full of bubbly liquid and lie back on the love seat. Good arm over my eyes and holy fuck, I stink. For a second, that distracts me.

Then the crushing pressure I felt last night grips my chest again. I try re-playing what happened, but it's fuzzy. Like there's something blocking me from remembering in detail. When I try to, all I can see is...the blood.

Fuck. I make it to the bathroom on time—barely—and spend the next ten minutes lightheaded from my shoulder and my headache. There's a big cut in my mouth, on my cheek, and some soreness by one of my molars.

I don't want to use Leo's toothbrush, but I borrow some mouth wash. *Stings.* One glance at my bruised face and I know that I don't want to look again.

I get a shower, do some clean-up. My shoulder hurts so bad my head is spinning.

On the love seat...I sit down with a towel around my waist, and my throat's so fucking tight and sore.

Now I'm standing up. Remembering. I was by the stage. I tried to climb up—but I was too slow. I squeeze my fucking shoulder till tears prickle my eyes.

I can see the thin slats that made up the old stage floor. I can see the way the blood came, dark ink with a gelatinous quality like blood always has.

Cold sweat pops out all over me. I can feel the gunshot in my bones. I can see the blood. I hear the screaming. *My* screaming.

I don't know how I got home, and I don't like that. I don't know why I got Dad's bat. Something's wrong with me. It's not the normal stuff, the floating feeling. It's like...I'm not working. My brain. I feel...off. Like time is off.

I know how I ended up in Leo's house. Though I don't remember it. I was at a bar. Drank the whole place dry. I think my friends took me to the strip club.

What day is it? How long has it been since I've seen Elise?

I want her. I need her. Need to hold her. And when I do I'll probably cry like a damn baby, but I don't care. Thinking of that almost makes me cry right now. I focus on my shoulder.

I must have hurt the collarbone pretty bad, because the pain is nothing like before. Every time I move my upper body, I feel sick from how much it hurts.

I eat a cracker, drink the ginger ale, and then have to get up to get some water from the bathroom faucet. Distantly, I try to think of something smart to say to my pals. Giving them a hard time for serving up some ginger ale in a kid cup. But I don't care enough. There's like space between me and everything. Like a solid layer of...I don't know. It's kind of a silence. Maybe like a blanket.

I take the pills they left and get some clothes from Leo's drawer and sit down on the old brown love seat. I spot my sling around the bathroom doorknob. Makes me feel sick just thinking about moving my arm into the thing.

But I will. I need it because I'm going into Manhattan.

Gotta be at my best. Like a joke almost, my hands start shaking. My heart races. I feel sick and spacey, like I can't focus—not even on Elise.

It can't be real.

My chest tightens as my blood roars in my ears. Tony shot him. I was right there, and he fucking shot him right in front of me. I let it happen. Did I stop him? Steal the gun away? No. I let him shoot my dad and now my dad is dead. My dad is dead and Tony killed him. I watched Tony kill him.

Some sound comes from my throat. I think a scream. It sounds like someone else. I'm on my feet now. I need to walk. I don't know where. I put on the black basketball shorts I'm borrowing from Leo. Then I've gotta do the shirt. It hurts so bad, I think it kind of grounds me.

My eyelids feel heavy, my eyebrows sort of heavy—like my brain is falling forward. I wish it would fall out.

I work my arm into the sling, gritting my teeth as I see black spots for a second.

"Jesus."

Then I look around. I don't know what for. Keys. My keys are on the table by the note. I look for a pen, find one, and scrawl a new note.

Catch ya later. I'm okay. Borrowed some clothes, Leo. –

I feel warm and sweaty, hyper-focused in a drifty way as I reach for the door to Leo's bedroom. Pain meds working. Dad's drugs. I gotta say I understand the appeal. I walk to the train and I can do it, although my arm and my mouth and head hurt. It's just hurt instead of agony.

Although there's plenty of that on the inside.

I try to not think about it, but I'm on the train, and I feel weird and sweaty, and when it comes into my head, I don't believe it: Tony shot my dad. I didn't think that it was real but it *was* real. Now it's done, and I just can't accept it.

I get up and pace the train car. I shouldn't because it hurts. I stand by a window, looking at myself in the glass.

Why would Elise want you?

Then I think of something that hasn't crossed my mind till right now: How will I tell Mom? And when?

"You're so fucking stupid, Luca."

"When I'm dead, it will be your fault. You drew his attention! This is all because of you!"

Rage burns through me. It wasn't my fault, some part of me argues. But it *is* my fault; I was there, I'm eighteen years old—today. I should take responsibility. I wasn't able to stop Tony. He got what he wanted, and I lost my dad.

The only thing that's bigger than my fury is the awful, clawing pain in my chest. Wanting to go back. But I can't. I can only go forward.

❧

Elise

I feel like I'm moving through a dream as I step out of the Belluccis' black car onto the sidewalk in front of Max's house. Dani dips back into the car, murmuring something I can't hear to Fil. Ree takes my hand, peering down at me with her eyes wide and careful.

"Are you sure about this?"

I nod.

"If you decide you want to go, we'll go. No questions asked."

"I just want to see if Luca's here."

Dani takes my other hand. "We won't say a word to anyone. This is a quick in-and-out operation. We find Luca, bring him back to Ree's if you want. Whatever you want," she emphasizes.

I nod. "Thank you." I want her to know how much I appreciate it, but I can barely whisper. Everything about me feels so small and quiet.

Dani hugs me, and I smile a little at the difference in her five-foot-ten frame and my five-foot-two one.

"What if he's not here?" I murmur as we follow the cobblestone walk. Max's home is a white two-story set back from the road, rising behind big trees that line the driveway.

"If he's not here, we'll go back by his house or keep calling," Ree says. "I'm sure he's okay. Maybe their house always looks like that."

I swallow hard. It doesn't—there's no way—but I don't want to think about that. I don't want to cry again. So I just nod.

Max's house is hopping, with music bumping, a big crowd on the second-story rooftop deck, and the front door thrown open wide to welcome everyone. Max's parents are on a cruise. He and his sister were going to go, too, but something happened at the last minute. So I guess they're not worried about Mr. and Mrs. Romano finding out. Maybe they wouldn't care anyway. Mrs. Romano is vibrant and funny, and Mr. Romano never struck me as particularly uptight.

We reach the front door and it opens wider for us. Then Max steps into the doorway. He looks gorgeous in what seems like the last threads of a tux. He's wearing a starched white shirt that's rolled up to the elbows and a pair of black dress pants. His dark hair is messy, flopping in a breeze that smells of grass and cologne. Dangling from his lips: a Camel menthol in an Audrey Hepburn-style cigarette holder. When he takes a drag, he tips his head back, showing off his thick, smooth throat. He blows the smoke away from our faces and gives us all a villainous grin.

I watch as the grin fades and his brows scrunch over his hazel eyes. He steps out onto the porch and shuts the door behind him.

"Hey...did something happen?"

A tear drips down my cheek despite a lot of effort.

"Oh, shit." He's all eyes. "Is it your sister?"

I nod, and he wraps his arms around me, pulling me against his warm chest. "Jesus, Elise. I'm so fucking sorry."

The hug feels good—but not as good as one from Luca. Still, I'm grateful for Max.

"You're going to be okay. You know that, right? She would want you to be completely happy. Eventually."

He steps back so I can look up at him, and I nod. Max has known my family forever. He remembers Becca before, when she was small and feisty, doing cannonballs into his family's Southampton pool to annoy my friends.

"Thank you, Max." More tears spill down my cheeks. "Maybe I shouldn't even be here, but..."

"No way." He gives a shake of his head. "Galante's in there." He tilts his head at the house. "Does he know yet?"

I wipe my eyes and shake my head.

He nods once. "You guys still...?"

"Yes. We are."

His hand gently claps my shoulder. "If you need anything, Elise— anything at all—you come and find me."

I don't want to be this person tonight. I don't want to be in tears, to feel fragile as a sheet of glass. *I don't want my sister to be dead!* I feel knotted inside—my chest, my throat, my head all tight and sore—but I go through the motions to act normal out of sheer necessity—to get to Luca.

Dani and I find a shadowy nook in one of the sitting rooms and settle on a cozy couch while Ree goes off to locate Luca. A second later, Jace walks over to us. He's got on well-fitting jeans, a snug, pale green T-shirt that's flipped up at the sleeves, and expensive-looking boots, and he looks stunning as he always does. He keeps his curly hair trimmed short, so it's just a little longer than a buzzcut, but he's got big gray eyes, dramatic cheekbones, and an angel's lips—which means hiding his pretty hair doesn't change his pretty looks. I've kissed those lips before, in sixth grade, but there was no spark. Jace is like a brother to me.

So I feel my stomach flip-flop when I see how angry he looks. The look fades some as he approaches, crouching down in front of me and hugging me against him.

"Elise. I'm so sorry. Mom told me a little while ago." So my mom's telling people. I nod mutely against his shoulder.

He pulls slightly away so he can look into my eyes. "You okay?"

I shake my head. "But I know I will be." Tears start flowing again.

"Was it last night?"

I nod.

"Ree said you were trying to link up with Luca?"

"Yeah," I rasp. "Do you know where he is?"

He frowns. "I think I saw him upstairs. Let me go check. You want something to drink? I'll have someone bring you something," Jace says, like he lives here.

"It's okay."

Jace and Dani exchange a look, which makes my pulse quicken. As soon as Jace is out of earshot, I frown at Dani. "Hey...is something wrong?"

"Oh, I don't think so. I mean...besides the obvious, you know." She looks like she's not sure if she should smile or cry, so I roll my eyes.

"Besides that."

Dani wraps her arm around me. "Maybe Jace is trying to shield you from too many eyes. Or help you rest."

"Maybe." But why didn't Jace take me to Luca? "I just want to see him."

"I know you do."

Dani's arm around me stiffens, and I look up to understand why. Lorenzo Missanelli is striding toward us, holding two champagne flutes and smirking with both dimples showing as he locks his eyes on Dani.

"Jesus Christ," she mutters, pulling her arm out from behind me. "Look at bozo the clown."

"Dani," I hiss. "He looks nice, I think."

She snorts.

Loren is tall and lean, wide up top but not as bulky as Luca or Jace. Tonight he's got on pale jeans that are ripped on one knee, a white Nirvana shirt, and he has a purple mohawk. No one had seen it until graduation, when we all assumed he had it done specifically to piss off his father, Senator Serg Missanelli. "Serg the Sarge"—as Loren calls him—is almost always in Washington, D.C., but when he comes home, Loren always gets weird. Well, weirder.

Seeing him with crazy hair gives me a little boost. I can't help smiling when he hands Dani and I our drinks and grins right at her with those killer dimples.

"Daniella."

"Lorenzo," she says pertly.

Loren runs a hand back through his purple hair—self-consciously, I think, but then he realizes the tell and grips a tuft of his hair. "So whaddaya think about my new do?" He smirks as if he's got the upper hand, even under Dani's withering stare.

"I think you look like Tinky Winky." Dani lifts her chin, now smirking back up at him.

"Tinky Winky." He looks totally affronted. "You saying I look like a fucking Teletubby?"

"I'm saying you look like the president of the Teletubbies. The grand leader. Chancellor, prime minister. Really might as well just get the full-on Tubby suit because that would make me laugh, and I need to laugh. We all need a laugh, Lorenzo. So thank you for that tonight."

I'm surprised when Loren halfway sits on top of Dani, wrapping both of his hands around her ear to whisper something.

I watch Dani's nostrils flare, and then she leans away. She gives him a *fuck off* look and says, "You can go now, Lorenzo. Thank you for the alcohol."

She holds her flute up and Loren arches his brows, like he's not happy but not sure what to say.

"You're welcome," he says finally, and he goes.

"C'mon." Dani sighs as she stands. "Let's go somewhere else so I don't 'accidentally' run into him again. It's been happening for weeks now, and I'm over it."

I follow her, holding my own cool glass flute. "Has it?"

She nods. "You know he's dating that girl from Horace Mann. I even think she'll be here with him tonight. But he can't resist fucking with me. It's insane."

I'm kind of surprised to hear Dani go off on him. Not really, because those two have been at each other's throats since we were all in diapers. But a little. Last year she decided "Lorenzo"—she's the only one who calls him that—was "dead to her," after he came to her house to hang with her brother and the two of them set up a bike ramp on a hill, which had them jumping over Dani's car. She never drives the car, but she was none too pleased when Loren crashed into the windshield like a bird into a slider door and left blood and little Loren hairs all in the glass.

"Boys are morons," she mutters now.

Her hand is at the small of my back, and I note she's walking pretty quickly as we head down the hall toward a side door that leads onto the back porch.

"Are we going outside?" I ask, feeling a kick of panic at the idea we won't be where Ree expects when she returns with Luca.

"Just for a second. I'd like to smoke. If Ree doesn't see us, she can just call." She holds up her leather clutch, where I assume her cellular is.

I nod. My chest is aching, but Dani seems so flustered that I don't want to make things harder for her. I'll stay for the cigarette and then I'll strike off on my own to look for Luca.

Everyone is sardined on the porch, so much that I can barely see faces...so I don't know if we know anybody out here. Dani finds a spot against the railing and lights up a Marlboro.

"Thank you," she says, apologizing with her eyes.

"It's okay. What is it about 'Lorenzo' that you think does this to you?" I force a small smile.

"What *isn't* it about him?" She looks genuinely angry...and also gorgeous, with her dark hair in a French braid and little baby hairs fluttering over her flawless eyebrows.

I'm formulating a reply when Dani's eyes pop open wide. I glance behind me, hoping for Luca, but it's Ree, looking pissed off as she elbows her way through the crowd.

Her eyes find Dani's; I notice she doesn't look at me. She throws her hands up. "We should go, girls. Mia Arnoldi is upstairs snorting coke and so are lots of other people. Some girl from Trinity saw and said she's calling her dad if they don't stop. He's a cop and hero that she is, she doesn't want people to die." Ree rolls her eyes. "Luca's gone already," she tacks on at the end.

Her eyes barely meet mine.

And then I understand why.

Something catches my eye on the second-story balcony that hangs over the deck. Isa Arnoldi loves to fasten up her blonde hair with jewel-studded clips...so it's her slim, pale form I notice first. And then I see something I'll never unsee.

Isa's head is leaned back, her pale hair falling over the rail. Someone's moving over her. Someone's making out with her like they're drowning and she's oxygen.

It's Luca.

CHAPTER TWENTY-SEVEN

Luca

She's like an octopus. I have to fucking peel her off me. I blink down to find her smiling coyly as my heart beats like it's trying to break out of my chest.

"Was that good?" Her voice is soft. Her eyes are heavy-lidded, and I think she's on something because her pupils have that glassy look I know way too well.

My throat feels so raw that I don't think I can reply. I swallow hard, still frowning down at her, and choke out, "Sure."

I want Elise. Every second I'm away from her feels like an injury. I don't know how long I can go...but what this blonde girl has, I needed.

She throws her long braid over her shoulders. "We both know I'm better than 'sure,' Luca Galante. That would be the best kiss of your life if you weren't hung up on Elise O'Hara."

Hearing her name feels like a knife twisting behind my pecs.

"I love her." I don't think before I speak; the words, like all my actions tonight, feel automated.

"You must want to know about this Tony Diamond pretty badly, then, because Elise was down there on the patio. I saw her friends all pointing at us. See right down there?"

"*What?*"

She leans over the rail, pointing. "Over there. I'm pretty sure I saw her."

"Max said she's not coming." I asked if he'd heard from Elise and her friends the second that I got here.

Isa shrugs. "I guess she changed her mind."

There's a geyser of panic pulsing somewhere way down, but I don't trust Isa Arnoldi enough to really worry. "Are you gonna tell me now?"

She walks inside the bedroom where I found her a few minutes ago. I watch as she pulls some lipstick from a handbag, starts to paint it on her mouth, then opens a small, round mirror.

"At the Columbus Building." She snaps the mirror shut. "It's my father's place. It's got twenty-something stories and it's—"

"Used for parties."

"How'd you know?" She steps closer. "Have I somehow missed you at one of my father's parties, Luca blue eyes?"

"I don't know." I try to hide it from her, but I end up sort of gulping down some air because my head is spinning.

"Well, that's where they are tonight. But listen: My family is fucked up. Well, Gabe's actually okay—I think one day he'll get out of here—but my father is...someone I would be careful around." She blinks a few times, frowning as she pops open the mirror again.

"What's the event?"

Her lips curl, dark magenta from the lipstick. "It's a wedding of someone in my dad's...organization. But your guy will definitely be there." She wrinkles her nose. "He's new."

"Yeah."

"Seems...doltish. What'd he do to you?"

My head is definitely spinning...and I can't get enough air. I'm too warm, this room too small. I lick my lips and taste her lip stuff, and I think of Elise seeing what I just did even though I know she didn't. My heart throbs in my eyes. "You sure he's going to be there?"

"Yes. I heard my mother complaining that that group of guys would be there tonight."

"Thank you," I say to the girl. Isa.

Then I get the hell out.

Everything feels weird as I move downstairs. It's like the air—the atoms all around me—are…not normal. Or I'm not. I don't fit into the world the way I used to.

I flex my right hand. All the fingers shake. Downstairs is really crowded. I see a glass of liquor on a table, toss it back, and make a beeline for the front door. I'll walk to someplace I can hail a cab.

A fresh-cut grass smell almost overwhelms me as I step outside and start down the cobblestone walk.

I'm thinking ahead, thinking of the passcode on the yacht, when someone grabs my shirt from behind. It's the motion, I think—being pulled backward. It sets something off, and I'm shoving Jace before I even see his face. There are grunts—from both of us—a "what the fuck" from him. I think he calls me a bastard; I don't know. He's in the grass. I'm looking down at him.

"What the fuck!" He's clutching his mouth. Blood drips through his fingers.

"Sorry." I can't look at blood, don't understand what's happening, so I leave his ass on the ground and walk. I can't think straight. I need to run. I'm gritting my teeth, bracing for the pain a sprint is going to bring my shoulder, when I hear her screaming, "Luca!"

It's like being dunked under the ocean. Everything goes quiet. I can hear my blood roar in my ears as I turn toward her, my whole body moving like a magnet.

I'm so focused on her, every atom in me fixed on the relief I feel—

But…is she crying? She sounds furious as she shouts, "*Where* have you been?"

"What?"

"Where have you been?" She's maybe ten feet from me. I can see her face now, see the rage all on it. "I've been trying to find you!"

I can't stand to see her upset, so I start toward her, but she throws her arms out. "No!" She's panting like she's hurt.

"What—" *happened*, I'm going to say, as she sobs, "What were you doing with her?"

"With who?"

"With Isa!"

I know how a log feels under a blanket of snow. I can't move, can't speak, can't even think. It's like I'm insulated from the moment. I take a few slow breaths as she cries into her hands.

"It was…nothing." My voice doesn't sound right.

Her eyes rise to meet mine, and they're wide and teary.

"Isa...like. Elise, I don't even know her."

"What does that mean?" She's near shrieking.

My dad died. I goad myself to fucking say it. *My. Dad. Died.*

There's another universe that's rolling like a film reel, layered right on top of this one, and in that world, this is when I tell her. I can whisper it, just a hoarse whisper, and she'll have her arms around me.

My dad died. Those three awful words, and her face will crumple in empathy and understanding. I can hold onto her, and afterward I'll explain Isa. She won't care.

Instead, I'm looking at her. I'm watching her horror-stricken face. She's so furious...about Isa, I guess. She looks like she's losing her shit. I think how she doesn't look like Elise.

I see Tony and I see my hands almost around his gun. I'm numb in the bathtub, running like a man on fire, screaming through the streets. Tearing up my house and leaving Mom and Soren at the hotel. And I feel so heavy. I can feel the weight of what's in my head. I can taste the cool metal and see the paper with the story. Not a story, just one sentence. That's all I am.

I look at her face, and I don't see my heart, my rose, the other half of my soul who restores me.

I see someone young and hurt and fragile. Sensitive, responsive, beautiful and giving. She needs me. Elise.

I could step to her right now and hug her. I could hold her like I always do and keep her safe.

But it's all bodies on cold floors. Tile and wood and squishy mats like at the salon. I can see the blood on the stage. I can see the red-soaked fibers of his jeans.

She's upset—she's devastated—over Isa. That's because she doesn't know. She is crying over paper cuts and I'm going to blow my head off.

I can't touch her. I can't even talk to her. It's like I saw the meteor. She doesn't know it's even coming. She could live a nice life.

For me, there's nothing left. I saw the inside of my father's head. I'm not going to college.

She steps closer to me, hugging herself as her wide eyes beg me to do or say something that will make things normal. She's begging me to be Luca.

Now's the time to rip the Band-Aid off. Now's the time to wreck this shit before she ends up on a salon floor. Now's the time to make the printed sentence in the paper not hurt.

I look at her, and I try to get my thoughts to come out of my mouth. I observe that I've started to shake all over, and internally, I want to bow down to that power, to the power of Elise. She is my heart. Forever.

So it's fitting that I rip it out.

I say, "I think that I need a change."

I see the horror I should feel reflected on her perfect face. "What do you mean?" she whispers.

When I'm dead, I'll haunt you in the best way. If you lose your keys, I'll move them somewhere you can find them.

I'm breathing so fast I can't speak to answer.

"What the hell do you mean?"

I blink, and she starts to weep. "Luca, are you breaking up with me?"

I nod. I'm like a puppet with a hand inside. The nod means nothing, but her face tells me it's not the same for her.

I'm breaking up with Elise. I laugh at the insanity.

"What's the matter with you?" she cries.

"Nothing." I sound hoarse, but my voice steadies as I look at her and realize that she'll never be the wife on the salon floor.

Something warmer rushes up my throat and burns my cheeks and stings my eyes as her lips tremble. Then she locks her face down, nods just once, and spins on her heel. She runs all the way to Max's as I watch the moonlight move over the crown of her head. Then I turn and walk toward a street where I can hail a cab.

CHAPTER TWENTY-EIGHT

Luca

The cab driver says he'll wait at the dock. I get out, surprised by how steady I feel. Lights and water. Everything smells like the water. I don't like the dock now. Elise—everywhere, a ghost—and I just want to detach from it.

I know I owe Soren, but he'll be all right. Soren's smart. My mom... I think my dad had life insurance.

"I love you, Elise O'Hara. Always."

"I love you more."

"It hurts for girls. Close your eyes and take a few deep breaths."

The passcode is the same. The gun is in the bathroom, in a drawer. I know it's loaded because I checked when we were here on prom night.

It's cold in my hand. I can't tell if it's heavy. I sink down to my knees in front of the toilet. Blue water. It smells like soap.

"Your dad's a rat. He's been squealing to the FBI."

I don't like this floating feeling. I stand up and I make myself check the gun. Still loaded. I don't want to hurt Tony. *I do want to,* but I wouldn't. I just want to tell him he's a piece of shit and maybe scare him.

I want to talk to Roberto Arnoldi. I just want to know why.

After that...

❧

Back inside the cab, where it smells like popcorn. The cab ride feels too long. The gun's handle is grooved, like tiny diamonds in a rough rub pattern. I rub my thumb over it. It's shoved into my pocket. I try to smile at the driver in the rear view mirror. Not a smile, but that thing you can do with your lips that's like a greeting.

Don't worry; it's not for you.

My heart is still beating too fast. Racing. My heart's racing. I just want Elise. Knowing that it's over *burns*. I have to stop the burning, but I don't know how.

Everything about the building is the same. I don't like how I'm different.

Maybe I just want to see him. Maybe I do want to kill him.

I don't want to kill him.

I'm a nice guy. There's only one person a nice guy can kill.

The elevator takes me up, and she was right—the daughter, Isa. It's a wedding party. Lots of people, and I don't know how to find him. I guess I'll just walk around until I see him.

I should have told him to shoot me. Maybe I'd be dead, but I'm dead anyway. Diamond's got no balls, so maybe he wouldn't have done it. Dad might be alive if I had gambled.

I don't like the noises at the party. I don't like the people.

I think of Elise...the way her hands would feel on my face. I like how she rubs my hair back. Sometimes she traces my eyebrows, and it's sort of weird, but it feels good.

Max said Elise wasn't at the party. Elise loves me. Even though I want her to move on, I kind of hope she always loves me. I need to be loved by someone.

My bounty is as boundless as the sea, my love as deep; the more I give thee, the more I have, for both are infinite.

It's so terrible how this is turning out.

I spot him standing in the doors between the food room and the dance room. He's wearing a tuxedo. He looks like a dead man. But I see him older. Tony will get older; he'll kill other people. He'll mop blood up. He'll harass old men, and the old men will be addicts who can't walk home from their store. Tony is a poison.

I'm poison.

Tony is poison, too.

I start walking toward him—all the people...pushing past them—and he drifts into the other room. The dancing room. My throat is so tight I can't swallow. Soren is smart and my mom is always okay. It's Elise that's in my head. She is my head.

I stalk Tony through the dancing room and into the hall. Crowded and it smells like flowers. He's with other people, and I recognize where they're all going. They go up the elevator, and I keep my distance. Wait my turn. I'm so sweaty with my hand inside my pocket, I feel like there's a light over my head that's flashing: danger, danger.

I'm not danger.

I was never danger, that's the funny thing. *I let Dad say those things and hit me because I knew he was sick.* I hardly hurt most times and words don't mean much.

Her lips, brushing my cheek... Her eyes as she looks up from between my legs. For a moment, I can feel her, I can feel us, I can feel the fortifying weight of all the love that lives between us, and it makes a whole world.

I'm about to shatter that world.

The coat closet with the door into the hidden hallways is a front. Alesso told me. Coats aren't ever hung there. It's just an entryway to all the other parts, the hidden places no one should be going.

I wonder if anyone will think that this is worth it. I will think it's worth it. Even if my dad was a narc.

A second slips through my brain, this one shiny second where it's clean and there's no badness. I could turn back. That's the message. But the second isn't real, it isn't right. I can see the blood on the stage, creeping over the uneven floorboards. I got Dad's wallet somehow—don't remember, but it's soaked in blood. It smelled like blood, and little blood circles like faint stamps were smeared atop his debit card. I rubbed them off with my thumb.

Worthless. What is worthless? Only that which has no worth to you. It matters to me.

And I know how to do it. I know how to get to Tony. Same as anything else: you just do it.

I walk through the door behind the stairs. The Elise door, and I remember that still. I stoop low and then stand fully in the larger hall. I can hear them in one of the rooms. Maybe the black room. I don't want it to be that room—but if it is, that's okay.

I hear them talking in some room, and I'm relieved to find that it's some sort of library. It looks a little like the dinner room, the steak room, the just the way I like it elemental room. See, I remember that. Even though I still feel really sick. I remember everything about that night.

Once I'm in the doorway it'll be a train that's taking off: no stopping. So I stand in the hall for some time.

I don't feel good. Maybe I can still find some way to hold Elise. I would really like to do that.

I reach my hand back into my pocket. A breath that's not enough, that goes by too quick. I'm aware of how cold my feet are as I move into the doorway.

A hush falls over the small group that's gathered in there. Tony's face is all I see. His eyes are wide as he looks at me. He says, "Hey, man," but he's scared. He looks at me like he's scared, and then he looks around.

I take another small step toward him. "Tony—you're a monster."

Then I pull the gun out of my pocket, point it at him, pull the trigger.

You can feel a gunshot in your bones. In every cell, in every atom. There is no sound and no vision. There is no mind. In the silence after, everything starts on fast-forward. And it's not real.

You can't tell me that this is real. Maybe it was never real.

Someone tackles me. I hit the floor hard. I'm staring at the fancy ceiling. I smile at it, feeling proud.

Nobody's ever going to hit me again.

Someone stands over me. "Go ahead and do it."

"Do what?" the voice says sharply.

"Shoot me. I'm not scared."

I think I'm ready to be free of all this.

Someone crouches down beside me. It looks like Elise's dad. He's telling me that I'm okay.

"Get up." I open my eyes to Roberto. *"Alzarsi,"* he orders quietly.

I do—even though it hurts. I want to stand in front of him, to be more real when it happens. I look at him and then around the room, at all the tuxes.

"He shot my dad," I offer.

Roberto moves toward me. For a bleary moment, I expect him to walk right through me. Then there's hot fear as I wait for pain in my chest. Something presses to my ribcage. I look down, and it's his hand. His hand goes around my side.

"C'mon." He presses me backward. *"Usa le tue gambe. Inizia a camminare. Tu vieni con me."*

I go with him. Trying to breathe. Trying to make my limbs do what my brain asks. He takes me into a yellow bedroom.

"Get on your knees," he orders. He pulls out a handgun.

I look at it, at him. And then I laugh. I don't mean to. It's only one soft laugh that slips out.

"Do I seem like I'll do that?" my voice says.

"You won't get down on your knees for me?"

"Never."

A hot tear slides from my eye and down my cheek. *I love you, Elise.*

He looks at me for a long time with his hard eyes. They seem hard and then they don't. They seem curious and maybe worried. They seem surprised.

"Sei pieno di sorprese."

"Yeah."

My brain picks that moment to short out. Black spots dance in my eyes, and he urges me toward the bed's side. I lean against it.

"Stay there," he says in raspy English.

I hold my head as time passes like long, slow waves around me.

"Here."

I look up. My blinks feel a few beats too slow. He's holding a glass out to me.

I drink all of it, and then I look down at the rug and his shoes on it.

"Am I going to jail?" I can barely breathe, but somehow I look up at him to read the answer from his face.

"What you're going to do," he says slowly, his fingers clasping my shoulder, "is come with me."

❧

Pre-order *Dark Heart* Volume 2, releasing October 14[th:] http://bit.ly/DarkHeart2

❧

Turn the page for a sneak peek of *Covet*, A Sinful Secret Series Romance.

SNEAK PEEK

COVET: A STANDALONE FORBIDDEN ROMANCE

One
April 2018

Declan

Smoke seeps from my lips, drifting out over the boat rail like a curl of fog. Tonight, the water's placid, an inky black with smears of pastel starlight. Out here in the middle of the Atlantic, the sky at night is more glitter than darkness. Hazy swaths of purple, peach, and green sky twinkle with diamond-bright stars, their reflection gleaming on the curve of wave that runs alongside the boat.

I curl my hand around my cigarette and bring it to my mouth again.

I'm standing atop the cargo ship's flat hull, hidden from most vantage points by the twenty-foot-tall boxy structure just behind me: the navigation post and captain's quarters. At this hour, both are likely empty. The crew is down below deck, playing poker. Still, I turn the cherry toward my palm.

Better to stay hidden.

That's been my game since I boarded *Miss Aquarius* back in Cape Town: wear my cap low, keep my mouth shut, and help out where I'm needed till I reach my destination.

I close my eyes on a long drag and lean against the railing. That'll be tomorrow. Fuck.

I finish off the smoke and light another one.

It's fucking cold out here. My T-shirt's not enough, even with jeans. South of the equator, we're headed into fall—in early April. Strange stuff. I swallow hard and look down at the deck under my feet. Then I cast my gaze up to the sky and fill my lungs with salty air.

When I feel something in my hand, I look down, finding a line of ash in my palm. I bring the Marlboro to my lips and take the last drag with shaking fingers before pinching the cherry out.

I should go below deck. Play some solitaire in my cabin. Instead I light a third smoke, and, with my free hand, rub my arms. Even after just a few months off, they're smaller than I'm used to, making me feel like someone else.

Laughter trills into the quiet, voices rising as footfall thuds inside the stairwell to my left. Before I can turn toward the sea, figures spill onto the deck. I whirl around, snuffing my smoke out against the rail. Then I turn the other way, aiming to sneak around the navigation post, but there's a loud "Hey, man."

I turn slowly. Half a dozen guys are lined up in some kind of formation, making a semi-circle between the stairwell they just came out of and me.

I nod, meeting the eyes of the one who spoke. Kevin is his name. I think. He's only an inch or two shorter than me, with blue eyes and close-cropped brown hair. He's one of the Americans on board.

I step toward the stairwell, but Kevin catches my arm. "Hang on a sec. We wanna talk to you."

I hear another say, "We barely know you," at the same time as a third—not an American, judging by his accent—is saying, "been six days."

I nod. Hold up a hand. "George," I say, as I step between two of them.

"That's the thing, though," he sneers. "We don't think it is."

"No?" I look behind me.

They're all grinning. "Hell no."

"We been watching."

"We've got an idea about you."

My stomach pitches as a hand claps my shoulder.

"You can tell us."

"We know you're not George."

One dude jerks a thumb at the captain. "You know Bo, don't you? He's the cap'n. No good lying to the captain."

Bo steps closer. He's older than most of the crew members, but still young. If I had to guess, I'd say no older than forty-five. He's wearing khaki-looking shorts and a stained Costa tee. "I know what your papers say. But take your hat off, mate, and help me win a wager."

I shake my head, stepping backward toward the stairwell. "Night, guys."

"I told you it's not him." Someone's in the stairwell, lighting a cigar. He grins around it.

At that same time, I lose my hat. I spin around and snatch it back, glaring at the fucker who took it. His eyes widen at the clear view of my face.

Gasps chorus around us.

"Holy shit."

"I fuckin' told you, Bo!"

The one in the stairwell spreads his arms, chuckling as he blocks me.

"That's some damn good camo, brother. I need something, though, before you get to pass."

He holds a slip of paper out, and the men gather around.

"Homer Carnegie on our boat, we're gonna need some autographs..."

I fake a grin and take the paper. Six thousand miles from Boston, and I'm fucking outed.

❦

Finley

I clutch the bottle to my chest and cross myself. Then I shut my eyes, bring my arm back, and throw it hard over the cliff's edge. With my eyes shut, I picture its trajectory as it plummets toward the ocean. I inhale, feeling dizzy as birds caw above my head, and far below me, waves break on the rocks.

Vloeiende Trane, these cliffs are called; it means "cascading tears" in Afrikaans. The highest peak is two hundred meters above the ocean's ragged waves. Midway between the cliff-top and the sea, water pours out of the rock in three long streams that look like tears from further out.

Standing atop Vloeiende Trane, the white caps look no bigger than a fingernail, the ocean's swirling cauldron just a gentle dappling of greens and blues.

Deceptive.

I wipe my eyes and fold my arms over my chest. *I won't throw another bottle*, I promise myself as I step toward the cliffs' edge. I search the waves for a flash of glass, for something that will give me satisfaction, but of course, I see nothing.

That's the point, though, isn't it? Throwing letter-stuffed bottles into the void. It's like a prayer. That's its magic. Still, it hurts to know no one will ever read my words. I wipe my face again and whisper, "Give me courage."

I lick my lips and stand with my eyes closed, thinking of Mum. It's something that I almost never do, because I can't bear it. Today, though, I can't seem to help myself.

When my eyes feel puffy and hot, I walk back across the stony plane that forms this small plateau and look down at the field below, its tall grass pressed flat by the wind. At the edge of the field, a cottage. Beyond that, the village valley—an expanse of lush, green grass framed by the cliffs that form the border of the island.

Three gravel roads stripe the valley where the village lies. Scattered along them are sixty-seven cottages, topped by roofs of thatch or brightly colored tin. My gaze runs over the island's few landmarks: the yellow roof of the café, the bare dirt of the baseball field, the green roof of the clinic near the village's east side.

The church's small, white steeple looks thin as a toothpick from here. I squint, but I can barely make out the blue tin roof of my dear friend Anna's house. I lift my hand to my eyes and stretch my thumb out sideways, and the village disappears—the whole world, gone.

Climbing down the plateau's steep side into the field behind Gammy's house takes half an hour. I move carefully without a harness, slow and steady in the warm glare of the sun, until my soles press into soft grass.

The wind-flattened field—Gammy's backyard—is big and round, hemmed in on one side by the dirt path that leads from the lower slopes of the volcano down to the village, and on the other by the rocky cliffs that overlook the ocean.

Before she passed, we built a table from wood scraps and set it near the field's center. I climb onto it and peer up at the sky. Early autumn now, its blue is almost violent. Today, for once, there are no clouds except some wispy tendrils behind me, wreathing the volcano's peak.

I watch the kingbirds fly, swooping off the cliffs and out of sight, and my heart aches for Gammy. She would have righted my course. Gammy would have told me to say "no" when I was asked. Probably "hell no," I admit. My stomach knots.

I shift my gaze to the cottage, to the stone kiln beside it and the blue sky spread above it, and the cliffs that rise out of the grass beside it. I inhale the salty air and tell myself *just stop*. Now is not the time for despair. Gammy would tell me to keep focused. There are options yet.

I swipe the hair out of my face and carefully re-braid it as my shoulders tingle from the sun's heat. When my damp shirt has dried in the breeze, I get up and walk to the kiln.

There's a small door on the front and two shelves in its slightly rounded belly, where I set my pieces. I haven't done enough of this lately. I'm not even sure I retrieved my last load. I open the door and find indeed I didn't. Two hunter green bowls and a thin, black vase with golden flecks wait inside. I gather them carefully into my arms and follow the stone path to the cottage's front door.

When I first moved in with Gammy, I called this the Hobbit cottage. She didn't know, of course—I wasn't speaking—but it reminded me of a Hobbit's house: the south side built into a hill; one small, round window punched into the grass; the rounded, dark wood door and beige stone facade in front; a thatched roof tilting low; chimes affixed to several spots; and a flower garden growing wild about the stoop.

The door opens with the old, familiar creak. I step into the tidy living area. I run my hand over the well-worn armchair and try to look at it through his eyes. The green and blue rug—woven by my great-grandmother—that's spread across the cement floor. The slouching navy love seat, with its tiny, beige polka dots. The boxy TV on a tiny cedar table in one corner. The wild banana plant dominating the other. Grandma's needlework adorns one wall. A fern hangs in a basket near the TV. The wall to my right, which divides the living room and kitchen, sports a horizontal bookcase.

It smells like rose and lemon here, and the lovely musk of aging paperbacks. I rip my eyes from the bookshelf and walk into the kitchen. Small and standard, I suppose, with a pale blue laminate countertop, a small, round table; some wall-mounted shelves; and a wooden cabinet/pantry in one corner. Wallpaper in a faded, fruit basket pattern adorns the walls.

I scrub my arms and hands with the same lemon pumice soap I use to get the clay grit off after I finish a new piece, and then unpack the bags of food I brought before my hike. I arrange apples, pears, and peaches in a small, wooden bowl and leave a shrink-wrapped loaf of friendship bread atop a matching wooden platter. I check the refrigerator again, as if the eggs, butter, chicken, duck, and various sauces I left there a few hours ago might have walked away. They didn't.

I line jam along the wall beside the sink, double-check the seal on three bags of homemade potato chips, and check the pantry for the pasta, canned goods, Pop-Tarts, and bags of popcorn I already know are there. I re-fold the towel on the oven—Home Sweet Home it says, in faded blue script—and drift back through the living room, picturing him walking down the short hall to the first door on the right, which I'll leave slightly ajar.

It was my mum's room, but when my parents passed, it became mine. It has one window, covered with a lace curtain and facing the ocean. When I was young, it held a full-sized bed, a bookcase, a dresser, and a rocking chair. Now I've moved the bookcase into Gammy's old room, where I store my pottery and package it for shipment on occasions when I sell a piece.

I step in front of the vertical, wall-mounted mirror by the dresser and peer at myself. Still no wrinkles, no more freckles than I've ever had. I don't look older than twenty despite my twenty-seven years. I pull my hair down from its tie and spread the long, rust-colored locks around my face. I blink my yellow-brown eyes, purse my lips, and study my cheekbones…the smooth skin of my throat and collarbones.

Will I look like an islander to him? Or just a woman?

I laugh. Does it matter? I suppose that shall depend on what I choose to do. The mere notion of that possibility brings about a need for smelling salts, so I move on from the mirror and my thoughts, stepping into the en suite washroom to pull open the curtains.

I look out at the vast, gray sea and smooth blue sky, and I try to imagine any other life for myself than the one I have. Could I have been happy here? *If Mum had lived.* The answer floats up from my bones, a truth too potent to quash.

The sea breeze slaps against the windowpanes and whistles through the thatched roof as I tidy up. Will our cottage be comfortable to him, or will this place appear pitifully lacking? The pristine American homes I've seen were all in magazines or movies, so I'm not sure they were the regular sort. Then again, neither is he. As my mum's stories alluded, he's more king than commoner.

I set my favorite eucalyptus bath crystals on the table by the claw-footed tub and arrange lavender fizzies in a wee bowl. These things were mine, once—but they haven't been for a while. Anyway, I don't mind sharing.

I stroll back into the bedroom, leaving a pack of Doublemint on the night table. I step over to the dresser and reach for the framed photo of Mum and me, twin flower halos on our twin red heads...but then I draw my hand away. I can't say precisely why, but it seems important that I leave it in its place, that I let her stay here—perhaps especially now.

Another spin through the house with the duster, and I call it ready. I linger in the living room, my chest aching and my head too light. On a whim, I turn back to the bedroom. I fetch a small bottle of rose water from the top drawer and spray the living area, tucking it into my pocket as I go.

❧

Two

Declan

I press the power button on my phone and squint at the bright light.

2:49 AM.

I stuff the phone under my pillow, roll onto my side. A bolt of pain sears my right shoulder, sending me onto my back again. Dammit.

I've gotta quit forgetting that. Left side it is. Except the left side has me facing the door to my matchbox-sized stateroom. There's a little window on it.

There's no paps here, asshat.

I made headlines in November, but nobody besides my team at Red Sox headquarters and a bunch of folks in white coats know the worst of it. I've been out of the press since the TMZ video shit, in no small part because the Sox have taken care of me. I try to find some comfort in that. I think about my agent, Aarons; my publicist, Sherie. Even the Sox board was more than generous with me, more than forgiving.

Instead of making me feel better, remembering everyone's kindness makes my throat knot up. I run a hand back through my hair and tug until my eyes stop stinging. Nothing's fucking wrong. It's always this way, I remind myself. I fold my knees up toward my chest and cover my eyes. I just need to sleep. Even an hour or two would help. A nap before breakfast…

After my identity was revealed, the ship's cook demanded to know what I wanted for my last breakfast on board, and he's now planning to cook omelets starting at six. He wants me there while he cooks —"to make sure I get it just the way you like it." The chief navigator and the captain plan to join us in the kitchen. After that, more autographs. And pictures with the crew.

Fuck me.

I don't know what to tell them. "No" makes me sound like a dick, and "yes" means I'll end up trending on Twitter.

I sit up and rub the shoulder. Useless. Without my usual concoction keeping me numb, the fucker hurts every time I breathe. My Sox trainers pushed for surgery before this trip, but my med team pushed back. Of course they did.

I lie back down and shut my eyes and focus on my breathing. In and out…and in and out. Behind my eyelids, I see sunlight stretched in gold webs on the sand and on the underside of waves.

❧

My phone's alarm wakes me at 6:05 after one snooze. I throw some clothes on, climb the stairs on legs that shake, and step onto the deck, stopping as a soft breeze feathers my hair back. Fog settled sometime overnight, blanketing the ocean in a haze that's tinted sepia by the rising sun. It's so thick I can barely see beyond the deck's rail.

I know I should haul ass to the dining room, but we're close to the island now. I can't resist climbing up onto the deck atop the nav post. The damp stairs squeak under my shoes as I hasten my steps. The stair rail is cool under my palm. I step onto the upper deck, feeling my pulse quicken at the thought of being here again. At that moment, a breeze pushes the fog aside, revealing a sight that I haven't seen since I was six: Tristan da Cunha—a massive chunk of dark brown rock that rises to a cloud-swathed peak.

Of all the islands in the world, this one is the most remote—the most isolated patch of land where humans live. These thirty-eight square miles of land are 1,700 miles from South Africa and 2,000 miles from South America. With no airport and no safe harbor for large ships, no GPS or cell phone towers, people here live cut off from the world. Mail comes every two to three months, the birth of a baby is a rare occasion, and if someone has a medical emergency, it's flag down one of the fishing vessels or cargo ships that travel back and forth from Cape Town to Antarctica and back, and hope it's headed *back*.

My throat tightens as I squint at the island, searching the grassy valley at the foot of the volcano for cottages that I don't see from here. Somewhere, maybe on the other side, there's a little village. If the guidebooks are to be believed, there are just a dozen or so shy of three hundred people—fishermen and farmers, mostly descended from a handful of British.

I remember them packed in their church, their heads all bowed in prayer, some cheeks wet with tears. I can see the women clutching rosaries, the men pulling on jackets and stepping into boats. I remember the lights at night as boats arrived and departed. Each time they came back empty handed, more tears.

Despite the circumstances, Dad and I were welcomed right into the fold. I remember helping an old lady knead the dough for bread while my father went out in a boat and helped search. I remember all the misty rain. I shut my eyes, seeing Dad's face when he stepped back onto the dock for the last time. His eyes were closed, but hers were open. That's what I remember most. This little girl wrapped up in blankets, with a dirty, sunken face and ropes of tangled red hair. And weird eyes.

I remember how they stood out in her pale, grimy face. Unlike all the other eyes I saw, hers hadn't leaked with tears. They seemed as depthless as the sea itself, and hot, almost like brownish-yellow fire. I think they stuck with me because I couldn't pinpoint the emotion in them. Not for years.

A gull caws, bringing me back to the moment. I can hear the swish of waves against the boat, can feel the wet fog on my face.

I did it. I'm back here. I laugh. Genius or crazy?

I don't have time to decide before someone slaps my back. I turn around and give the captain a smile. For the next hour, I'm Homer Carnegie—household name. I tell myself to buck the fuck up, try to act like the record-breaking Red Sox pitcher they expect. I sign everything from baseballs to a woman's sports bra, telling jokes and answering a bunch of questions while the chef serves me two omelets I can't taste.

"Thanks, man. Real good."

I sign his apron, listen to someone's account of a record I broke last summer. When I can, I steal away to have a smoke and hide my shaking hands.

I close my eyes and try to feel the warm sun on my face, but all I feel is pressure in my throat and chest, behind my eyes.

"Hey, dawg." I look up and find one of the crew lighting his own smoke. I think his name is Chris. He's kind of short and wiry, with brown hair hidden beneath a gray beanie. He's another one of the American crew members. "Just want to tell you thanks. My kid loves the Sox. He's gonna be so happy when he sees that ball."

"Yeah—no problem, man."

"If you don't mind my asking…whatcha doing way out here, in the middle of the ocean?"

I smile tightly. "Here with the Carnegie Foundation. We're laying new phone lines. Maybe internet, too, if we can find a way to make it work."

He nods once. "Riding back to Cape Town with us?"

"Yeah."

"Damn, that's eleven weeks. I'm surprised you can be gone that long. Aren't things firing up?"

I guess this guy's an actual fan. I shrug. "I'll miss some, but it's a one-time thing."

He nods. "Yeah. It's cool you're doing what you're doing. It was nice to meet you." He holds his hand out. I shake it, squeezing harder than I have to so he can't feel my fingers shaking. "You're an idol to so many. Don't forget it."

I give him a small smile and a nod, and, thankfully, he turns and goes downstairs.

I spend the next half hour packing up and helping haul wooden crates—full of supplies provided by the foundation—to the boat's ledge. From there, they'll be lowered in an elevator type of apparatus that's hooked onto the boat's side, and eased into a boat from Tristan.

Since the island's coastline is mostly rocky cliffs, with just one tiny harbor, ships dock out about three hundred yards, and islanders come out in small boats to get visitors like myself.

Morning crawls toward noon. The fog burns off, and I can see the island more clearly. Is that a seal? Fuck, there's a bunch of seals or sea lions on the cliffs. I reach for my phone, snapping a few shots. I remember those guys.

Finally, I spot the smaller boat—a nickel-sized brown dot moving from the island toward *Miss Aquarius*. The crew shuffles around me. I step closer to the rail, stopped short by a hard lump in my throat.

Meanwhile, two crewmembers go overboard on rope ladders to attach the smaller boat from Tristan to the side of this one. After that, the crates are slowly lowered.

I fill out some departure forms, toss my pack over my shoulder, and move to the boat's edge, where my gaze falls down a rope ladder to the waiting boat. It's pretty small, maybe even smaller than a cabin cruiser—the smallest of all yachts—and looks like it's powered by a single motor on the back. I'm watching two guys strap down the crates when the captain's voice startles me.

"Pack off," he says. "We'll lower it. Just climb down and you'll be on your way."

Then I'm over the boat's side, clinging to the ladder as I inhale salt and brine and the scent of wet rope. I can feel the dim sun on my shoulders, the boat's slight rocking underneath my boots. One rung at a time, and I can see the sea shifting between my moving feet. Then I step into the boat and turn to greet my island escorts—two ordinary-looking, middle-aged men in ordinary, working-class clothes. One—in a pair of oil-smudged coveralls—reaches to shake my hand as the other tips his ball cap.

"Homer Carnegie," the hat-tipper says, as the hand-shaker says, "I'm Rob."

"Mark," the one with the cap says. "You got everything?" His face is creased with sun-lines, and his pale brown eyes are kind.

"Once you're here, you're here to stay," Rob chuckles.

I nod. "Good for it."

Rob nods to the wooden bench behind me. "Have a seat."

I sit, the motor rumbles, and we're off.

The sea looks like a sheet of black glass as we zip over it. A fine spray arches up on each side of the boat, dotting my arms and cheeks with cool water. The breeze lifts my hair off my head as we move along the island's rocky coast.

I look up at the grassy cliffs with eyes that sting. From down here on the surface of the water, I can't see the valley that covers most of one side of the island; Tristan da Cunha simply looks like grass-covered cliffs that stretch to an unseen plateau.

I'm wondering where the boat will land when its nose points slightly inland, toward the cliffs, and I see…yeah, that's penguins. A bunch of little dudes on a low-lying, flatter-looking rockface, hopping up and down and doing penguin shit. As we pass by, I swear one looks right at me. A cold sweat flushes my skin, but I shake my head and laugh and rub my hands together.

I'll feel better by the time I leave this place, if everything goes right. Until then, penguins.

We curve around the island's edge, and finally I see it—Edinburgh of the Seven Seas, the long name of the little village I remember.

From here, it looks like a smattering of brightly colored buildings in the shadow of a mountain. Fuck—it looks like almost nothing.

I wrap a hand around the top of my pack, take a deep breath. I rub my forehead. Christ.

We're headed toward the jagged shoreline, which has dipped down lower, rising only ten or fifteen above the crashing waves. I tighten my grip on my pack and try to look alive when Mark glances at me.

Soon the motor's noise softens, the boat slows slightly, its nose tipping up, and I see we're coming up on the strange dock—two lines of cement jutting outward from the shore like two arms forming an almost-circle. Waves crash into them, shooting toward the sky in a wall of frothy white. As we edge closer, spray slaps my cheeks. I push a hand back through my now-wet hair and smile as my escorts grin back at me.

As we idle into the gap between the arms of the dock, the waves beneath the boat smooth out some, so we're bobbing lightly. I can hear birds caw above us, smell the thick, salty air. A wave hits the dock behind us, and I see a flash of rainbow just ahead of the boat. I'm looking at it when I notice people standing at the shoreline— blurry figures through my wet eyelashes. They're clearly here to greet us. To greet me.

Fuck, I'm really here again. And suddenly I feel like I can breathe.

❧

Continue reading *Covet* now:
bit.ly/EllaJamesCovet

FOLLOW ME

Keep in touch!

Sign up for my Newsletter.
Keep in touch on Facebook.
Join my Facebook Group, Ella's Elite.
Follow me on Amazon.
Follow me on Bookbub.
Follow me on Twitter.
Find me on Instagram.
See my bookshelf on Goodreads.

ALSO BY ELLA JAMES

Manhattan Monsters:
Dark Heart, Volume 1
Dark Heart, Volume 2
(Coming October 14, 2020)

Contemporary Romance Standalone
Hate You Not

On My Knees Duet
Worship
Adore

Sinful Secrets Romance
Sloth
My Heart For Yours
Covet

Off-Limits Romance
The Boy Next Door
Fractured Love
The Plan

The Love Inc. Series

Made in the USA
Coppell, TX
09 June 2021

57076732R10146